East of Aden

East of Aden

Elisabeth McNeill

ROBERT HALE · LONDON

ISBN 978-0-7090-9245-2

Robert Hale Limited
Clerkenwell House
Clerkenwell Green
London EC1R 0HT

www.halebooks.com

2 4 6 8 10 9 7 5 3 1

Typeset in 11/15pt Palatino
Printed in Great Britain by the MPG Books Group,
Bodmin and King's Lynn

LONDON, APRIL 2004

'Where's that?' Jess asked the radio set in her kitchen as an announcer said something about Mumbai.

When she realized that he meant Bombay she said aloud, 'Oh I hate all this political correctness!' Mumbai would always be Bombay to her.

That night she could not settle to read or watch television because her mind was full of memories. The next day would be her 65th birthday and she resolved to give herself a present.

She was going to find Joan and Jackie, the other two of the Three Jays from Bombay forty years ago, and if possible meet them again.

Joan

On the way home from the swimming pool at Breach Candy, Joan Ridgeway's three year old daughter Liza started to plead for a bag of humbugs from the Gymkhana Club shop and would not stop whining.

'Oh, darling, the sweets in that shop are horrible,' protested Joan weakly.

'They're not horrible, they're *lovely*. The sticky striped ones are the best. I want some of them.' Tears followed so, in spite of Joan's misgivings, a bag of bright green confectionery was purchased – and eaten. Next morning, however, Joan was horrified to see that Liza's pee had turned a virulently viridian colour. The anxious mother poured some of the pee into a bottle and rushed her child to Breach Candy European Hospital's out patient clinic where she waited to see the English doctor who looked like the actor Rex Harrison in *My Fair Lady*.

When he called her into his consulting room he was kindly and reassuring, but did not seem to be taking the problem very seriously as he examined a boisterous Liza and sent the bottle of sinister-looking urine to be tested. There was another wait and when Joan was called in again, the doctor told her, 'Don't worry, it was only food colouring. What's she been eating?'

Joan said, 'Normal food – except that she made me buy her a bag of mints from the Gym shop yesterday and she ate the lot before supper time.'

'That's it then,' he said with a laugh, tossing the sample bottle into his waste paper basket.

'But isn't it dangerous? I was afraid that she'd been poisoned,' she said, and the doctor, whose name was Alex Paisley only laughed though he was battling a hangover that made his eyes ache.

In spite of his headache he looked at the worried mother sympathetically and noted her trembling hands and the frown line between her eyebrows. There's more to this than green pee. She's the one who's in need of treatment, not the daughter, he thought. She had never consulted him before and she was very different to the usual American wives who turned up to consult him. This one had unusual style and, unlike some of the others, she hadn't tried to flirt with him.

The few Americans he saw were connected with one of the two big oil companies which were extending their enormous landing jetties and refining plants on the far side of Bombay's cluster of islands. When their expatriate employees fell ill, they rarely came to Breach Candy but preferred to consult the company retained doctors who worked exclusively in specially built, closely guarded and very private American housing communities beside the plants. These places were like small towns with walls around them. They even had guards on the gates and visitors needed permits to get past them.

Some of the Americans Alex treated came to him because he had acquired a good reputation for diagnosing the many gastro-intestinal illnesses that plagued foreigners living in Bombay. For some reason Americans seemed to suffer worse than other nationalities and Alex suspected that this was because of their over-zealous attempts to avoid the ever present infections.

One worried woman had told him that she even made her servants boil all the cutlery before meals, but she had overlooked the fact that when her bearer laid out the forks and knives he did so with his bare hands, so, in spite of her efforts, she and her family succumbed to every bug going. Another patient who seemed to be suffering from malnutrition admitted that she rarely ate solid food and lived exclusively on vitamin pills and invalid food supplements. Alex advised these people that it was better to live more dangerously and expose themselves to India and its infections so they could build up some immunity, but he feared that this advice would be ignored.

Today, however, he found himself sympathizing with the angular blonde woman on the other side of his desk and said, 'Go home, Mrs Ridgeway, and don't worry about Liza. Her urine will be clear now. She'll have pissed out all the colour. Keep her off the Gym sweets for a bit if you can, though.'

Joan thanked him, but still only half convinced, and to make sure that what he said was right, she took Liza into the out-patient lavatory to check before she left the hospital. When the pee was clear she considered Alex Paisley a gifted physician.

In relief she said to Liza, 'You've been such a good girl, would you like to go for a swim now?' Beautiful Breach Candy pool was almost next door to the hospital. Joan, who was liberal minded, was shocked when she discovered that it only admitted white people. All Indians were banned. Unfortunately for her conscience, it was very convenient and a favourite place of Liza's so she had paid her subscription and joined. Being members they had their own lockers and kept swimming costumes there. Inside its privileged, green surroundings, the members, mainly women, sprawled in the sun beneath enormous striped umbrellas on well-watered, closely cropped grass. Some of them were grossly fat Russian women and Joan thought it would be far more aesthetically pleasing to be swimming with beautiful lithe Indians than those ugly specimens, but, like so many things in Bombay, rules made during the days of the Raj were still rigidly enforced.

There were two beautiful pools, one large and kidney shaped with a floating platform in the middle, and the other smaller and more shallow for children. Joan always found a quiet place between the pools where she could lie in the sun while Liza played safely nearby in the shallow water. They stayed there happily till the sun began sinking and it was time to go home, but in the car Liza began chanting again in her most irritating monotone, 'I want some more of those nice mints like yesterday, I want mints, I want mints, mints, mints, mints.'

Joan put a hand to her forehead. The sun had made her feel faint and unable to cope with her daughter. She tried, but could not withstand Liza's bombardment.

'All right, all right, I'll buy them for you, but only if you ration them to one an hour,' she bargained, knowing that at the rate of one an hour Liza could only eat three at most before bedtime and anyway, what harm was sugar-dyed pee causing her child? None obviously, for the doctor had made her realize that there were worse things to worry about.

Amazingly the one mint an hour bargain appealed to Liza who, of course, had no clear idea of time. 'One an hour! All right, Mummy, one an hour,' she cried.

Their driver stopped at the main door of another European enclave, the Gymkhana Club on the edge of the Maidan. It was slightly more liberal minded than the pool because it had the grand total of one Indian member among several hundred whites. The Sikh doorman, splendidly turbaned and uniformed in white, scarlet and gold, stepped forward to open the passenger door for Joan.

'Is the shop still open?' she asked, weakly hoping that they were too late to buy mints, but he nodded, 'Yes, but closing time is in fifteen minutes, *memsahib*.'

'One an hour, one an hour,' shrieked Liza, running along the open veranda to the little shop in the middle of the building. She knew exactly what she wanted and where to get it.

When the purchase was made, Joan felt so sun struck and feeble that she sat down for a bit on one of the cane chairs that were arranged in sets of four along the first half of the club's long veranda. The other half of it was for men only. Women and children were confined in the first stretch. This caused Joan more misgivings because she hated the idea of women being considered less than men, but none of the other members' wives seemed to object to the out-of-date arrangement. Like everything else in Bombay, it was a hangover from the past.

A barefoot waiter in a frayed white suit approached her chair and she told him, 'Bring me a coffee please – black.'

Liza stood beside her mother with her eyes fixed on the paper bag of mints so Joan opened it and took out one, unwrapping it and anxiously noting the dark stripes along its surface. They looked as if they had been made with green ink.

Which poison is green? Isn't it arsenic? she wondered, as she handed over the sweet, inwardly resolving to renege on her bargain and flush the rest down the lavatory as soon as they got home. Liza could yell all she wanted because Theo would be there then to back her up and also the *ayah* who would hurry Liza away so as not to upset her father.

While Joan was sipping her coffee, Liza was diverted by the arrival of some other children who ran onto the rugby pitch in front of the Gymkhana building to play with a striped ball. The grass was still green and soft under foot because it was early October and the monsoon rains, which had been pelting down for weeks, were only beginning to peter out. The constant rain and grey skies of Bombay's mid-summer months had driven Joan almost to the point of suicide. *Thank God that cooler, sunny weather is coming back*, she thought.

A couple of women hurried past her table and one of them smiled at her. She smiled back weakly because she recognized an Englishwoman, Ginny Baldwin, who she'd spoken to at the pool a few days before. Ginny was whippet thin, and her skin was so deeply tanned that she looked like a mulatto though she had a broad Yorkshire accent.

'Hello, Mrs Ridgeway. Have you come to join our show too?' she asked.

Joan looked surprised. 'What show?' she asked.

'The Rugger Revue of course, what else? Your husband's in it this year, isn't he?' called Ginny, as she passed on.

Joan had never heard of the Rugger Revue, but she was aware that there were a lot of things in Theo's life that she didn't hear about these days. A wave of homesickness overwhelmed her and for a moment she wished that they had never come to this benighted place. She stood up quickly and recklessly handed out another mint to Liza to coax her away from her friends. As they were leaving the club she heard a piano starting up in a distant part of the building that was forbidden to women.

There's no business like show business, no business at all.... was the tune that was being played.

Ginny was entering into the all male part of the club and heading for the large central dining room which had a stage at one end. On it stood a grand piano with its lid open and a handsome, dark-haired man was strumming away at the keys. This was Donald Maitland-Smith, a public relations executive with a large pharmaceutical company. Because most of his work was done by able Indian assistants, his job gave him ample time to pursue his many hobbies and flirtations. As well as being a serial seducer, he was a skilled pianist, much in demand at rugby club parties because he could play any popular tune without sheet music. Every year he took over as director of music for the rugby revue, an event that was looked forward to even by people who had never been near a rugby field in their lives.

Donald half turned on his stool when he heard the two women arriving and grinned as he called out, 'Ah, the talent arrives! I should have guessed you'd be signing up, Ginny. And who's your beautiful friend?'

'Lucy Allan, a new arrival,' said Ginny, with a sweep of the hand as if she was producing a rabbit out of a hat.

Donald stood up and bent over Lucy's hand, pressing his lips onto her skin. '*Bellissima!*' he sighed, and Ginny giggled as she said, 'Watch out for him, Luce. He's Bombay's biggest seducer. Every woman is fair game for him, isn't that true, Donald?'

'Only the pretty ones. I'm very fussy. It's a compliment to be seduced by me,' he said, straightening up, 'and I've never had any complaints and I'm a quick worker. You can vouch for that, can't you, Ginny? How long did it take us to get together?'

'About two days,' she said flirtatiously.

'*Two* days! My goodness, I couldn't have been on top form that week,' he replied with a laugh.

The women stepped out of their cotton skirts to reveal that they were wearing tiny shorts and black fishnet tights which had been specially ordered from England for this occasion. He sat back on his stool and watched them critically. Ginny's so tanned she looks mummified and her legs are stick thin, he thought, She's gone off a lot since she first arrived three years ago. Some women don't wear well in this climate.

Her friend, however, was a different proposition. In contrast to Ginny's dark looks, she was blonde and verging on plump, like a well-fed chicken, and was obviously avid for an adventure. He'd felt the tremor in her hand when he kissed it. She'd be easy, too easy really. He preferred them to be reluctant and need winning over.

Ginny was prancing theatrically across the stage. 'Who do you think will sign up for the chorus this year?' she asked him.

He began to play, *I could have danced all night…*' and said over his shoulder, 'Lilias as usual and all the other regulars, I expect, though some of them are growing a little long in the tooth – I don't mean you of course, darling.'

'Is Marcia volunteering?' asked Ginny. Marcia was Donald's wife, a woman who was as big a sexual predator as her husband.

Their marriage was a battle ground with most of their skirmishes fought out in public, though in fact they had no intention of leaving each other. Constant fighting and mutual recriminations were food and drink to them.

He shook his head. 'Come on! Marcia gave up high kicking years ago. She needs to keep her energy for her other activities. Anyway she's too stunted, not tall enough,' he said and played a long trill of Oklahoma.

Ginny was five foot eight and she drew herself up proudly as she said, 'I saw that new American woman, randy Theo's wife, having coffee outside and I wondered if she's waiting to volunteer. I heard Theo's in the show and if she has any sense she'll be wanting to keep an eye on him. He's rampant,' she said.

The idea of Joan joining appealed to Donald and he looked up in interest. 'I know the girl you mean. I hope she's coming. She's very classy looking.' Lifting his hands off the keys for a moment, he then launched into a new tune *Getting to Know You...*

Ginny demurred loudly. 'Oh, Donald, surely not! That straight hair of hers is awful and her clothes are so drab. She's probably frigid too, because Theo propositions every woman he meets. I heard he's working his way through the secretaries in the oil company he works for. He's out to match your record.'

'I beg your pardon, I don't go for secretaries. I concentrate on club wives like you,' he said sharply.

Ginny scoffed, 'At least we're not frumps like Joan Ridgeway,' she said.

'You're not like her at all,' agreed Donald, playing on, for Ginny and Lucy had their hair curled and tinted but Joan's poker straight hair, though fair was not flaxen enough to be described as blonde, and it was usually held back from falling over her face by a long Kirby grip. Her day-to-day clothes were pastel coloured cotton shirt-waisters buttoned down the front and, unlike most of the other Gymkhana Club wives, she did not buy sequin studded sandals from Bata on Colaba Causeway, but usually wore navy-blue tennis shoes with thick white soles and laces.

'She's a frump!' exclaimed Ginny again, turning to Lucy for confirmation and asking, 'You saw her out there. As plain as a pikestaff, isn't she?'

Donald teased them. 'That's where you're both wrong. She's a very sexy woman and a Boston Brahmin to boot.'

'A what?' They gaped at him.

'A Boston Brahmin. You know what an Indian Brahmin is, don't you? Very well bred and clever. She's the American version. In fact, she's a typical example of an upper-class ex-college girl, a fish out of water here, I'm afraid.'

'You fancy her, don't you? Well, I bet she's the one you can't catch. She'll be your only failure,' sneered Ginny, who resented being compared unfavourably to a woman she considered insignificant.

Donald laughed as he turned back to the piano and started playing *Jealousy*!

'Let's have a bet on it, five hundred chips, or are you afraid you might meet your match with Mrs Iceberg,' she persisted.

He struck a discordant chord on the piano. 'All right! You're on! Five hundred rupees it is,' he said.

When she stepped into her air–conditioned flat on the twelfth floor in one of the most select apartment buildings in Bombay, Joan stood in the middle of her enormous drawing room and lifted her damp hair onto the top of her head with both hands in the hope that cool air circulating round her neck would soothe her headache. Then she flopped onto the white sofa, pushing off her shoes with her toes and closed her eyes.

Yusuf, her discreet bearer, slid into the room and said softly, 'Martini, *memsahib*?'

She looked up and shook her head. 'No, Yusuf, I'd rather have water, but get the Scotch, ginger ale, ice and soda ready for *sahib* returning from work.'

Yusuf looked down at the empty tray in his hands and said, 'But *sahib* has been in already and gone out again.'

She knew very well that if she asked where Theo had gone, the bearer would be able to tell her but she did not want to reveal ignorance of her husband's movements.

'Oh, good,' she said, and closed her eyes again, waiting for the arrival of iced water with a slice of lime floating in it. Ginny, the woman in the Gym, had said that Theo was in the show they were rehearsing so he was probably there already. As he hadn't told her about it, he obviously didn't want her to join him.

They had been living in the teeming Indian city of Bombay for nine months because Theo Ridgeway was being groomed for high office in a major oil company in which both his and Joan's family had large shareholdings. They had arrived in India young, handsome and in love, believing that their lives were set on a clear course to happiness and success.

Twenty-eight-year old Theo was a typical ex–college boy with an open face, splendid American teeth and curling fair hair. He had been sent abroad to 'work his way up' because his family expected that he would in time sit on the board of the company and then go into politics – Republican, of course.

He was not one to sacrifice his high standard of living while abroad and from the beginning he set out to make his family's stay in Bombay as comfortable as possible. He absolutely refused to move into the gated enclave of executive houses beside the company's refinery on Trombay Island and demanded to be housed in the best part of the city.

'Joan and I can't live with a lot of rednecks. We're not used to mixing with couples who call each other "Hon". We want to meet the best people, rajahs and nawabs, people like that,' he said.

Joan, too, was glad that they did not have to live in the oil company compound even though every house there had a large garden and a private pool and the compound was provided with its own school, a shop stocked with specially imported American goods, a medical centre, and a private hospital staffed by doctors trained in USA. She thought that it would be like being shut up in an American ghetto especially because the company wives she'd met were afraid of Indians, preferring to do their own household chores rather than hire native servants. In fact, many of them avoided going into Bombay at all and some families lived in the refinery enclave throughout their two-year-contracts without ever setting foot in the city. Joan thought they might as well have stayed on in some small town in a remote Mid-Western state, but she was more adventurous and curious. She wanted to get to know India and meet Indian people.

Because he had such important connections, Theo's housing demands were satisfied and the company installed them in a luxurious air-conditioned penthouse with a roof garden in the most exclusive block on Malabar Hill. For Liza, there was a little nursery school nearby run by a very genteel Englishwoman and she loved going there in the mornings because it was housed in a large concrete yellow boot with little rooms inside where the children played.

Before she arrived in Bombay Joan had made a list of the historic sites she wanted to see, but when she tracked them down on the map she was appalled by the distance away most of them were and by the difficulties of travelling to such remote places.

'I'm here to work, not to sightsee,' Theo told her, so, with her travelling list cut back, she reconciled herself with the hope that she would be able to make Indian friends in their apartment block where the door plates displayed enough titles of rajahs and nawabs to satisfy even Theo.

Joan had gone to Vassar and would have liked to have studied anthropology, but that was vetoed by her parents who had other plans for her. Specifically they wanted her to marry the only son of their closest friends and business associates. Both families were old established, rich and influential. and a marriage between their children was what both sets of parents wanted.

The young couple fulfilled these hopes – danced, flirted, made out in his convertible at drive-in movies and, when Joan was nineteen, they married in great style. Liza appeared within ten months and Joan happily accepted her destiny by settling down to playing tennis and bridge like her mother, hosting dinner parties for friends and dutifully having Theo's favourite cocktail waiting for him when he arrived home in the evening.

In Bombay she intended to continue with that domestic routine but found it difficult. She made no friends among the other American wives who shied away from her because they feared she would be a snob like her husband who threw his weight around among the men. In an effort to extend their social circle, Theo joined the Gymkhana Club but everybody she met there seemed to know everybody else already and had no time to waste on a stranger whose shyness made her appear remote.

The company provided her with a big tail-finned car and a uniformed driver called Ali who drove her through the thronging city, and she was filled with incredulous wonder at everything she saw. She would have preferred to explore by herself, but that was out of the question because the company advised against it. White women like her, the wives of important men, risked being kidnapped and held for ransom, they told Theo.

So they provided her with Ali as a driver and bodyguard, who was big enough to be intimidating to any would-be kidnappers. He spoke good English so when she told him that she wanted to read about Indian history, he took her to a well-stocked bookshop called Thackers where she bought armfuls of books on Hinduism, the Mughal Empire and the British Raj. Soon her mind was teeming with questions that she felt only educated Indians could answer. Her neighbours in the block of flats all looked extremely sophisticated and were exquisitely polite when she met them in the lift, but no one offered her any hospitality. She was never invited to call or to drop in for a cup of coffee.

'Perhaps they expect us to throw our own party first,' she suggested to Theo.

'Probably; just go ahead if that's what you want to do,' he said casually. After consulting the door name plates, she wrote out embossed invitation cards and sent Yusuf to deliver them to the other flats. Replies trickled in slowly and most were refusals. Previous engagements were the universal excuse and when the special night came round only four couples out of an original guest list of twenty turned up and it was a stilted occasion.

As she saw her last guests to the door, Joan could barely blink back her tears. 'It was very kind of you to come,' she said, to an exquisitely beautiful Indian rani who was dressed in a shimmering purple sari fringed with gold, and enormous diamond ear-rings that swung down to her shoulders.

The rani saw that she was upset and touched her arm gently. 'Don't worry. It's not your fault. Indian people can be reserved, you know, and lots of them don't drink so they avoid parties where there might be alcohol.'

'But we're not heavy drinkers. We only want to make friends,' said Joan pitifully.

'I know that, my dear, but I went to a finishing school called the Monkey Club in London and I've been to the States. Most of the other wives in this block have never left India. Lots of the men have, but not the women.'

'Did they refuse our invitation because we're not Indian?'

The beautiful woman nodded. 'I'm afraid so.'

Joan was surprised because on several occasions she had seen white men and women visiting her neighbours' homes. 'But they have other European friends; I've seen them coming in,' she protested.

'Some have *English* friends,' she agreed.

'You mean it's because we're Americans?'

'Yes. It's only a silly prejudice. Don't worry about it.'

'But I've been reading about the Raj. The British were horrible to the Indians. How can you overlook that?'

The woman in purple laughed, 'Some Indians are more British than the British. They think like them, but they can't understand Americans.'

The failure of their drinks party did not bother Theo as much as it bothered Joan because he made friends in the Gym through his prowess on the rugby field. At Yale, he'd played American football and he was as tough as any rugby player so when the rains began he was in his element on the Gymkhana playing fields getting thickly smeared with mud and playing as dirty as he could. He always arrived home full of high spirits on practice nights and told Joan it was his ambition to be given a place in the first team which played most of its games against the Bombay police who were notoriously ferocious players.

On the evening of the day that Joan visited the doctor to investigate Liza's green pee, Theo was very late in arriving home. She was reading one of her history books on their long white sofa when he came in, and she looked up to ask, 'Do you want any dinner?'

'No, I had a sandwich at the Gym,' he said.

'I was there this afternoon. A woman called Ginny told me the rugby club is rehearsing some sort of show and that you're in it,' she told him.

He took a glass of whisky off the tray Yusuf held towards him and said, 'I am. The show's called the Rugger Revue and they put it on every year.'

She put her book down and said as pleasantly as she could, 'That's interesting. What are you doing in the show?'

'I'm in a barber shop chorus.' Theo had a good singing voice.

'Why didn't you tell me about it?' she asked.

'I wanted it to be a surprise, anyway I didn't think it would be your sort of thing,' he said in an unconvincing tone.

'I might be able to do something in it too. I get so bored here doing nothing all day,' she said wistfully.

'Do what? I certainly wouldn't want to see you in tights, high kicking in front of the lechers of the rugby gang,' he said, finishing his drink and holding the glass out for another.

'Perhaps I could paint scenery, or do props or something.'

'There's not much scenery or props. It's not that sort of a show. It's more like vaudeville.'

'But surely there would be something for me to do. I'm so lonely, Theo. I don't know anybody.' She sounded as desolate as she felt and his conscience pricked him. If truth were told he preferred keeping his time in the rugby club away from his wife because he could behave as badly as he liked and not worry about her finding out. Now contrite, he sat down beside her and said, 'I'm sorry, baby. I know it's lonely for you here. The rugby club is holding a curry lunch party on Sunday for people taking part in the revue. Would you like to go? But I don't really think they're your kind.'

'I'm ready to accept any kind of people,' she said, not realizing that she was about to launch herself into saturnalia.

The party was held in a ground floor flat off Napier Sea Road. Recently the roads of Bombay had been given Indian names by the government, but nobody used them and the old British names were still used by all, even the taxi drivers.

Every guest took their own alcohol to the party because of prohibition laws that had been enacted by Chief Minister Morarji Desai to try to cut down drinking in the city. As a concession, if expatriates declared themselves to be alcoholics and acquired a medical certificate to say so, they were issued with government liquor permits which allowed them to buy three bottles of spirits or twelve bottles of beer each a month, but that was woefully inadequate even for the most modest drinker and there was a thriving black market masterminded by a fisherman nicknamed Pedro who was distinguished by the amount of gold he wore round his neck. Pedro brought liquor in by dhow from the gulf and buried the bottles on Marvi beach, sending them out by order to customers in the city. Some hard-up people tried to make their own liquor in their bathtubs out of pineapples and potato peelings but most of the hard drinking rugby club members had their own bootlegger who delivered Pedro's goods by bicycle. Some of the bootleggers had to be closely watched because they tried to cut out Pedro and passed off cold tea as whisky or home-made toddy liquor as gin. Toddy gin smelt so foul it could clear a room.

Theo, being flush with money, soon found a reliable bootlegger and when he and Joan arrived at the party they were armed with a bottle of imported Gordon's gin which had cost ten times more than liquor store prices at home. Its elegant yellow label with black juniper berries printed on it caused a sensation when Theo laid it on the drinks table. It was handled amid cries of admiration because most people reckoned themselves lucky to get Parry's Indian stuff that was made in Madras.

'Gosh, real Gordon's! Good bloke! Put your bottle down on the table and give me a slug and tell the bearer who you are so he doesn't let anyone else drink it. Make sure you write your name on the label or you'll lose it,' said the host, a fat, amiable banker who played prop forward in the first team to which Theo aspired.

Pleased to be greeted so enthusiastically Theo poured drinks for Joan and himself, and then, to her dismay, introduced her to the first couple they met and promptly disappeared into the throng. She held her drink tightly and sniffed it. Theo, who knew she was not fond of gin, had poured some brightly coloured orange squash into her glass to take away the taste. I'll be back at that doctor complaining that I'm peeing orange tomorrow, she thought ruefully.

Looking around she saw that the flat was large, but sparsely furnished which was just as well, because there were well over a hundred people crammed into two reception rooms and couples were jiving in the middle of the floor to records playing on a gramophone.

She felt panicked and needed room to breathe so she excused herself from the strangers and went looking for a lavatory where she could hide, but though there were two, both were continually occupied. She hung around watching for a door to open, but no one ever came out of either of them.

Eventually she saw Ginny in a group of women and went over to whisper, 'Are any lavatories ever available?' Ginny laughed. 'Eventually they are! Can you hold on for a little while longer? Colin and Pam'll be having it off in one of them, but it never takes them long and they'll be finished soon. The other one's out of bounds because I saw some of the boys putting Bill Lethem into its bath till he sobers up. Don't go in there because he's starkers and it's not a pretty sight.'

'Is there really a couple having sex in the bathroom?' Joan was astonished by Ginny's *sang froid*.

'Yes, they do it at every party, but they're usually quite quick. I'll bang on the door to hurry them up for you if you like,' said Ginny, obligingly.

The door banging worked because in a few minutes, the latch clicked back and a rangy-looking woman with a mop of curly auburn hair appeared, followed in a few moments by a dishevelled man in a colourful shirt with parrots printed on it. They went off in different directions as if they had nothing to do with each other and never spoke again as far as Joan could see.

Ginny saw her surprised face and said mischievously, 'I'll introduce you to them if you like. He's Colin and she's Pam. She's over there now with her husband Hugh.'

Joan asked, 'Does her husband know what goes on in the lavatory with the man in the parrot shirt?' She realized she sounded prim but couldn't help it.

'Oh, yes; Pam and Colin have a go at every party. She picks up other people too sometimes. She's quite proud that her three children all have different fathers. There's a bit of a nympho problem there, I'm afraid.'

'Doesn't her husband mind?'

'No, he plays around too. They get on well together actually. She told me that when they go home after a party they discuss their conquests and laugh about them.'

At that moment, Joan looked over Ginny's shoulder and saw to her horror that Theo was starting to dance with red-haired Pam who draped both arms round his neck and was raising her face to his. Oh no, he isn't going to kiss her, is he? she thought. Yes he was. Yes, he did. Then Pam pulled at his hand and led him off onto the terrace where cane chairs were set out among huge potted plants with sinister-looking yellow trumpet flowers.

Ginny saw what was happening between Theo and Pam and a smile crossed her lips that she didn't bother to stifle, but when Joan took a step towards the pair on the floor, she became suddenly sympathetic and held her back saying urgently, 'No, don't do that. Act cool. Pretend you don't see them. It's not important. With Pam it doesn't mean anything. If you break it up she'll scream and make a scene and you don't want that, do you? Come with me and I'll introduce you to some other people.'

She pulled Joan over to a sofa where two women were sitting chatting and laughing. 'Sit down here with Jess and Jackie, they'll tell you who everybody is,' she said, as she patted the sofa cushion and made her own escape.

Though she felt like weeping, Joan smiled at the strangers but had little to say and soon made her escape to barricade herself in the bathroom. It seemed that everybody did it.

When she emerged twenty minutes later plates of curry were

being served, and Theo, whose hair was soaking wet as if he'd been swimming, sought her out where she was sitting in a corner pretending to eat and listen to the music. In a falsely jolly tone, he asked, 'Having a good time, darling? Made any interesting friends yet?'

She felt herself quaking inside with rage but managed to control her temper and say, 'You look as if you've been swimming, Theo.'

'Yes, there's a private pool out there and people are skinny dipping. Do you want to have a go?'

She shook her head. 'No. I want to leave now in fact. I've had enough of this Hogarthian scene.'

He'd been drinking heavily and he shrugged. 'Hogarthian? Very erudite and disapproving. Please yourself, but skinny dipping is wonderful. Go home if you like, our car's outside and I told the driver to wait. He'll take you back.'

'Please give my thanks to the host and hostess,' she said, as she picked up her purse and walked to the door. In the car going back to her own flat, she sat dry eyed and grim faced, longing to weep but determined not to give way to tears in front of Ali, the driver, who she knew was watching her in the rear-view mirror.

Jess and Jackie

Back at the party the two women on the sofa where Ginny had tried to dump Joan had been watching the tense exchange between the American husband and wife.

'I feel sorry for that woman, she's agonized with shyness and insecurity,' said Jess Grey nodding at Joan's departing back. Her friend Jacqueline – usually called Jackie – Innes agreed, 'So do I. She was terribly awkward with us, wasn't she? I saw her in Alex's surgery last week with her little girl and she looked then as if she's on the verge of a crack up.'

'Hardly surprising if she is. That husband of hers is said to be running wild among the women here like a little boy turned loose in a sweet shop. You saw him with Pam just now – and so did she.'

'She has a very nice face and doesn't dress all frilly and fluffy like some of the American women you see around. Funnily enough I've been reading a novel by a woman called Mary McCarthy and our American could be one of the characters in it,' said Jess.

'Is it any good?' Jackie wanted to know.

'Yes, it's fantastic. It's called *The Group* and it's about some American college girls who all know each other. One of my friends at home posted it to me because he knows I'm starved for reading matter here. I'll pass it on to you when I finish it.'

'Maybe you should lend it to our American friend first,' suggested Jackie.

'Yeah, in fact I was thinking about trying to make friends with her because she looks so lonely. I see her sometimes at Breach Candy with her daughter and she's never with anybody else. Next time she's there I'm going to talk to her,' said Jess.

She sat back on the sofa and clasped her hands round her knees as she eyed the dancers. Her husband Sam was nowhere to be seen and God knew what he was up to. 'Anyway, perhaps we should worry about our own husbands instead of hers. Where's your Peter?' she asked Jackie.

Jackie sighed resignedly. 'Playing cards, I suspect. There's a game going on in the flat next door I think, and Alex said he'd bring his roulette wheel today. If he has, Peter'll be there. He loves gambling. He's sure he's going to make our fortune one day,' Jackie told her.

'Has Alex really got a roulette wheel?' asked Jess in surprise. She couldn't imagine the doctor as a croupier.

'He brought it back from his leave last month. He and Mary are going to hold roulette parties at their flat in the hospital. We went to their first one and Peter lost five hundred chips, but at least roulette stopped Alex and Mary fighting with each other,' said Jackie.

'That's a miracle,' said Jess, 'Last time we had them to dinner they ended up pelting each other with the bread rolls and they were throwing to hurt! God knows why they stay together. If one says black, the other says white.'

Jackie sighed, 'Sometimes I wonder why most of the couples out here stay together. Love's not like it is in novels, is it?'

Jess laughed, 'Especially not out here. Sometimes I think I don't believe in love at all but perhaps it's easier for people to settle down together at home. Another thing I think is that we all marry far too young. Where I come from if you're not engaged by twenty-one, you're in danger of being left on the shelf.'

Jackie smiled, 'I fell for Peter the moment I saw him at a party in London.'

'How old were you?'

'Twenty.'

'Too young,' said Jess dismissively.

'How old were you when you got married?' Jackie asked.

'Twenty-three.'

'Is that a better age to get married?'

'I'm beginning to wonder if any age is the right age to get married, especially when you see the couples out here,' said Jess solemnly, 'There's an interesting old man who's always in the Ritz bar. He's a Polish Jew and somehow he escaped from a Nazi concentration camp and made his way here. All his family disappeared and he's terribly lonely. He talks to me and the other day he said that European women shouldn't pass through the Suez Canal.'

Jackie laughed, 'Why? That's crazy.'

'I'm not so sure it is. He says that coming east of Aden makes European women go to pieces and shed their inhibitions. He says they recreate themselves, sometimes for the better but usually for the worse. They begin to feel capable of doing anything they want without restraint. Think of the people we know and you've got to admit he has a point.'

As she listened, Jackie's face went solemn. 'I know what he's getting at. India has a peculiar effect on some English people – women especially. My father's family were Indian Army for generations and so was my mother's. He drank like the men at this party are drinking and my mother had dozens of affairs. So did her sisters, my aunts. I remember watching it all going on when I was a child – the drinking, the fighting and the lovers – and I decided that I wanted my life to be different if I married. I was born here, but I never intended to come back after I went away to school though I love this country. It's the expatriate society that bugs me.'

'Why did you come back then?' Jess asked.

'My cousin offered Peter this Bombay job. He couldn't get

anything that suited him at home. He didn't believe me when I told him that though the English have given up governing, they still try to live here as if nothing has changed. Thank God, he's not like most of the rest of them though. He actually prefers Indians to Brits.' Jackie's voice rose and she visibly grew agitated as she spoke.

She went out of her way to defend Peter against people whom she was afraid did not like him or might look down on him because of his working-class background. She herself came from a snobbish family with Indian links going back for two centuries. In fact, with her lustrous black hair and high-cheekboned face, she looked as if there might be a strain of aristocratic Indian blood in her, perhaps from a long dead Mughal princess. She'd told Jess about being born in Darjeeling, a military hill station, and going to her first school in the south near Ootacamund. That her parents lived in the same sexually casual way as the people they knew in Bombay had never been mentioned before however and it obviously upset her.

'You and Peter are OK together. You're lucky. Hold onto it,' Jess said soothingly. Privately she thought that her friend made too many excuses for Peter for he was an idle layabout who took lots of time off from his office. His excuse for not going to work was unspecified illness which always excited Jackie's anxious sympathy. Fortunately his boss in an old established import and export company was Jackie's cousin and nepotism had prevented Peter from being fired long ago.

'I'm very glad I married when I did and I don't think I was too young. I believe in love because I love Peter,' said Jackie simply, and Jess's heart went out to her friend whom she hoped would never be disillusioned.

'What about you and Sam?' Jackie asked the question that Jess did not want to answer. In fact she tried to avoid thinking about it.

She frowned as she replied, 'I honestly don't know. We first met years ago when we were at school and we met again when he came home on his first leave. It was all very sudden. After only six weeks we got married in a registry office and I came back here with him. My family were all very disapproving and boycotted the wedding. I think I love Sam, but I might not have married him if Bombay wasn't part of the bargain. I certainly wouldn't have settled down in some city suburb with him – or with anyone else. I wanted to travel because I've always had terrible wanderlust. When I was three I ran away from home and walked nearly four miles before they found me sitting under a tree on the main road out of Dundee with my pet dog Toby.' She laughed and went on, 'Dogs and the open road are my real passions.'

Jackie laughed too. 'You're always joking, Jess, but I think you and Sam make a great couple,' she said.

'I suppose we do. He amuses me a lot and we have good sex,' said Jess, but she was thinking, What you don't know is that we have a triangular marriage. Two's company and three's a crowd and I'm number three.

After she landed in Bombay with her new husband, she discovered that his salary was so low that he could not afford to rent a flat himself and they would have to go on sharing a bungalow in the suburbs with his bachelor friend Perry. From the beginning Perry hated her and tried every way he could think of to make her pack her case and go home. But she was determined to stay to spite him. The atmosphere between them at home was always tense. She was about to tell Jackie about that when her friend suddenly changed the subject, and gasped as she nodded towards the doorway.

'Just look at that. It's Marcia the menace. Who's the poor innocent she has with her?'

Jess looked over too and said, 'I've met him in the Ambassador's Bar. He's called Jack Bradford, and he's the latest arrival at Globe Insurance. He seems to be a decent chap and Sam and the rugby club gang welcomed him with open arms because he played rugby for Durham University – in the first fifteen no less!'

'Rugby! It's a religion with the men here. Thank God Peter doesn't play,' said Jackie.

'I caused chaos with Sam and Perry the other night because I said it's a homosexual game, with all that grappling for each other's balls and the communal bathing at the end. They were horrified. It was as if I told them on good authority that God doesn't exist,' Jess told her.

Jackie laughed. 'You're lucky they didn't pin you to the wall with their steak knives,' she said.

'It certainly put an end to polite conversation.'

'How do you think Marcia's always the first to get her hands on any new arrivals?' Jackie asked.

'The way Marcia gets her hands on everything – by grabbing,' was Jess's reply and they both sat forward on the sofa with their eyes fixed on the couple in the doorway.

Marcia Maitland-Smith was a tiny woman with a head of highly teased, yellow-dyed hair and an expertly made-up face. No one knew her real age – not even Donald to whom she had been married for nearly twenty years. They had two sons, both of whom stayed in London with Donald's sister and never came to Bombay.

No matter how long she lived, Marcia was going to remain blonde because she was really dark haired with a very Anglo Indian look, but her local blood, even if there was as much as her detractors claimed, was a few generations back. Anyway, she denied its existence vehemently.

Her father had been managing director of a large tea exporting company in Calcutta and she'd always lived like a princess, looked after devotedly by an Anglo Indian nanny who had been caring for her since she was a child and was with her still. Nanny, as she was called by everyone, conducted an ongoing war with Donald and she always won. She and Marcia gossiped together in Hindi when there was no one else around to overhear them.

Marcia never got out of bed before noon but attended every party and was famous for always having a new dirty joke to tell – where she found them all was a mystery. She was also notorious for the amount of gold jewellery that she hung around herself – heavy hoop ear-rings, several chunky necklaces and lines of elegant bangles up both arms. Her most prized piece hung round her right wrist. It was a massive gold charm bracelet dangling with miniature hearts, cupids, flowers, shamrocks, Scotty dogs, models of the Taj Mahal and the Eiffel Tower, a tiny trumpet, a galloping horse, a spinning top and a Jaguar car. The bracelet weighed so much that Marcia always seemed to walk slightly tilted to the right. She never tired of showing off the charms and telling about the various lovers who'd given each one to her.

None of them came from Donald, her husband.

As always she made her entrance to the party deliberately late, clinging to the arm of the embarrassed young man who looked about twenty years her junior. Donald was already at the party with a spectacularly busty Anglo Indian girl called Zoe who claimed to be his chief mistress and tolerantly overlooked his other affaires, which were many and which he made no effort to hide. Some of them ended in either blood or tears and the most recent finished when the woman's husband attempted suicide. They had been shipped home to Australia but Donald sailed on regardless.

When he spotted his wife's arrival, he walked across the floor to kiss her on the cheek and say, 'Ah, my ever loving spouse! Welcome to the party. Who's your new friend, my dear? Have you been out cradle snatching?'

Jack Bradford stammered, 'Your wife asked me for a lift to the party. I was having a lunch-time drink in the flat next door to yours with my boss, Mr Goddard, and Marcia came in to join us and asked me to bring her here because you'd gone off with her car.'

'I believe you, I believe you, I bet she took you back and gave you another drink first, didn't she?' said Donald clapping him on the back.

'Yes, she did.' Jack's blush deepened as he remembered Marcia sitting next to him on her sofa, running a hand appreciatively over the fly of his trousers and saying, 'Let's see what we can do with that little fellow first, shall we?'

He'd jumped to his feet and backed away from her, gabbling about wanting to get to the party because he'd arranged to meet friends there. He was a virgin and eager for experience but definitely not with the terrifying, fast talking Marcia.

Fortunately she accepted defeat. It was enough for her to be seen arriving at the party with him and make people think she'd taken his virginity. She hoped Donald would be furious and so would the other predatory wives because she'd beaten them to the prize of this latest young bachelor. Nobody would be able to prove anything different.

Jack managed to slip out of her grasp when she and her husband began to argue. He fled into the crowd massed round the drinks table where he found his Globe Insurance colleague McCallum reading the names on the bottles.

'Bloody hell, this is Gordons! It says Ridgeway on it, that's the American. I'm going to help myself to a slug of it because Americans are all so rich they can afford crates of the stuff and he'll never know the difference,' McCallum said, pouring himself a healthy measure before he turned to Jack and joked, 'I see Marcia grabbed you. I bet when he gave you your first pep talk old Goddard told you to watch out for the women. He did, didn't he?'

'Yes, he did,' agreed Jack, producing his bottle of beer and pouring himself a glass.

'Save your beer. Have a gin on the Yank,' said McCallum, but Jack ignored him and turned to watch the dancing as his mind went back to earlier in the week when he had his first interview with his new boss, Mr Arthur Goddard.

'The best advice I can give you about living in Bombay is stay away from other men's wives,' had been Goddard's opening words.

Jack laughed as if that was a joke but soon realized his mistake. Goddard was deadly serious. He leaned forward and fixed the new recruit with a bleary stare as if sensing insincerity. His breath smelled of gin though it was only half past eleven in the morning, and he was sweating so heavily that there were yellowing semi circles of wetness under both his arms. In London they'd told Jack that Goddard could be tricky and had been known to send men home after only a few weeks if they did not suit him. The last thing he wanted was to be shipped back home because he was glorying in the brilliant sun and the colourful throngs of people he'd seen on the streets.

He was jolted out of remembering his first day in Bombay when McCallum slapped him on the back and said, 'You've made a good start by getting off with Marcia. Is she as wild as they say?'

'Pretty wild,' said Jack.

'I made a set at her but she said she doesn't like moustaches. I'm not going to shave it off for an old tart like her. It took me months to grow it,' McCallum told him.

'Hard luck,' said Jack, looking around for a way of escape. He wished he could go back to having his peaceful drink with Goddard who wakened his sympathy for some reason.

As he scanned the crowd he saw a girl that he'd met at the Ambassadors Bar. She was sitting on a sofa with a dark haired, very beautiful woman, and he walked across to say, 'Hello. Can I talk to you? I don't know anyone here except McCallum.'

They laughed and the beautiful one said, 'That's no great advantage, is it? Sit down and we'll fill you in with who everybody is.'

He sat between them and began to enjoy himself. The girl he'd met before was Jess Grey, a slim, short, brown-haired girl with unusual tawny coloured eyes that seemed to transfix anyone she stared at. He remembered being struck by her eyes and her curiosity when they first met, for all she'd done was ask him questions. Though usually reticent, he was surprised to find himself answering as if she bewitched him.

Her friend Jackie was tranquil looking with a striking, film star-like face.

'Where are you living and how are you settling in?' Jess asked. She was starting her questioning early.

'I'm settling quite well in a chummery at Apollo Bunder with McCallum and three other fellows from insurance companies. They're good company.'

'You're not a solitary then? Are you from a big family?' Jess wanted to know.

'There's three of us – me and two sisters. Can I ask you something? Why do you ask so many questions?' he said.

She laughed and so did Jackie who said to him, 'Good for you! She quizzes everyone she meets.'

'What did you work at before you were married? Were you a policewoman?' he asked Jess.

'God no! I was a newspaper reporter. I'm sorry, I suppose I'm used to asking questions, but people don't need to answer or tell me the truth, do they? Do you mind me asking you things?'

When you fix those eyes on people they'd probably reply to anything you ask, he thought, but he said, 'No, I don't mind.'

'Good. Now tell me who you'd like to know about and Jackie and I'll fill you in,' she said with a grin.

He looked around and saw a worried looking angular woman in a white pique dress bustling about from room to room picking up glasses and empty plates. 'Is that the hostess?' he asked.

Jess grimaced. 'She'd like to be. She's after the host, the rugby team captain. She's Gloria Morton, Bombay's Number One

Gossip because she's sister in charge of the maternity department at Breach Candy hospital and goes about gossiping about how women react when they're giving birth – she tells who cries, who screams, who swears, who yells for their mothers, who can't pay their bill, and who has tatty nightdresses. She has no discretion. If I had a baby I'd sooner go to one of the native hospitals than let her get her hands on me.' As she spoke she saw her friend's face change. Jackie suddenly looked scared. Why? Jess wondered.

Jack's interest had moved on however, and he nodded at a curly-haired man in a bush shirt with brightly coloured parrots all over it. 'Who's the guy in the brilliant shirt?'

Together the girls chorused, 'That's Colin' and Jess called out, 'Colin, come and meet a newcomer.'

Colin came weaving over and said, 'Sorry, girls, I'm a bit pissed. I'm going home to Florrie and Raju.' And without stopping he headed for the door. Jess smiled as she watched him go. 'He's crazy but I like Colin,' she said.

'I do too, but I wish he didn't feel it necessary to have it off in the loo with horrible Pam at every party,' said Jackie.

'At least today he didn't take off all his clothes, or stand on his head naked in a corner like he usually does,' Jess added, and they laughed again.

'He sounds like a menace,' said Jack.

'He's not. He's more like a naughty schoolboy, and he's actually very kind,' said Jess.

Jackie nodded, 'That's true. He's been out here for about seven years and has an old bearer called Raju who adores him. Colin is paying to put Raju's son through medical school and he's the only white man I've ever heard of who goes to the cinema with his bearer. They don't sit together because Raju won't allow it. He sits in the cheap seats and makes Colin sit in the gallery, but then they walk home together like father and son chatting about the picture they've seen.'

'I like the sound of that. He said he was going home to Florrie and Raju, is Florrie Raju's wife?' asked Jack.

Jackie shook her head. 'No, she's Colin's mistress. On his first leave he went home to Bournemouth and proposed to a girl he met on the tennis courts there. They got married quickly and he flew back here to get their flat ready while she came out by P&O, but on the boat she met an Australian ship's officer and when they docked in Bombay she told Colin she wasn't getting off but was going on to Australia to divorce him and marry the other guy. Florrie was a tart working on Colaba Causeway and she moved in with him after his wife baled out. She never goes anywhere with him but she's always there if you're invited to his place for a drink. They're a family, the three of them – Colin, Raju and Florrie.'

Jess added, 'I was once moaning to Colin about missing British newspapers and especially the *Daily Telegraph*'s crossword puzzle. It turned out that his mother sends the weekly *Telegraph* airmail edition to him and he insists on passing it on to me. He likes the puzzle too, but he leaves it for me. He's a good bloke.'

Their conversation was interrupted by the arrival of McCallum who stood in front of them and said to Jack, 'You can't sit here with those two witches all day. You have to meet McLean, the captain of rugby. He might give you a trial for the first team before the ground gets too hard. Come on.'

When the men left, Jess turned to her friend and asked, 'Why did you look so scared when we were talking about Gossiping Gloria? What has she got on you?'

'Nothing yet, but I didn't want to think about it – I'm pregnant again.'

Jess stared at her friend's anxious face and wondered if congratulations were in order. 'I never guessed. How far gone are you?' she asked.

'Six months. I'm lucky because I never show till near the end. It's my primitive hips, you see.' Jackie sounded bitter.

'You hide it well, but why did you keep it to yourself all this time?'

'I was stupid and kept hoping it would go away. Two children are enough for me and I've had other alarms in the past but this one's hanging on. I haven't gone to check it out with Alex yet but I don't really want another baby. We're completely broke. The company won't give Peter a rise because they don't appreciate him. My cousin Tony, his boss, is a snob. Because Peter didn't go to a good school and his father's a postman in Portsmouth, Tony thinks I married beneath myself.'

'But Peter must be getting a reasonable salary. He's working for a good company,' said Jess.

'He won't ingratiate himself so raises don't come his way. And because his health's not good, he has to take time off which doesn't go down well. The worst thing is that he keeps getting into card schools hoping to make some extra money for us but it never seems to work out for him.'

'He'll have to stop gambling now that you're pregnant,' said Jess.

'I've told him and he's promised he will but somehow....' Jackie's voice trailed off.

She's always making excuses for him, thought Jess as she took her friend's hand and said, 'Listen, go to your cousin and ask him to pay some of Peter's salary into a bank account in your name. He can't gamble if he doesn't have the money.'

Jackie stared at her miserably. 'That would look as if I was treating him like a child.'

'Rubbish! You have to look after yourself and the children, especially now. Do it. Your cousin might be a snob, but I know him and he's a decent bloke at heart. Promise you'll do it.'

Jackie only nodded and stood up to go, saying, 'That's made up my mind. I'm going to find Peter now and take him home before he gambles away any more.'

'Off you go. I'll wander around and find someone else to

needle,' said Jess. The person she found was Jack who rushed back over when he spotted her sitting alone and said, 'Come and dance with me. They're playing "Let's Twist Again". I love that.'

She laughed and stepped onto the little floor saying, 'I love it too.'

They danced together for the rest of the party and she ended by enjoying herself more than she had done for months.

Jess

When she was in bed that night, she lay sleepless with her arms behind her head and staring up at the moving ceiling fan – they could not afford an air-conditioner, but Perry had one.

She was worried about Jackie because she had heard rumours that Peter's employers wanted to fire him and all that kept him in a job was the family loyalty of Jackie's cousin Tony. But even he wouldn't put up with Peter for ever. And now Jackie was pregnant again. Her other children were six and four and she found it difficult to give them everything they needed already.

Poor Jackie, she refused to accept that her beloved Peter had faults. Until she became tougher and more realistic, he wouldn't change. Jess had not known he was also a gambler and probably betted heavily or Jackie would not have talked about it so despondently.

Everybody in this place has secrets, she thought. I have them myself. Like Jackie she never talked about her deepest secrets. Even Sam did not know them all.

She'd married him because he appealed to her physically and made her laugh. He was good-looking, cheerful and easy to get along with. She thought she'd fallen in love and he said he was in love with her too.

Another reason for her marrying was because she needed to get as far away as possible from Edinburgh where she was trapped in a painful love affair that had obsessed her for two years.

The man involved was a philanderer and after much agonizing she eventually accepted he would never stop cheating on her. The trouble was that he kept coming back and she always accepted him. Eventually she decided that the only way to put a stop to it was by marrying someone else or running away as far as possible. It was like a miracle – by marrying Sam and coming to Bombay she was doing both.

But when she took her marriage vows she meant every word of them, swearing to be faithful and supportive, determined that she wouldn't let Sam down, but there was a strong strain of cynicism in her character that made her sceptical about the lasting power of romantic love. She thought poets and novelists rhapsodised too much. To her marriage was more of a legal contract than something sent from heaven.

In Edinburgh she'd worked as a reporter on a busy evening newspaper and was one of a strongly competitive group of young journalists who would almost cut each others' throats for a story but nonetheless were friends. 'You're crazy taking off for Bombay,' said her friends when she resigned, 'You should be aiming for Fleet Street.'

'Fleet Street isn't far enough,' she told them.

Her first few months in Bombay however had proved to be a miserable disappointment. When Sam went off to work in the city every morning in the car he shared with Perry, Jess was left alone in an isolated suburban bungalow where none of the servants spoke English and the only books were a few tattered American pulp novels. *Peyton Place* was the most intellectually stimulating of the selection.

Without realizing how much she needed kindred spirits, she scribbled airmail letters home describing her new life. It was a surprise when a reporter friend called Andrew wrote back saying, 'I'm worried about you. You sound miserable. Why don't you come back?'

She was genuinely shocked when she read this letter. It had

not been her intention to reveal unhappiness because, in fact, she had not realized till then that she was unhappy, but Andrew's letter made her face up to the truth and it rallied her.

If I'm discontented, it's my own fault, she told herself and after much internal debate, she decided to stay.

Her biggest problem was snobbish Perry, an ex-Haileybury public schoolboy, who took every opportunity to make her feel ill bred and unsophisticated, but after Andrew's letter arrived she started to stand up for herself and be sarcastic back. Their relationship then worsened because when she set out to be cutting, she could wound for she had a better command of words than he did.

An unfortunate discovery turned out to give her a major advantage. Every time they went to the local petrol station to fill up the car, she was surprised by the insolent behaviour of the proprietor. Most of the tradesmen they dealt with were polite but this man always spat on the ground just clear of their feet and smeared their windscreen with a dirty cloth so that it was more difficult to see through it afterwards than it had been before he started on it.

'Why do you always use that filling station? The man's so horrible,' she complained to Sam.

He shrugged as he said, 'We've always used it.'

'If I'm driving the car, I'll go to his rival. It's only a hundred yards away.'

He looked alarmed, 'Oh don't do that. We have to use him.'

'For God's sake, why?'

'Because Perry and I owe him money.'

Debt was anathema to Jess and she was shocked. 'Let's pay him off then,' she said.

'We can't. It's rather a lot.'

'How much?' Unknown to Sam she had a small sum of money hidden away. Something had told her she might need it.

'Quite a lot.'

'*How much?*'

It'll be about ten thousand chips by now. We've been running it up for over two years.'

Ten thousand rupees was well beyond her secret fund. 'Dear God! No wonder he spits at you. What are you going to do about it?' she demanded.

'There's no way that we can find that kind of money. I only earn two thousand a month.'

'And out of that you pay half the rent, half the servants' wages, two thirds of the food bill, your cigarettes and all the beer you can drink!' she said bitterly. Even by a rough reckoning, Sam's basic outgoings added up to more than two thousand rupees a month.

She was furious. Her father, who owned several hotels, was well off and the sudden suspicion hit her that, when he married her, Sam might have been hoping she would come with money behind her. What a disappointment for him when her father washed his hands of the match and told his daughter that because she was making a mistake, and disinheritance would be the result if she went through with it.

'Come home whenever you've had enough,' he told her, 'Just send me a telegram and I'll buy you an air ticket.'

Her mother backed him up. 'I don't like that man you're marrying, he has a mean mouth,' she said.

Mean mouthed! thought Jess bitterly. The petrol station owner would probably agree.

There was a thriving black market for imported items in Bombay and one of Sam's friends was an Indian dealer who was always eager to buy and sell. Swearing him to secrecy, Jess sold her portable typewriter, her 21st birthday gold and diamond watch, a gold chain necklace and her cameo ring. They raised 10,100 rupees, a fraction of their real value. She knew as she handed over her jewellery that she would never put a sentimental value on any possession again.

When she walked onto the petrol station forecourt with a wad of notes in her hand, the proprietor almost fainted with shock and actually offered her a free bottle of Pepsi Cola.

That night at dinner she produced a grubby receipt and told Sam and Perry what she had done. Then she stated her terms. 'Till Perry's share of the petrol bill is paid off, Sam and I will pay no more rent and I'll never settle any more bills for either of you. Also, I want to drive into the city once a week and have the use of the car to myself for the rest of the day so I can go wherever I want.'

Perry raised an eyebrow and asked, 'You don't happen to have any Jewish blood, do you?'

'As a matter of fact I do and I'm proud of it,' she said, 'Do I get the car?'

Perry cut into his buffalo steak and said, 'If you drive around Bombay on your own, you'll probably get your throat cut.'

'I won't be so obliging,' she snapped back.

He pretended not to hear and said, 'You shouldn't have worried about that bill. Gentlemen never pay bills on time. The petrol wallah knows that when I finally go home my company will settle any bills I've run up. Everybody out here lives like that.'

'They may, but I don't,' said Jess.

Their car was a grey, round-nosed, tank-like 1948 Studebaker, which one of the older lady members of the Gym always referred to as 'the sturdy bugger'. Driving it, Jess explored every area of the city of Bombay, unaware that she was intruding into districts where unescorted white women were never seen. She felt invulnerable.

Her best discovery was the Thieves' Bazaar, several square miles of closely packed, urine-stinking rat-infested alleys around the city's biggest mosque and she spent many hours walking up and down rubbish-strewn lanes edged by open drains, poking her nose into stalls that sold heavily carved Portuguese furniture, musical instruments, tattered paintings of long dead *sahibs* and their *memsahibs*, rusty swords, glassware, mercury mottled mirrors, Victorian decanters, and old military uniforms, including a magnificent red coat that looked as if it had been worn by an officer in Clive's Company Army.

She rarely bought anything unless it was very cheap, never more than ten rupees which was the price of a couple of chocolate bars, for the exchange rate was thirteen rupees to a pound. The stallholders ignored her because she obviously had no money, which meant that no one was tempted to rob her. In fact, she was never challenged or insulted in any way and felt completely safe in the bazaar though she was well out of shouting distance from another white face or any policemen.

Getting to know the bazaar and its people gave her a longing to explore parts of the city that were avoided by the other white women she knew. She also longed to set foot on mainland India and after her weekly drives of discovery, she stopped the car at Chowpatti Beach and got out to stare across the bay at a jagged outline of misty hills on the horizon. These were the western *ghats* and she longed to drive over them, to see what lay on the other side.

'Let's go driving off the island this weekend,' she often pleaded with Sam, but he always had an excuse, usually because there was a rugby club party to attend. He and his friends spent almost every weekend drinking in one of the two favoured hotels in central Bombay, the Ritz or the Ambassadors, or, if not in the bars, they held riotous parties in each others' flats or houses.

Though rugby was only played in the monsoon, the parties went on all the year round and Jess hated them. What annoyed her most was when the wives and girlfriends joined in the communal singing of smutty songs.

At one party she snapped when the women linked arms with the men round the piano and started singing a song about a monk having sex with a nun. *In and out, in and out, he went,* they sang and Jess banged her fist on the piano top, shouting, 'How can you sing that smut? Aren't you aware how it denigrates women? You should have some pride in yourselves.' The singing didn't stop and everyone thought she was either crazy or drunk.

'Poor old Sam has landed himself with trouble there,' male rugby club members said to each other, and their wives gossiped that Jess was very peculiar for she'd been overheard saying she was an anti-royalist! Nursing sister Gloria, who seemed to be able to pick up more news than anyone else, also suspected that Jess was a Communist because she had been seen going into a bungalow that belonged to Krishna Menon, an important local M.P. and a rabid Communist.

'What was she doing there?' Gloria asked, but could not find out because when tackled on the subject Jess denied it. Gloria then set out to find out as much as she could about Sam's wife who was definitely *Not Quite Our Sort*.

Jess's disgusted outburst at the singing of smutty songs had two results however. First it won her Jackie's friendship, and second, it made Sam realize that she was near breaking point and he agreed to drive onto the mainland with her on the following weekend.

She was thrilled. 'Where will we go?' she asked.

'I haven't any maps, but we'll just take the main road and head for Poona,' he said.

'You'll never make Poona. It's too far and the road is horrific, full of potholes,' said Perry who was listening to them.

She ignored him. 'Please let's go to Poona,' she pleaded. It was a name for her to conjure with. 'When I was in Poona' was a favourite phrase of the comedian Sam Costa whom she used to listen to on the radio at home.

She and Sam got up at three o'clock on Sunday morning and loaded the car with a cool box full of ice and some bottles of beer, as well as a pack of tomato sandwiches and fruit that Jess ordered from their cook the night before. At four o'clock, when they were about to set off, to Jess's outrage, Perry, still in his pyjamas, appeared from his bedroom and climbed into the car's back seat.

Mohammed the bearer, who was more Perry's servant than Sam's, put a pillow and a small suitcase of clothes and a plastic box of his master's medicines and phials of citronella oil to deter mosquitoes, on the seat beside him. Perry was a hypochondriac who took salt pills, iron tablets, Veganin tablets for headaches, plus vitamin pills and various draughts to combat dysentery daily. Before they could leave, he had to be covered up with a blanket and then settled down to sleep.

Jess looked at Sam and asked furiously, 'Did you say he could come with us?'

'He wanted to.'

She said nothing, only stared stonily ahead until the multi-coloured glory of an Indian sunrise over a jagged range of hills called Wellington's Nose made her cry out in sheer delight, all anger forgotten.

They made it to Poona, which was unchanged since the days of the Mutiny when the roads of the cantonment had been deliberately re-laid in long straight lines so that cannons could be fired down them to decimate any screaming mutineers coming up to kill the inhabitants of the big military bungalows set back among now overgrown gardens.

When they returned to the city it was four o'clock in the morning, and Jess's longing for India was raised to fever point, but her temper was much improved. She could even laugh to herself at the memory of Perry unpacking the picnic and shouting with rage because the cook had omitted to put in any French dressing or a proper salad.

Joan

When the telephone rang in Joan's sitting room, Yusuf glided through the kitchen door to pick it up and say importantly 'The Whitehead residence' as she had taught him.

The voice of an American woman came rasping over the wires, 'Is my daughter there?'

'Yes, madam, she is with the little girl. I will fetch her,' he said, and carefully laid down the precious instrument from which an agitated voice was still squawking.

There were few private houses in Bombay with telephones in the 1960s. Immense bribery or very influential connections were necessary before one could be installed and even then there was no guarantee that there would be a regular service. Making quick calls abroad was impossible because they had to be booked days in advance and even when you got through the line was always crackly.

Theo's company bought him a phone but they could not buy reliable service with the result that making or receiving calls from America were rare occurrences.

'Your mother is on the telephone, *memsahib*,' Yusuf said, when he went into Liza's playroom where Joan was reading her daughter a story.

'My mother!' Joan jumped to her feet in a panic, sure that some catastrophe had hit her family if her mother, who was obsessed with her high blood pressure, was risking the frustra-

47

tion of trying to make an international call to India. When she picked up the receiver, she gasped, 'Oh Mama, I'm so worried, are you all right?'

'Of course I'm all right. It's you who's the worry. I've just received your letter and felt I had to talk some sense into you. It's taken me three days to make this call, so just listen and don't interrupt.'

Joan's mother had a clear, penetrating voice and Yusuf was standing in the kitchen doorway unashamedly eavesdropping. Joan walked over and closed the door with him on the other side. 'Mother, please modulate your voice. People can hear you,' she said when she returned to the phone.

'Listen to me, Joan. Your last letter has really annoyed your father and me. You never used to be a whiner. What's got into you?'

Joan felt anger rise in her. 'I wrote you about how unhappy I am. There's no one else I can tell. I had to get it off my chest. You're my mother and I thought you'd understand.'

'What· have you got to be unhappy about? You have a wonderful way of life and plenty of money. Your daughter is a delight and your husband has a brilliant future, if you don't spoil it for him.'

'What do you mean spoil it? He's playing the field, Mother. It's so obvious that people are talking about it.'

'Joan, every attractive man worth having plays the field. According to your letter Theo's been thrown in amongst some very immoral women. Who can blame him if he succumbs? He'll get it out of his system and end up a pillar of rectitude, mark my words.'

'Mother, I feel so betrayed! I love him and thought he loved me, but now he's making a fool of me.'

'Don't be stupid. You must rise above it. Pretend you don't notice. Between you and me I have had trouble with your father in the past, but I kept my dignity and he grew tired of the women eventually.'

Joan was astonished. She remembered one elegant woman who could have been her father's mistress and knew how much her mother hated her. 'So there was more than one!' she exclaimed.

'Four at least,' said her mother bitterly.

'How could you stand it?'

'By realizing what the alternative would be. We're not the kind of people who divorce. We have standards.'

'You mean you wouldn't give up your Manhattan duplex and the house at Martha's Vineyard, the country club membership and the charge accounts, the invitations to Sotheby's private viewings, the glittering parties and the family's Sunday church attendances. Didn't it strike you that you were behaving like a whore?' said Joan bitterly.

Her mother was shocked. 'I'll forget you said that,' was her cold reply. 'But I have advice for you. Our family and Theo's family have high hopes for him and so should you. He'll almost certainly be a senator one day. He might even be President. His great grandfather was President after all. If you cause scandal and try to divorce him as you threaten to do in your letter, it could smear his name and his political career would never get off the ground. You and your daughter will be consigned to the dregs of society. Your father agrees with me and we forbid you even to think about it!'

Then the conversation was cut off, either by accident or design, leaving Joan with the receiver in her hand and a stunned look on her face. What a fool I was to imagine for one minute that my mother would sympathise with me or take my side, she thought bitterly.

She was still standing looking shocked when Liza came flying along the corridor. 'You said we could go swimming, Mummy,' she cried, and grabbed her mother round the legs almost knocking her down.

The *ayah* gently pulled Liza back and said, 'Wait, baby,

Mummy will be ready soon. Come into the kitchen and Yusuf will give you some chocolate.'

The servants spoil Liza, Joan thought. If she stays in this country much longer, she'll be out of control completely. Bloody Bombay! she said to herself. But because Liza wanted to swim, to Breach Candy they would go.

It was Saturday afternoon, the schools were closed and the baby pool was crowded, so Joan called a boy to put up an umbrella for her on the side of the big pool where she settled her possessions before plunging into the deep water with her child on her back and striking out for the floating platform in the middle of the water.

Liza loved riding on her mother's back like the boy on a dolphin, and squealed with delight all the time. She was almost able to swim herself by now and Joan coaxed her to jump off the raft into the water, and start thrashing around with her doggy paddle. When they were both tired, they made their way back to their umbrella and Joan was disappointed to see that another had been put up beside hers.

Two women in dark sunglasses and bathing suits, one red, one green, were lying on towels on the grass reading paperbacks. One of the books, she noticed, was Mary McCarthy's *The Group* that she'd read about in newspapers her mother sent out from home.

She was changing Liza into a dry pair of pants when the red-suited woman sat up and said, 'Hi, we met at the rugger revue party, didn't we?'

Joan bristled. Any reminder of that party was painful to her. 'Oh, yes, I do remember you. I was only at the party for a little while,' she said shortly.

'Very wise. They're pretty awful affairs and they end up the same way with headaches all round. I especially hate it when the women sing dirty songs with the men and that makes me look like a pursed mouth old lady. But my husband is one of the boys so I have to put up with it,' said red suit, who was called Jess something, Joan remembered.

'I wasn't there when there was any singing,' said Joan.

The woman in the green suit sat up too now. She had a towel draped around her waist and the book she was reading was *Seven Years in Tibet*.

'You got out in time then,' she said, with a sweet smile that made Joan's hostility soften.

Red suit was leaning back on her arms and grinned too as she took off her sunglasses. She had a sharp, intelligent face and strange golden coloured eyes that seemed to bore into Joan.

'Remember us? I'm Jess and this is Jackie – Jacqueline if she's being formal. We're rugby club hangers on because we love to watch the way the world wags its tail out here.' Both girls laughed and Joan's face tightened up, fearing they were getting at her about Theo's exploits.

Jess saw the American girl becoming defensive again and said in a friendly way, 'Have you been roped in to do anything in our famous revue?'

'Good heavens no. I'd be hopeless. What do you do?' asked Joan.

'We're just dogsbodies. We help the chorus line dress and put out the props. If you want to, you could come along and help us.'

Joan was surprised to hear herself saying, 'That would be fun. It wouldn't mean giving up a lot of time, would it? I spend most of the day with my daughter Liza when she's not at the nursery school.'

'Just a couple of hours at night and, like my two, Liza'll probably be asleep in bed by then,' said Jackie, 'It's good we've met up here today. Your little girl's about the same age as my Anna, I think.'

'Liza's three. Have you other children?' Joan asked, looking first at one woman and then the other.

Jackie replied, 'I've two – a boy and a girl. Anna's four and Simon's six. He's in the baby pool looking after Anna but I can keep an eye on them from here.'

'I haven't any,' said Jess shortly. She had been married for over two years and was fed up getting letters from her widowed grandchild-hungry mother-in-law asking if there was any 'news' yet. Her problem was that she could not make up her mind whether she was glad or sorry that she had not conceived though she was taking no precautions against falling pregnant. It was in the lap of the gods and the longer she lived in India the more convinced she became that the gods called the tune.

'I see you're reading *The Group*. I haven't managed to get a copy yet,' Joan said to Jess, who lifted up the book and said, 'Yes, it's great. I'm loving it. It's about women standing on their own feet – or at least trying to.'

'I'm all for that,' said Joan wishing she could act as confidently as she sounded.

'I've nearly finished it and I'll pass it on to you if you like.'

'That would be wonderful. I go to a bookshop in the city but it's rather scholarly. Popular fiction is a bit beneath them, I think. I'm looking forward to reading *The Group* because I went to Vassar.' She sounded as if she was ashamed to admit it, just as some men Jess had met were ashamed to admit to having been to Eton. It was less famous public school boys who boasted about their educational background. One of the first questions new male arrivals to Bombay were asked was 'Where did you go to school?'

'As an ex-Vassar girl, you'll love this book. You'll probably know the people in it,' Jess said to Joan and all three of them ordered Colas and sat laughing and talking for another hour while Jess shot questions at Joan – where did she live in America, what did her father do, what were her hobbies, what sort of music did she prefer, how old was she when she got married, did she believe in God, what sort of books did she like?

Under this barrage of questions, Joan opened up and when it came to talking about books, she positively flourished.

'I brought a box of books out with me from home, but they're mainly classics. I have Jane Austen, Dickens, Thackeray and lots of Trollope but every now and again I want to read other writers, like Steinbeck.'

Her voice trailed off and she looked at them apologetically as if she was afraid of being boring but Jess was sitting forward eagerly and saying, 'I'm mad about Steinbeck, especially *Cannery Row*. Last week I found a copy of it in the second hand bookshop over the road from this pool beside Bertorelli's ice cream parlour and I'll lend it to you if you lend me Trollope's *The Eustace Diamonds*. It's the only one of his Palliser books I haven't.'

'I have a copy!' cried Joan delightedly. For the first time she looked young and carefree.

'Bring it here tomorrow afternoon and we'll do a swap,' said Jess.

When Joan took Liza away soon afterwards, Jackie looked at Jess and grinned. 'Well, your constant questioning seems to have pulled it off again. I bet she told us more about herself this afternoon than she's told anyone in one sitting for her entire life.'

'Unless she's been to a shrink,' said Jess, 'And I'm not sure that she doesn't need one.'

Back in her flat, the sight of the white telephone brooding on its little table beside the sofa reminded Joan of the conversation with her mother, but she knew there was nothing to be done. She had to conform and turn a blind eye to Theo's behaviour. Perhaps her mother was right, he was only getting it out of his system. She had made her bargain and must stick to it but she wasn't going to give him *carte blanche* to do as he pleased.

When he came in that evening, she said, 'I'd like to help with the rugby revue, darling. I made two friends at the swimming pool this afternoon and they've offered to let me help out with dressing the dancers and putting out props. I'm going to do it.'

It wasn't a request, it was a statement.

The trouble was that there was not a lot of dressing nor prop procuring to do in the early stages of rehearsal and Joan spent the next few evenings listening from the veranda while the acts inside the big hall were dragooned by the director, an effete gentleman with an impeccable accent and a disdainful attitude. His name was Tom Shackleton and he claimed a distant relationship with the explorer, but, as Donald the pianist said, the only exploring this Shackleton had ever done was cottaging in public lavatories in London's West End.

Donald and Shackleton hated each other and Shackleton also hated women. If he could have mounted a show without a single woman in it, he would have been happy. Donald, on the other hand, only took part so that he could pick off the best and most complaisant women in the cast, and the selecting of the chorus line was up to him.

When the cast and the hangers on held their regular parties, Shackleton never attended. He was a surgeon in private practice who'd started working in Bombay the year before the war and stayed on after British rule ended. He lived off Colaba Causeway in a beautiful walled bungalow with an immense garden where it was said he had a collection of snakes, particularly pythons which he loved. Exactly what type of surgery he specialized in was not generally known because he looked down his nose at Breach Candy Hospital and worked in a special private section of the vast J.J. Hospital, the layout of which had been designed by Florence Nightingale. His fees were rumoured to be astronomical and none of the rugby crowd knew anyone who had ever consulted him, far less been cut into by him.

His only known friends were a couple called Meadows, a solemn-faced banker in his forties and his sallow-skinned wife

Daphne who claimed to be Greek though some of the Anglo Indian girls who attached themselves to members of the rugby team insisted that she was Anglo Indian like them and had even been at school with their mothers.

She was not as beautiful as most Eurasian girls, but made up for it by being intimidatingly intelligent and ambitious. Not only had she managed to snare a British husband, and persuaded his employers in the bank to swallow the story of her Greek background (otherwise he would have been sent home rather than allowed to marry a chi-chi as the other expatriates called Eurasians) but she was an unashamed flatterer of important people, especially Shackleton who made her his second in command when directing the revues.

He was totally stage struck and went home every winter to collect ideas and sheet music for his next production. Even people who disliked him intensely had to admit he always turned out a magnificent show, as good as revues in London's West End. Working with unpromising material, he could turn out stars.

Listening to the thump, thump, thump of dancing feet and the repeated singing of one song till the chorus got it right – which seemed to be never – Joan soon grew bored and stopped accompanying Theo every night.

'How long is this rehearsing going on?' she asked him eventually.

'People say about seven weeks. Shackleton's a stickler. You needn't come every time there's a rehearsal because back stage helpers aren't needed till the last week or ten days. The show is staged in early December, just before people's children come back from their boarding-schools for the Christmas holidays,' he told her.

She laughed. 'By that time you'll all be able to apply for Equity cards, but it seems unfair to stage a show when the children can't see it.'

He grinned. 'There's a reason for that. Wait till you hear the script.'

Though she stopped attending every rehearsal, Joan still forced herself to go to the parties, which were more bearable now that she was friendly with Jess and Jackie.

Almost overnight it seemed that Jackie began to show her pregnancy and, as her stomach bulged, her complexion glowed and she radiated a kind of inner happiness that affected people who came within her orbit.

'You've obviously overcome your reservations about having another baby because you look wonderful,' Jess told her.

'When it started to move, I began to love it and I do feel wonderful now. I've always felt well when I've been pregnant and I've stopped worrying about money and stuff like that. Things will work out because Peter has met a new man who's come out to join one of the big trading companies and he's renting part of our flat. You know how huge it is – five bedrooms and five bath-rooms. We're giving him two big rooms and his own bathroom so he has a kind of flat inside a flat and he's paying us a good rent.'

'Do you have to feed him?' Jess asked doubtfully. The food provided by Jackie was always peculiar. One favourite lunchtime dish was a jelly made of pureed tomatoes which was frankly disgusting.

'No, he has his own cook and bearer. It seems to be working very well and I suspect that my cook is giving us leftover food the lodger's cook is making. It's very tasty.'

'What's the lodger's name?' asked Jess.

'Daniel Sullivan. He's related to some earl or other and went to Eton. That's the only thing about him that Peter doesn't like. It offends his socialist principles.'

But it won't stop him taking the guy's money, thought Jess cynically.

'I'm glad things are easier for you. Did you talk to your cousin about paying part of Peter's salary direct to your account?' Jess asked, and to her surprise Jackie nodded, 'Yes, I did and he thinks it's a good idea. In fact, he gave Peter a rise without telling him and is paying the extra money to me.'

'That cousin of yours is a good bloke,' said Jess wholeheartedly.

At that moment Joan arrived to join them, nodded at Jackie's burgeoning belly and said, 'I'm sure I saw it jump just now. You must be quite far on.'

'Yes, I am. I closed my eyes to it for ages, but now I'm very pleased and looking forward to it being born.'

'Aren't you scared of the delivery?' asked Jess, who shied away from pain. She did not even like having an injection.

'Oh no. I'm lucky. Both my other babies came quickly. I have the right kind of pelvis apparently.'

'And you start to forget the pain as soon as your baby's in your arms,' agreed Joan.

'In that case Gloria the Gossip won't be able to dine out on your agonies,' said Jess. As she spoke she was suddenly filled with a peculiar longing to share this secret that her friends knew. She wanted to join the community of mothers, to experience the sensation of a baby turning inside her. What on earth is happening to me? she asked herself in alarm.

The disquieting longing persisted and two days later she took herself along to Alex's surgery and said to him, 'I'm wondering if there's something wrong with me, Alex.'

He leaned back in his chair and eyed her critically. 'You look all right. A bit pale, but most people are after the monsoon. I don't think you're a heavy drinker, are you?'

'I don't drink at all. Sam uses up both our alcohol allowances.'

'Do you smoke?'

'We can't afford for both of us to smoke either and I gave up because I never inhaled anyway.'

'So what do you think is wrong with you?' he wanted to know.

'I've been married two years, we have sex regularly and I don't get pregnant.'

'Are you worried about that?'

'Not really. It's only just struck me recently that I might like to have a baby.'

He frowned and asked, 'Can you afford one?'

She shook her head. 'Not really. Sam's company is Indian owned and they won't pay medical bills for me, only for him. In fact, they were thinking of firing him but when he got married they decided to give him a second chance because they thought marriage would sober him up. The Indian owner and his wife came to visit us at our bungalow a little while ago – to have a look at me I suspect – and the wife told me about them wanting to fire Sam. Apparently they had his horoscope cast and it said that he would be lucky for them in the end so they decided to give him six months to pull himself together or he'll be out. They're very pleased that he's working much harder now and not taking as much time off as he used to. In fact he's just got a contract for work at one of the American oil refineries so he's the blue-eyed boy, but that hasn't brought us any more money yet,' she told him.

She knew that when Sam had graduated with a degree in mechanical engineering he'd answered an advertisement from a small Bombay engineering company that specialized in piping work. The only other European employed was the managing director, a Dutchman who had been a Nazi sympathizer during the war and hated the British. He would not have protested if Sam was fired, but was taking a different attitude now that the order book was looking different because two giant American oil companies were planning expansions on Trombay Island.

'Having a baby out here will cost you at least two thousand chips even if there are no complications,' Alex warned her.

'I could find two thousand chips but I must admit I don't

particularly want to,' said Jess, thinking how much she'd have to grovel to get the money out of her father.

Alex said, 'Perhaps you should think about it a bit more then. In the meantime, because you're a bit peaky, I'll prescribe you a course of vitamin B injections. They won't cost much. In fact I'll put them down as being prescribed for Sam. His company will pay that, won't they?'

She nodded and said, 'Thanks Alex.' His kind heart and cool capability made him one of the people she liked best in the rugby crowd because, though he drank as much if not more than the other men, he never seemed to become totally incapable. Several times she had seen him snap into awesome efficiency when there were accidents or injuries. Once when the horrible McCallum went for Bill Lambert with a broken bottle and slashed an artery in his wrist, Alex instantly changed from being a semi-comatose drunk to a miracle worker. He staunched the bleeding, stitched the wound with a darning needle and saved Lambert's life though he was to have a slightly crippled hand forever. Alex also kept the information of the attack from the police which was more than McCallum deserved.

'What will vitamin B do for me?' she asked. She hated injections.

'Perk you up mainly; you do look a bit anaemic. Has it occurred to you that you're not ready to have a baby yet? Sometimes children are conceived in the mind before they are conceived in the body, you know.'

She shied away from him, pushing herself as far back as she could in the chair before his desk. In fact she was ambivalent about having a baby and almost resented the trick she felt her mind was trying to play on her body.

Alex scribbled a note for the injections and passed it over to her. 'OK, start the jags tomorrow if you still want them,' he said, and stared at her in a contemplative way, all the while thinking, What an odd girl you are. He'd already noticed her peculiarly ironic sense of humour because things that left most people cold seemed to make her laugh.

He remembered that a *sadhu* recently had himself buried in a pit dug in the sand of Chowpatti Beach to prove that he could survive underground for a week by controlling his mind. Bombay's English language evening newspaper ran front-page stories about him every day – HOLY MAN IN THIRD DAY OF ORDEAL – *SADHU* IN FIFTH DAY OF ORDEAL – *SADHU* TO EMERGE TOMORROW! – it trumpeted. On the seventh day the *sadhu* was dug up and he was stone dead. Apparently he'd been dead for days.

Alex remembered Jess reading the newspaper story aloud while sitting in the Ritz Bar and laughing fit to burst. He'd walked over to her and said, 'Jess, I'm very worried about your state of mind.' For some reason that made her laugh even more.

'Do you remember that *sadhu* who died in the sand pit a couple of weeks ago?' he asked her suddenly.

She stared at him, obviously surprised. 'Yes, what about him?'

'My mother wrote to tell me that a British newspaper ran a story about him. She thought it very bad form. It was as if they have nothing better to write about, she said.'

Jess stared back at him. 'Who ran the story?' she asked.

'According to my mother some paper that working-class chaps read. I don't know how she found out. Probably from her daily,' he said.

'Imagine!' said Jess sarcastically, and hurriedly rose to leave. In fact she wanted to laugh as she remembered that Alex had been to school with Perry at Haileybury – working class chaps' newspapers indeed! But, as she left the hospital, she wondered if Alex was a mind reader. What made him think of the story? What did he suspect? She wished she could have told him not to worry about putting the injections on Sam's bill. If her story had appeared in print, a dead *sadhu* would pay for her vitamin B.

*

Sam was ebullient when they met up in the Gym that evening. 'I've just been introduced to a great bloke who's been sent over from Texas to help with the planning of one of the new refineries. We got on really well and I've invited him to dinner,' he told Jess.

'What's he like?' she asked.

'Unusual. One of the other guys on the installation told me he has a medal, a Purple Heart or something, for smuggling guns up the coast to Naga tribesmen in Burma during the war. He did it under the nose of the Japanese when he was only a kid apparently.'

'When's he coming to dinner with us? What will we give him to eat?' Jess worried because she wanted Sam to make a good impression on such an important man.

'I've asked him for Friday, the day after tomorrow,' was the reply, and she groaned. It usually took their kitchen days to prepare for dinner parties. She'd better get fit, so next morning she steeled herself to go for her first vitamin B injection and to her surprise it seemed to give her such an immediate boost that she was able to contemplate the dinner with confidence. When she told Mohammed that an important business contact would be eating with them, he beamed because he loved occasions. On special nights he always looked immaculate in a long jacketed suit that was whiter than white and a carefully tied turban. When he chose, he could out Jeeves Jeeves at his most deferential.

'Tell the cook I'd like an *interesting* menu. This dinner is important for my husband's career,' Jess told him.

'The cook will do his best,' said Mohammed.

His best was not what Jess wanted however. 'Perhaps he could make a cream soup? And what about a fish course?' she suggested. She was still slightly intimidated by the servants who made it obvious that they knew more about running the house than she did.

'I'll tell the cook and it will be a good dinner,' Mohammed reassured her.

On Friday night, to her relief, Perry was dining with friends in town, so she and Sam waited alone on their veranda till a large glittering American car, of a much more recent vintage than their Studebaker, drove into the compound. Sam rushed off to greet his visitor and when she heard their voices coming round the corner of the house, she wondered what this important client would be like. Probably a sharply suited, well groomed executive like Joan's Theo, she guessed.

From the darkness of the lawn, two figures climbed onto the veranda and the visitor was revealed. He was not as tall as Sam and more stocky, as well as being almost twenty years older. He was probably in his forties. In the flickering lamplight she saw that his hair was fair and a tuft of it stuck up at the back like the hair of Oor Wullie, a popular cartoon character in the Scottish *Sunday Post*.

Unlike Sam and most European men who went out to dine in Bombay, their visitor was not wearing a white dinner jacket and a black tie but a plain grey suit with the jacket slung over one shoulder. His tie was tied squint and his trousers held up by a battered looking leather belt. This can't be a director of one of the world's biggest oil companies. Sam must have made a mistake, she thought.

Unaware of her surprise, he walked across to her chair and bent down to shake her hand. The moment she looked up into his face she felt as if she had been hit in the stomach. The pain was real and shocking, like a bolt of electricity. The strange thing was that he must have felt it too because he seemed to freeze with his hand held out for hers.

She was the first to recover. 'Hello, I'm Jess,' she said, and laid her hand in his. 'Erik Hansen,' he said, but words and names seemed unnecessary. He was not a handsome man, the way Sam was handsome and sexy-looking, but somehow everything about him pleased her and it was as if they had known each other for ever. Now I understand the meaning of *coup de foudre*, she thought.

Next morning all she could remember was how she'd sat silent, not asking questions for once, and listened to him talking about his work. He told them he'd started in the oil business working with a legendary man called Red Adair who was famous for his daring at fighting oil blazes.

'I learned a lot from him, but I'm not in his league. I'm more of a prevention man than a trouble shooter. When we build the new refinery, my job is to make sure there are as few hazards as possible in the installation. You and I will have to collaborate on that,' he said to Sam.

He never mentioned any medals but talked about his love for Nagaland where he'd lived on the run for three years. 'I hope that when I die I'll wake up in a village there with cocks crowing and smoke rising from the cooking fires,' he said.

She was so stunned by how she felt about him that she forgot to reprimand Mohammed and the cook for ignoring her instructions to serve cream soup and fish. As usual they'd eaten mutton and rice pudding.

When Alex saw her in the clinic a few days later, he smiled and said, 'Those jags must be doing you good already. You look completely different.'

I wonder if I look different because for the first time in my life I've fallen in love? she thought.

Joan

On his way to play the piano for the revue rehearsal, Donald spied the oddly attractive American girl sitting alone on the Gym veranda waiting for her husband. He paused by her table and said on impulse, 'I'm sure you can play the piano.'

She looked up in surprise. 'As a matter of fact I can, but I'm rather rusty. We have no piano in our flat at the moment.'

'Come into the hall with me now and have a go on the grand. It's a good piano.'

'I don't know any popular tunes.'

'You can read music, can't you?'

'Yes but—'

'I know. You passed all your exams playing Schumann and Chopin. So did I but people don't gather round at a party when you play *etudes*. Come in and have a try. I'm sure you can do it.'

Intrigued, she followed him and he pushed along the piano stool for her to sit on while he himself pulled up a wooden chair. 'Play me something,' he said.

It was a fine piano and she looked at the keys with yearning rising in her. She laid her hands on the keyboard and then shook her head. 'I don't remember anything,' she said.

'What about the Brahms Lullaby? Every piano student knows that.'

Brahms's Lullaby. *Guten Abend, gute Nacht* ... she used to play it to Liza at home in New York. The music ran through her head and seemed to trickle down into her fingertips. Tentatively she struck a note that sounded true. Then she struck it again and her hands moved involuntarily. Music flowed out of her and she was lost in the delight. Before she finished the piece, he leaned over and started to play a backing theme to it, then as soon as they finished, he teasingly launched into 'Tiger Rag'. The music echoed and re-echoed round the hall till people came running in from all directions with smiles on their faces.

'Well done. You have music in you. I knew I was right. Will you play "Tiger Rag" with me as a duet?' he asked her.

'No, I can't,' she said.

'Yes, you can. I have the music here. It's easy. Let yourself go and play. Like this!'

'I don't know if I can let myself go,' said Joan honestly, but she moved down the stool and soon they were playing together.

'I knew you could do it! I need another pianist and I hereby appoint you as my deputy,' he exulted.

'But I don't know your programme.'

'You'll pick it up. I'll give you the sheet music. Rent a piano from the furniture emporium in the docks to practise on and come along tomorrow night to the rehearsal. You have a job, Mrs Ridgeway.' From the corner of his eye he saw Ginny and her friend giggling. They thought he was launching himself into a seduction.

On the following afternoon when she met her friends Jess and Jackie at the pool, Joan told them about getting a piano and being enlisted to help with the music. They were delighted because they knew that she badly needed diversion.

'Just watch out for Donald,' warned Jess darkly. 'He's a terrible trophy hunter. Unattainable women appeal to him.'

Her tone was acid and both of the others looked at her sharply. She had been acting oddly recently, very distracted. Jackie remembered what her friend had said about wanting to have a baby and hoped she was not worrying about being infertile.

Joan was unworried by the warning against Donald however. 'I'm not likely to succumb to him,' she said.

'That's fine, just beware. He can be a real charmer when he chooses and charmers are dangerous,' said Jess, staring bleakly across the water of the little pool where the children were playing. She was hopelessly in love with Erik Hansen and though there was nothing of the Donald type charmer about him, she was beginning to wish they'd never met because there was no certainty she'd ever see him again.

She was wrong to doubt. On the following Sunday he returned with a full sack of oysters for lunch. Normally cautious about eating Bombay oysters, Jess found herself swallowing them down as he opened them: her trust in him was so complete.

Jess

As she sat at the edge of the swimming pool with her friends, pretending to listen to what they were talking about, Jess was startled out of her reverie by the sight of Ginny running towards them in such a way that it was obvious she was the bearer of important news. As soon as she reached them she began gasping,' Have you heard? Isn't it terrible?'

Jackie looked startled and asked, 'Heard what?'

'About Gerald Savage. He's been killed in a car crash in Hong Kong.' And without saying any more Ginny was off again towards another group of people.

Jackie was shocked. 'That's awful. He's a good friend of my cousin. They were at school together,' she said.

'Where?' asked Jess, who snapped into awareness.

'She said Hong King, didn't she?'

'I mean where did he go to school.'

'Does that matter? It was Winchester as a matter of fact.'

'How old was he?'

'The same age as Tony, my cousin. Forty-six. For goodness' sake, Jess, the poor man's dead....'

Jess was pulling on her shirt and wrapping a sarong round her waist, 'Sorry, but I have to go. I've just remembered something I said I'd buy in the city for Sam and it completely went out of my mind.'

The others looked astonished. 'You're leaving now?'

'Like I said, I forgot. It's some medicine he needs.'

'From the city?'

'Ayurvedic medicine.'

'What?'

But Jess was already running away and only turned her head to say over her shoulder, 'Sorry but I can't explain. I'll tell you tomorrow. Bye.' And she was off, leaving her friends bemused. On her way out of the pool she was waylaid again by Ginny who was brimming with more information and needed to share it.

'It happened yesterday. Gerald was in Hong Kong for some big business deal. He was being driven to the airport when his car crashed and he was killed outright apparently. The news has just come through and Lilias is devastated – devastated. The company is flying her out there for his cremation. She'll be a very rich widow, you know.'

'That's awful,' said Jess, but all she felt was pure excitement.

Back by the pool Joan said to Jackie, 'Who was Ginny talking about?'

'You'll have seen Savage's wife Lilias at some of the rugger parties but not Gerald – he never went to them but she's very much a party girl. She's in the revue too. Very dressy, very dashing, but a bit bosomy and barmaidy. People say she was a dancer at the Windmill when he first saw her and she still does the most spectacular high kicks.'

'But who is he?'

'The boss of British Oil! The biggest British oil company. Your Theo will know him. He is – was – a *very* important man and nice too. Quiet and cultured. Everybody thought he was a confirmed bachelor till he came back from one of his leaves married to Lilias and it caused astonishment because they seem to have nothing in common. I'm really sorry to hear he's been killed.'

She didn't say anything to Joan, but she was also astonished by Jess's strange behaviour. As far as she knew Jess had no connection with either of the Savages. She would have been even more surprised if she had seen what Jess was doing at that moment.

Bombay's main telegraph office was an immense Victorian building with two tall crenulated towers overlooking Flora Fountain where every evening turbaned men in *dhotis* led little children round and round the slowly trickling fountain on docile ponies.

The cable room was on the ground floor of the telegraph office and it was the domain of a khaki-clad, gap-toothed, skinny fellow called Babu who liked his job because he usually had the place entirely to himself and, when he felt sufficiently energetic he would go round idly dusting the eight rickety typewriters, most of which had several keys missing.

The only disruption to his untaxing routine was when that white woman came rushing in demanding paper and a typewriter ribbon without holes in it. Then she'd hammer out lines of words and demand he send them off to London at once – AT ONCE, she always repeated.

It was his job to transcribe her messages onto the telegraph machine and at first he took his time, but Jess had learned the art of bribery from her father whose by-word was 'every man has his price'. She gave Babu a hundred rupee note which she could ill afford and dangled the hope of more over his head by saying, 'My head office will let me know when this message reaches them. If it's quick, I'll see that you're rewarded.'

The judicious distribution of money made him her ally and he took as much pleasure as she did when she told him one of their despatches had actually appeared in the newspaper for which she worked as a stringer.

The paper was the *Daily Herald*, an old established, Labour-supporting publication, and she never saw her stories herself because though the British Council and the British High Commission both received airmailed copies of *The Times*, the *Daily Herald* was beneath their notice.

However, her friend Andrew had found himself a position on the paper's London news desk and it was he who suggested to the foreign editor that they needed a freelance representative in Bombay and his ex-colleague would be ideal for the job. Andrew wrote her a letter every now and again listing which of her pieces appeared in print so she knew what to claim for.

A stringer's position carried no fixed salary, but she was paid good freelance rates for anything the paper used and she could also claim expenses. She was given an official press card and, wonder of wonders, a telephone was installed in her bungalow – that was the biggest perk of all. When other Europeans heard that Sam and Perry had acquired a phone they assumed that Perry's father had arranged it for him because he was managing director of a big paint firm in Calcutta and had lots of contacts.

It never crossed their minds that the phone was Jess's and she did not put them right because it suited her that no one should know she wrote for the press. The *Herald* never printed her by-line: it was easier to find things out and say what she liked if she was anonymous. That was why she was troubled by the fear that Alex seemed to suspect she had something to do with the *sadhu* story.

Most of her communication with head office was by cable, but when the foreign editor gave her the job he sent her a note that said, 'Remember I don't want to hear if ten thousand Indians die in a flood, but if there's one Englishman among them, I need the story.' She grimaced with distaste when she read it for she was rapidly developing a genuine love for India and the Indians, but the man who paid the money called the tune and mostly she did as she was told. It was a victory to hear they'd used the story about the dead *sadhu*.

Another problem was that the foreign editor had no conception of the size of India or the problems of getting around the subcontinent. One night she received a cable from him saying that an Indian rajah from an obscure state in the middle of Bihar had died of a heart attack in London's Savoy Hotel and she should 'pop up there' and find out how the locals felt about his demise.

Jess knew a retired police inspector involved with the rugby team who had served in Bihar so she phoned him up to ask what sort of funeral obsequies would be practised, wrote it down, cabled it off via Babu and the story appeared, making it seem that she'd been present at the mourning ceremonies. She abstained from charging expenses for that one however.

When she discovered the depths of debt that Sam was in, her ingrained caution made her keep the full details of her lucrative connection to herself. Occasional cables came to her from London, and Sam accepted she still corresponded with old newspaper friends and occasionally sent information back to them, but he did not know how much she sent or what she was being paid for it. She opened a London bank account with the British Linen Bank into which her money was paid.

At her request, the bank only communicated with her once a year and she intended to take out as little as possible. Sometimes she wondered why she was taking so many precautions but in her secret heart she knew that the account could be her running home fund, though she hoped she would never have to use it.

When she rushed into the cable office to send off the news of Gerald Savage's death, she feared that Reuters would have the story first but she might be lucky and get it to the *Herald* before the agencies. After all, Lilias would have to be informed before the news was officially released.

'Hurry up, hurry up,' she urged Babu, hopping from foot to foot as he painstakingly transcribed her hastily typed words.

When he got slower, she delved into her pocket and produced a ten chip note, waving it above his head. It was all she had on her, but it worked and the cable was sent off in record time. She'd kept it short and succinct – giving Savage's position, name, age, education, marital state and childlessness, and circumstances of death. If they wanted more they'd get it from the agencies.

'Poor man, are you not going to say you are sorry for this poor fellow?' asked Babu as he read her words.

She looked at him in surprise. 'I'm a journalist, Babu. It's not my place to say I'm sorry for him.'

Out on the pavement a few moments later she realized she'd given away most of the money she had on her. How was she to get home? Pali Hill where they lived was miles away in the suburbs and a taxi there cost twelve chips. The best she could do was walk to the Gym and ask the manager of the shop to ring Sam at his office in Hornby Road hoping he could pick her up.

City centre offices were already disgorging their hoards of workers and though it was not far to the Gym the sight of a white woman making her way through the crowds caused surprise. The afternoon was hot, Jess's feet hurt and her flimsy sarong clung to her. Her hair was wet with sweat and stuck in tendrils on her cheeks. 'Bloody hell,' she muttered as she started to hurry along with her head down so as not to catch anyone's eye.

That was when she jumped and gave a little scream as a hand was placed on her shoulder and a voice said, 'I saw you when I was taking the air beside the Fountain. It's nice there in the evening. Where are you going?'

It was Jack, the young fellow who'd accompanied Marcia to the revue party.

'To the Gym. I've lost my money and can't pay for a taxi home.'

'I saw you coming out of that big office over there. What is it?'

'A sort of post office.'

'Not like our nice little post offices at home, is it?' he said with a laugh, looking up at the twin towers towering towards the sky.

'Not really,' she agreed.

'My car is parked here. I'll take you to the Gym. Is your husband waiting there for you?'

'I'm hoping to phone and catch him before he leaves his office. He and Perry have our car you see. They share it.'

'It's well after five,' he said looking at his watch.

'Oh God,' she groaned, 'He'll be furious if they get back to our bungalow and he has to come back into the city and pick me up.'

'I'll give you the money for a taxi,' he said, 'but I'd rather drive you home. I've nothing else to do and I like driving round Bombay. Where do you live?'

'It's miles away – about ten miles in fact.'

'Great. I haven't seen the suburbs yet and it's a nice night. Come on, let me take you home. I've nothing else to do except listen to McCallum talking about his love life. You can give me a beer when we get there,' he said.

'It's very kind of you. We might even manage to give you supper,' she said with a laugh and walked with him to his car.

Jackie

Jess can be very strange sometimes, thought Jackie. Recently she'd been behaving as if she was not in her right mind, and now she'd rushed off without any explanation when she heard about Gerald Savage's death. Like Jackie herself, Jess probably only knew Savage by sight though she was better acquainted with his wife who could be seen holding court with her bridge playing cronies in the Gym almost every day.

After Jess went off in such a hurry, Joan's Liza started to grizzle and her mother decided to take her home, so Jackie and her children were left alone at the pool. Everyone she knew seemed to have disappeared and she had visions of them rushing to each other's flats to discuss the latest news. Savage was arguably *the* most important British businessman in Bombay and speculation about his successor would be rife.

Though Peter was not due to be home for at least two more hours because he'd gone to play tennis, she decided to gather up their things and leave too. The doorman fetched a taxi and within twenty minutes she was drawing up outside her home.

The Inneses occupied the first floor of a big sea-facing house on Cuffe Parade that ran parallel with Colaba Causeway, which was not a very salubrious area nowadays though fifty years ago it had been a very smart address and their house would have been occupied by an English box-wallah, probably boss of a jute mill at the other, less salubrious, end of the island.

Now an Indian dentist had his consulting rooms on the ground floor and Jackie's family lived above him. Fortunately they had private use of the garden and it was full of the sort of plants she remembered from the army bungalows of her childhood – spikes of purple, yellow and white canna lilies, huge scarlet poinsettias like the illustrations on American Christmas cards, arching branches of purple and white bougainvillea, and a frangipani tree with its heavily scented cream flowers sprouting straight out of the bark of bare twigs. The flowers filled the air with a heavy sweet fragrance and she remembered her least favourite *ayah* telling her that you always knew if English people had planted a bungalow garden when there was a frangipani tree in the middle of the lawn.

'Indian peoples do not like it. They think it brings bad luck,' the *ayah* said.

The frangipani in her Cuffe Parade garden was very vigorous and stood at least ten feet tall and Peter liked its smell so Jackie put the disquieting condemnation of it out of her mind. Probably only anti-British prejudice, she thought.

From the garden gate she looked up at the long wooden-railed balcony that ran the length of her drawing room and saw to her surprise that two young and disreputable-looking Indian men were lolling over the rail jeering at people taking their late afternoon walks on the parade below. When they saw her, they stepped back quickly into the shadows, and as Prabu, her bearer, let her in to the house, she asked him, 'Who are those men on my balcony?'

He rolled his eyes in the way that she, Indian born, knew was the invariable accompaniment to the telling of a lie, 'What men, madam?' he asked innocently.

She walked past him straight into her big drawing room, but it and the balcony were empty.

'There were two men here when I got out of my taxi,' she snapped.

'No, madam, no men,' he insisted and she could tell that he was scared for some reason. He was a skinny shrimp of a fellow whose white uniform was threadbare and slightly grubby. She recalled the stately bearers who had served her parents when she was growing up. They were always immaculate and bore themselves like giants whereas Prabu scuttled around like a crab. Indian servants were tremendous snobs and the most important people got the best staff. She and Peter were so far down the pecking order they were stuck with shambolic Prabu.

'Is my husband home yet?' she asked next and he shook his head as she knew he would but volunteered, 'Sullivan *sahib* is here.'

'Get the *ayah* to take the children and please invite Mr Sullivan to have a cup of tea with me in half an hour.' The sun had not yet fallen below the yardarm so she would not have to offer her new lodger an alcoholic drink, which they could ill afford.

She was sitting in front of the tea tray when he walked into the room. He was about twenty-six years old, tall, languid and totally composed, with a lock of butter-coloured fair hair drooping over his right eye. In spite of his good manners and pukka accent, there was something disconcertingly louche about him. Jackie had met young subalterns of his type and was well able to manage the situation, acting the polite hostess as she poured tea from a silver teapot, and dropped sugar cubes into thin china cups with silver tongs while thanking God for traditional wedding presents.

'I'm Peter's wife. We haven't had a proper conversation yet. I'm sorry I can't rise to cucumber sandwiches at such short notice, but I came home early this evening and thought I'd find out how you're settling in. Is everything to your satisfaction?' she asked.

'Absolutely, I'm extremely comfortable,' he said, crossing one long leg over the other.

'That's good.' She passed him a plate of biscuits and he

accepted a piece of crumbling shortbread. She then took a leaf out of Jess's book and decided to start asking him questions. Which part of Ireland was he from, she wanted to know.

'None really. My Irish connections are only through family. I live in London and so do my parents.'

'Will you be staying long in Bombay?' she asked next.

'Not very long, I'm afraid. I work for the old John Company, now under a different name of course. When I've done about a year here, they'll send me on to Hong Kong, I hope.'

She knew that the John Company was the insider's name for the original East India Company that had been disbanded after the Mutiny in the 1850s. 'Many of my family were associated with John Company. Do you have family connections with it too?' she asked, putting them on a basis of talking the same language.

'One of my ancestors was on the board of directors in the 1760s,' he told her.

'So was one of mine! They probably knew each other. Was your ancestor's name Sullivan?' she asked.

'No, it was Roberts,' he said.

'Mine was Andrew James,' she told him. He leaned back in his chair and looked at her more closely. Her voice was cultured and her manners impeccable. He could see she was from the right box, but he wondered what she was doing married to that prole Peter who tried to put on a correct accent but only succeeded in sounding semi–strangled. He knew that he could condescend to Peter but would never dare to do that to his wife who was obviously a lady. In fact, in a way, she reminded him of his mother though she was about the same age as he was himself.

'You've only been living here for a few days and I want you to feel completely at home, but please ask your servants not to come into our part of the house or bring their friends into my sitting room when I'm out,' she said sweetly, putting down her teacup.

He was obviously taken aback. 'I wasn't aware that they did.'

'It might have been a mistake, but when I was coming in tonight there were two young men who looked like servants on my veranda and I have never seen them before.' She was accusing no one, making no protests, merely stating a fact.

'I'm sorry. It will not happen again,' he said and, as his cup of tea was finished, he made his escape.

When Peter arrived home in the evening, complaining as he always did of utter exhaustion and his superiors in the office as well as his opponents on the tennis court, she listened till he'd had his say and then told him, 'I took tea with our new lodger tonight. He seems very gentlemanly.'

'Eton,' said Peter, as if scoffing, but she knew he was impressed nonetheless.

'So I believe. I told him that his servants or their friends must not encroach into our part of the house.'

'Was that necessary? You don't want to start out being the heavy landlady with him surely. After all he's paying us two thousand chips a month for his rooms.'

'I wasn't in the least heavy. We got on well actually. I only told him that his servants must stay in their own part of the house. When I came back from Breach Candy tonight there were two men who looked like *goondas* out there.'

She gestured at the long wooden balcony that ran past their open drawing room windows. It was bliss sitting out in the evening when the breeze came in from the sea.

Her husband looked blankly at her. '*Goondas*?' he asked uncomprehendingly. She laughed. Sometimes she used Hindi words that she'd known from childhood without realizing that Peter did not understand what she was saying.

'*Goondas* are ruffians. Gangsters or bandits. Not the sort of people you'd want in your house when you're out.'

'What did he say?'

'He said he'd make sure it doesn't happen again – I think. I asked Prabu and he rolled his eyes and said he knew nothing about it. They probably had him scared out of his skin.'

'Anyway you dealt with it,' said Peter, as if he'd lost interest in the mystery.

Jess

Jack's car was a nippy locally produced little Fiat and, to Jess's relief, he proved to be a good driver. When she married Sam he did not have a British driving licence and had never sat a test but Indian licences were handed out if you filled out an application form and gave the clerk enough bribe money. Sam learned on the road so to speak.

Perry had a proper licence, but she hated driving with him because he was fond of driving close behind cars full of Indian families and scaring the wits out of them by hitting their boots with the formidable bumpers of the massive Studebaker. Jess noticed that Perry never tried the bumper trick on Sikh taxi drivers who were capable of rushing at him with a knife.

She and Jack drove in a companionable leisurely way through Worli and the outer suburbs, making a long detour to coconut palm-fringed Juhu beach where cream waves curled over golden sands. As they talked, she found she liked him very much because he reminded her of the happy friendships she'd enjoyed with some of the male reporters, particularly Andrew, in the newspaper office.

They talked about their families in a general way, and she desisted from quizzing him too much. 'What brought you out here?' she asked however.

'I wanted to see the world. A job came up in Bombay and I

went for it though my father felt it would have been more sensible to stay at home and work my way up to head office.'

She laughed, 'I bet you make head office anyway.'

'I hope so. I'm pretty ambitious. But this place is a surprise. My boss, Goddard, is a queer old stick. When he introduced himself to me all he did was warn me against British women. He seems to think they're all nymphomaniacs,' said Jack.

'I know him. He lives next door to Duncan and Marcia so no wonder he thinks that. But there's an exception to every rule.'

He slid a glance sideways at her and knew what she was telling him. He wished he could say to her, *It's OK. I think you're terrific and I'm not a woman hunter*.

When they reached the Pali Hill bungalow, he was surprised to see lights shining in the trees and hear Louis Armstrong music blaring from a loudspeaker relay system in the garden. 'It looks as if you're having a party,' he said, switching off the engine.

'Oh no. Sam and Perry do this almost every weekend we're at home. It's Sam's birthday and I've ordered a special dinner so you're in luck. I told the cook to buy some of those big crayfish and make a seafood salad. His mayonnaise is magnificent but almost every night he dishes up grilled steak or roast mutton. Tonight I want a change.'

He laughed. 'Mutton and steak are the staples of our chummery diet too. I'll enjoy a crayfish salad.'

'Chummery! What a weird word. Is it really chummy, all you boys living together in a company flat?' she said.

'It's more like a sexually charged monastery,' he told her.

They walked across the lawn and climbed the steps onto the open veranda. She looked around hoping that Erik might be there but only Sam and Perry were reclining in cane chairs with glasses sitting in the holes conveniently cut in the arms. 'Where have you been? I was just about to mount a search party for you,' Sam told her.

'I met Jack at Flora Fountain and he gave me a lift home in exchange for dinner,' she told him.

Sam liked Jack because he was a first-class rugby player. 'Good to see you. Have a beer,' he said, waving a hand at the hovering Mohammed who, as usual, appeared the moment he was needed. Jess hated Mohammed more than ever. He was so bloody perfect.

By the time dinner was announced, the men had downed most of the beer Perry had procured from somewhere. He always seemed to be able to afford drink even though he couldn't pay his petrol bill. They sat down at the round dining table and were served with clear consommé. Into each helping a thimbleful of sherry was ceremonially poured by Mohammed. When the soup plates were borne away, Jess was eagerly awaiting the crayfish salad but to her horror a roast leg of what passed for mutton but which she suspected was actually goat, was borne in.

She glared at it and then at Mohammed. 'I told the cook to serve crayfish salad tonight,' she said.

He straightened up to his considerable height and said equally loftily, '*Sahibs* like roast mutton, madam.'

You bugger, I am going to get you, she swore silently as she glared first at Sam and then at Perry, both of whom were laughing uproariously. They laughed even more when the dessert turned out to be rice pudding which Jess also hated and her instructions had been for lemon mousse. But, again, rice pudding was what the men liked.

She went to bed immediately after dinner and did not waken when Sam joined her later. Next morning, at breakfast, a bleary-looking Jack was at the table drinking black coffee. 'So you didn't make it back to Bombay. Heavy night?' she asked.

'Very heavy and that sofa of yours is not very comfortable,' he said. She laughed, thinking that he'd been enrolled in the fellowship of the boys.

In mid morning, after Jack left and before either Sam or Perry appeared from their beds, Jess called for Mohammed and told him that she wanted to see the notebook in which he accounted for the housekeeping money they gave him each week. It was a tatty red-covered school jotter and each day had a different page. The cook went marketing every morning and money had to be produced at night for whatever was to be bought next day – usually mutton and rice.

With her own notebook and a pencil, she went through the accounts meticulously, fighting back a laugh at some of Mohammed's spellings – 'for kleening trowser' and 'half a kilo of green piss' – but at least he was literate which was more than you could say for the rest of the staff and she herself couldn't have written even one item of a shopping list in Hindi.

It took her an hour but when she was finished, she had a list of queries and, when the men of the household appeared for lunch, she laid her papers on the table and said to Perry, 'Do you actually swallow two tubes of Veganin every week?'

'Of course not. I have one tablet every second or third day if my head gives me trouble.'

She put a slash through the Veganin entry on her list. Then she asked, 'Have you any idea what three pounds of butter looks like?'

'No,' said Perry.

'Mohammed,' she called, 'please bring out an unopened pack of butter from the fridge.'

It was produced on a plate and laid reverently on the table. 'It weighs eight ounces,' said Jess, reading the label, 'There is no way that we eat six of those packs every week but without fail we are buying them. I ask you, where do they go?'

No one had any suggestions. 'Now for the sugar,' she said, 'According to the accounts we buy four two-pound bags of sugar a week. I do not take sugar in my tea or coffee. Sam does not take sugar in his and neither do you, Perry.'

They were both staring at her as she sat back in her chair to announce, 'In future I am doing the marketing myself.'

'You can't. It's not proper for an Englishwoman to do her own household shopping,' gasped Perry.

'Listen, I am not English and neither am I a lady. I will do the shopping. Sam and I pay two-thirds of this food bill and we seem to be feeding a village instead of a household of three people.'

'If you persist, our servants will leave. What you don't under-stand is that the custom is for employers to allow their staff a certain amount of leeway. It's part of their wages, you see.' Perry was trying hard to keep his temper but his colour was rising.

'This is more than leeway, this is an ocean. And I don't think Mohammed will leave. He's either in a gold mine or practising downright robbery and has probably been doing so ever since he started working for you,' she said.

'Both Mohammed and Pasco, the cook, came to me with the very best references from a woman who ran a perfect house-hold,' said Perry.

'I know, I've heard the story. You told me that she was your father's ex–mistress and when you came to work in Bombay, she found your servants. However that doesn't influence me. I am doing my own marketing in Crawford Market. If Pasco doesn't like it, he can leave. There are other cooks looking for jobs,' said Jess. It was the first time she'd ever heard their cook's name and it gave her a good deal of satisfaction to spit it out.

Pasco left within the hour, driving off in a taxi that was called up for him from the main road. Jess watched him go and was amused and surprised to see that he was wearing a smart pair of brown and white brogues, the sort that used to be known as corespondent shoes.

Mohammed produced a candidate for the vacant cook's job that afternoon and, though Jess would have preferred to find a substitute herself, Perry and Sam insisted that he be taken on.

Mohammed's 'revenge' turned out to be very incompetent indeed. His rice pudding was almost inedible and Perry did not bother to hide his wrath. At meal times he complained about everything laid in front of him and delivered homilies into the vacant air about ill-bred people not knowing the difference between good food and bad food, and also about how some classes of people were not brought up to handle staff.

Jess did not care because she had discovered a new passion – Crawford Market. On the first morning she went there, she parked the car in the square opposite the market's main gate and entered another hidden wonderland. As she walked towards the gate a gang of small boys surged round her legs shouting, 'Carry your basket, *memsahib*, I will carry your basket!'

None of them looked more than ten years old and they were all desperate, but one in particular caught her eye. He was small, so black that his skin looked almost purple, and he had the most pronounced squint she had ever seen in her life. What does the world look like to that poor wee soul? Does it come up in duplicate? she wondered.

'What's your name?' she asked him.

'I'm called Sammy,' he told her. His English was good. Sammy! Great. Her husband was Sam and her market boy was Sammy. 'You'll be my boy then, Sammy,' she said.

She'd made a good choice. Sammy was quick witted and claimed to know the cheapest shops for everything she wanted. Of course she realized that the stall holders would give him a kick back of some kind on everything she bought but that did not matter. She and Sammy were doing each other a good turn. He took her to the fruit and vegetable stalls, and to a flower stall where masses of tightly budded roses were piled up, but when she bought a bunch she found out that each bud had been cut off at the seed head and stuck onto a long piece of wood. 'Why do they do that?' she asked in disappointment.

'They last longer,' Sammy said.

However she also discovered sweetly scented tuberoses, the flower that was to bring back her delight in Crawford Market for the rest of her life.

The stench of the meat and fish markets was too much for her however, and she resolved that the new cook would have to do the buying there. She ended her expedition by opening an account in a large grocery store just inside the market's main gate. When she and Sammy parted she tipped him a couple of rupees and he promised that whenever she came back to the market again, he would be her boy and get her 'best prices'.

The longer she lived in Bombay, the more Jess was coming to sympathize with and like the native working people that she met. She had also struck up a friendship with her postman who shouted out to her as he got off his bicycle at the gate. 'A letter from your father' or 'One of your friends in London has written to you'. He told her that he had a BA in English Literature and was passionate about the novels of Sir Walter Scott, but 'because I have no influence' the only job he could get was delivering the mail.

It was the postman who told her that Mohammed had been selling their overbought food to a small grocer's shop nearby. So her suspicions were fully justified, but her satisfaction was spoiled by the knowledge that she was making enemies and the chief of them was Mohammed who joined Perry in his efforts to make her give up on her marriage and go home.

Perry jibed at her lack of breeding and all the time tried to make her jealous about Sam's past. Every dinner time he would remember some ex-girl friend of Sam's and go on about how perfect she was, or how her well-to-do family stepped in to prevent a marriage. Photographs of parties would be produced and they always showed her husband with his arms round some beaming girl or other – usually blondes which Jess was not. 'You should tint your hair and wear a pink lipstick, not bright red,' Perry suggested.

'Why should I?'

'Because Sam prefers blondes,' was the reply.

When they were alone together, Jess accused Sam of not backing her up. 'Don't let it bother you. It's just old Perry playing the fool,' he said.

Mohammed was more subtle. One afternoon when he served her four o'clock cup of tea, he also produced a bottle of calamine lotion and put it on the table beside her.

'What's that for?' she asked.

'For Sam sahib's prickly heat. I forgot to give it to him this morning when he was complaining that the itch was coming back,' said Mohammed in a caring tone.

True, Sam had been complaining about prickly heat, a nasty red pimply itch that appeared under his arms and around his groin. She sympathized. 'The itch must be horrible,' she said.

'Put it in the bathroom, he'll use it there,' she told Mohammed.

He lifted up the bottle, 'I just wanted to show it to you so you can make sure he uses it. You see, when he was sleeping in the air-conditioned room with Perry sahib, he got no itch. It's heat and sweat that causes it.'

'I suppose it does,' she said, and lifted her book to go on reading but her mind was racing. Mohammed never said anything to her without a reason. He wanted her to know that Sam shared a room with Perry before he was married. In Perry's room there was only one large double bed. The room she slept in with Sam had two singles pushed together and there was no air conditioner.

'Don't be daft,' she told herself. The main problem she had with Sam was his habit of canoodling with other women at parties. In that respect he conformed with the rest of the rugby crowd and she'd given up protesting to him about it.

Mohammed was still standing by the tea tray and she looked up with a smile. 'Thank you for your thoughtfulness, Mohammed. I'll see he uses it,' she said.

*

As a gesture of sympathy for Savage's death, Shackleton decided to suspend the show rehearsals for a week – after all the man's wife was in the chorus and would surely want to go straight home after his cremation in Hong Kong. Another dancer would have to be recruited which was a pity, he thought, because Lilias was easily the best mover of them all in spite of the fact that she was edging on forty.

He wrote an elegant note to the widow expressing his deepest sympathy and saying that he understood that it would be impossible for her to carry on with the show now. 'You are irreplaceable for your contribution has been essential and you will be much missed,' he told her.

It was a surprise when she wrote back a few days later to tell him that she was coming back to Bombay from Hong Kong and would not be leaving immediately because she had a lot of things to do before she decided where she would spend the rest of her life. 'I know my dear Gerry would tell me to be brave and face up to the fact that life must go on. He was always so proud when I appeared in the revue and it would be my tribute to him to go on again for the last time. Because of my professional background I do not need the amount of rehearsing that the other girls do, and if you are prepared to let me have a couple of weeks off to deal with my grief, I would very much like to continue with the show!!!' She ended with three exclamation marks which approximated to how astonished Shackleton felt when he read her letter.

'You will not believe this. Lilias wants to dance in the revue again this year,' he said to Donald. By late afternoon the news was widespread and again it was Ginny who took it to Breach Candy and she sat down beside the three Js as Jack Bradford had started to call them, to say, 'Lilias is back. She's being marvellous, absolutely marvellous, and is going to dance in the revue as usual. She says it's her tribute to Gerald.'

Having spread her news she leaned back on her arms and watched their expressions. Jess laughed. 'If anyone can cast themselves as a merry widow, it's Lilias. She'll be multi rich because Gerald must be insured up to the hilt and she'll get the lot.'

'I suppose she will. That's why it's so surprising that one of the reasons she wants to stay on here for a bit is so she can sell off his things,' said Ginny.

The others stared at her. 'Sell his things? What things?' asked Jackie.

'She says he had a lot of expensive shaving creams, bath essence and aftershave lotions, things like that.'

'Was he stockpiling the stuff?' asked Jess.

'Of course not, but he always bought the best – Dior and brands like that. Most of the bottles have been opened but even then there's a lot of Indians who'll buy them. You know how difficult it is to get your hands on luxury goods out here. And he had some very nice clothes.'

'She's selling his clothes? She's not giving them away to charity or something?' Jess sounded as if she found it difficult to believe her ears.

Ginny was on Lilias's side. 'Why should she? They'll be worth a lot of money – golf shoes, panama hats, cricket whites, cashmere sweaters, cravats, silk shirts – *monogrammed*! What would charities do with stuff like that?'

Sell it, thought Jess, but she suddenly went solemn. 'When is this great event taking place?' she asked.

'She's put the word round that the things will be for sale in her flat next Friday. I want to buy my husband a cake of fancy soap for his birthday and I'll have to get there early because she's selling a couple of bars still in their wrappers for five hundred chips each and some that are half used for about a hundred,' Ginny said.

Jackie shook her head, 'You can get perfectly good Indian soap for three rupees a bar,' she said.

'Not French soap,' Ginny told her.

'I think I'll go to that sale,' said Jess slowly, and her friends looked at her in surprise.

'I didn't think it was quite your thing,' said Joan.

'You never can tell, can you?' said Jess.

Joan

In spite of the ferment of excitement about Lilias and Gerald Savage, Ginny did not forget the 500 rupee bet with Donald about seducing Joan. At every opportunity she made snide remarks asking how he was getting on with the American girl. 'Perhaps you're losing your power of seduction,' she suggested.

Donald's problem was a growing enchantment with Joan. For the first time in many years he was in awe of a woman and eagerly looked forward to her coming into the Gym to play the piano beside him which happened almost every day during the hiatus in rehearsing because of Savage's death. He even persuaded Shackleton to hire another piano so he and Joan could play together.

'I do hope you haven't any wild ideas about including piano recitals in the show,' Shackleton drawled.

'Don't worry, we'll stick to your usual honky tonk,' said Donald. It was his opinion that Shackleton had a tin ear.

For her part Joan was revitalized by the opportunity to make music. She was a skilled pianist, far better than Donald, and she had been tutored by excellent teachers. Sometimes when there were not too many people around, she would start to play with such feeling and fluency that Duncan felt a catch in his throat. What impressed him most was her rendering of Schubert's *Trout*. Enchanted he sat beside her imagining cool sparkling water running down a mountain stream as her long fingers flitted unerringly over the keys. 'Play it again, play it again,' he pleaded when she finished.

For the revue music, however, they would have to sit at their pianos and play tunes like 'The Lambeth Walk' or 'Tulips From Amsterdam', Donald banging them out in his inimitable style and Joan following. If she felt the music was beneath her, she never said so, and in fact she did not feel that. It was such a delight to be enjoying herself, to be out of her sterile flat and away from her anxieties about Theo. One evening the doctor, Alex, leaned over her piano and said, 'It's good to see you looking so well,' and she wondered how she'd looked on the day she consulted him about Liza's green pee.

When proper rehearsing began again, people began to notice Donald's courtliness towards her. He guarded her from the importunities of Bill Lethem and McCallum, and if she needed a coffee or a Cola, he rushed to fetch it. He sought her opinion on the show music all the time – 'Should we repeat the chorus, Joan, or is once enough?'

Sometimes if they had been playing for a while, she felt the need of a cigarette and it was always Donald who rushed to get one and lit it for her like a subject serving a queen. His devotion was not missed by Ginny who watched the exchanges between him and Joan with eagle eyes.

'Your husband has a bad case of puppy love,' Ginny said to Marcia, at the first party after Savage's death.

'He's always in love with somebody but he'll never leave me,' said Marcia.

'You're probably right because I don't think the woman he's drooling over would have him.'

Marcia bristled. 'I doubt any woman would refuse Donald if he turned the full force of his personality on her,' she said.

'This one's holding out well. He's trailing around after her like a besotted boy and I don't think she's even guessed he's infatuated with her,' laughed Ginny.

'Is she some sort of half wit?' snapped Marcia.

'Perhaps. She's certainly odd,' was Ginny's reply. She was delighted to realize that she had rattled Marcia.

'Who is it?'

'Oh come on, Marcia, you must have noticed,' was all Ginny was prepared to say.

Marcia began turning up at rehearsals and stood in the hall doorway scrutinizing the girls in the chorus with a hard look on her face. As usual Donald was up and about patting bottoms, brushing against breasts, but there was no sign of adoration, only lust, in any of his gestures. Then, when she was about to leave, convinced that the bitch Ginny was only trying to rile her, she saw her husband climb down from the stage and approach one of the pianos where Theo Ridgeway's wife, who had just arrived, was putting a sheet of music on the rack.

It was the look on his face that gave him away. She had not seen that look since she was eighteen and they had met each other for the first time.

Jess

Lilias Savage lived in an exclusive building like the one that housed Joan and Theo. On Friday morning as she drove up to the marbled main entrance, Jess found it difficult to believe that she was in the same city as Crawford Market and the Thieves' Bazaar. A swift elevator carried her to the top floor and the door swished open to reveal a softly carpeted hall with candelabra-style electric lights on the walls and skilfully arranged vases of silk flowers in the corners.

A hubbub of voices was coming from an open door in front of her and she went through it into a long hall that led to a curved reception room with a half-moon shaped balcony that commanded a panoramic view of Marine Drive and the ocean, far, far below them.

The room was packed with women, some European but mostly Indian, and all of them were scrabbling through items spread over a vast mock Georgian dining table. Surely, thought Jess, Gerald Savage did not own all that rubbish! Lilias must have invited her friends to offload whatever they did not want at this gigantic sale where the feeling of frenzy resembled the shopping horrors of sale days in Oxford Street when people queued up all night to buy something for a bargain price. Except that the prices here were not bargains. Jess stretched her arm over shoulders and grabbed a bottle of Trumper's pomade that was marked 350 rupees – about £25.

She held it up to the light to check the level of the liquid in it. The bottle was only half full and she was about to put it back on the table when an Indian woman wearing beautiful emerald earrings snatched it out of her hand saying frantically, 'I want that!'

'*Do* have it,' said Jess and stepped back towards Lilias who was standing at the open window surrounded by familiar faces. Tall Gloria, the maternity sister who looked like a giraffe was there, and so were Ginny, red-haired Pam and several of the females who sang loudly at rugby parties. Gloria spotted Jess first and her eyes narrowed as she turned to say something to Lilias, who glanced across at Jess and obviously dismissed her as insignificant. She went back to dabbing her eyes with a screwed-up lace-trimmed handkerchief, but it was obvious that she was watching everything that was happening, almost visibly adding up the profits in her head.

Gloria detached herself from their group and went across to Jess who was about to try on a golf cap that had Malibu Country Club printed on it.

'Are you looking for something in particular, Jess?' Gloria asked in a falsely sweet tone.

'How do I look in the hat?' asked Jess, popping it on top of her head.

'It doesn't suit you,' snapped Gloria.

'Pity it's red. Not my colour,' said Jess, putting it back on the table, before she grinned and asked, 'How's the sale going?'

'Very well. The local ladies are thrilled to have the opportunity to buy London toiletries for their husbands.'

'I suppose it's Lilias's good turn to them, sort of charity work,' said Jess. As she spoke she was heading for the group by the window, and to Lilias she said, 'I was very sorry to hear about your husband's death, Mrs Savage.'

'Oh do call me Lilias. Yes, it's a terrible shock. I haven't really accepted it yet. My doctor tells me it will be several months before it really sinks in.' The grieving widow wiped her eyes with the crumpled handkerchief and then noticed that it was smeared with mascara. When she opened her capacious handbag to find another handkerchief, Jess noticed that the bag was stuffed full of crumpled notes and most of them were 100s.

'You can buy mascaras that don't run these days. You'll be able to get some when you go home,' volunteered Jess helpfully.

'I've more important things to worry about than mascara,' sighed Lilias, with a break in her voice.

'I'm sure of that,' Jess agreed, but Lilias was walking away to speak to someone else so she went back to where the red hat lay on the edge of the big table. 'How much is it?' she asked Gloria who was still there.

'It'll be on the label.'

'It says ninety rupees. That seems steep 'cos it's a bit dirty, isn't it? I'll take it though. Don't bother to wrap it. I'll put it on.'

Gloria knew that she was being sent up but could do nothing about it. 'It's just your style but I didn't know you played golf,' she said nastily.

'I don't.'

'Sam doesn't either, does he?' asked Gloria.

'He hasn't the time these days. I might send it home to show them the sort of thing we can get out here.'

'Will you send it to your father?'

'Perhaps.' This time it was Jess who was wondering where the conversation was going.

'I heard from someone the other day who knows him,' Gloria said.

'Knows who?' asked Jess.

'Your father.'

'Really?' Jess raised her eyebrows under the eye flap of the hat.

'Yes, she said that he's a gangster.'

Jess laughed. She laughed so loud that several people turned round in disapproval to see what was amusing her. 'Gosh,

Gloria, you must have gone to a lot of trouble to find that out. My father will be really pleased when he hears that his fame has got as far as Bombay. But don't worry, he won't put a contract out on you,' she said.

In fact she really was amused. If that was all Gloria had on her she was not bothered. Her father was a man who believed in using useful connections, but gangster in the Al Capone meaning of the word, he was not.

Gloria turned on her heel and walked away, unsure whether she had scored a hit or not. It was difficult to read what was going on behind those yellow eyes, she thought.

Jess went back to rummaging on the table, reading labels and storing up information in her mind.

What a story, she thought. They'll be asleep in London right now but when they go back to work there'll be a good piece waiting for them.

When she headed back to the lift, Ginny was walking behind her and they both stopped at the lift door at the same time.

'What did you say to Gloria? She's fizzing at you,' Ginny asked. Jess remembered that when Ginny had her last baby recently, Gloria had spread the word that her husband had trouble settling the bill and was paying it off by instalments.

'Is she? That's good. I didn't say anything. I was interested in the sale, that's all. How much do you think it's made?' Jess said.

'Thousands! People have been grabbing things all day. It's not as if she needs the money either. My husband's company is handling some of the insurance claims and he thinks it'll come to hundreds of thousands – in pounds, not rupees.'

'Do you want a lift anywhere?' Jess asked.

'I wouldn't mind. I'm meant to be playing tennis at the Gym in ten minutes and I'll have to get a taxi but they never cruise up here because all the residents have their own cars and drivers,' said Ginny.

'I've got the sturdy bugger today. I'll get you there in time,' said Jess, and she did. Her reward was even more information about how rich Lilias was going to be when the insurance claims were settled and, as Ginny said, that was before you counted in the pension his company would pay her.

Babu was ooh-ing and ah-ing and clicking his tongue in disapproval when he read her story as hour later. After he sent it on its way, she took off the Malibu hat and popped it onto his head. 'Ay-ee Malibu,' he said, preening himself. He knew very well where Malibu was and what it represented. 'Wear it in wealth,' said Jess.

In the middle of the night a cable arrived at Jess's home and was on the breakfast table when she got up. By that time Sam and Perry had gone to work and she was alone when she read it. It was from Andrew and it said, 'Today's piece brilliant. Everyone here delighted.' Jess was delighted too because she had written the story in a feeling of genuine outrage. She folded the cable in half and hid it between the pages of one of her favourite books, one that she had brought with her from home and read over and over again: Hugh Cudlipp's *Publish and Be Damned*.

Joan

The atmosphere between Theo and Joan was becoming tense in the extreme. Mindful of her mother's advice, she tried hard to maintain the appearance of not minding that he was unashamedly running wild among the women in the revue. Many people looked at her with scorn or, what was worse, pity when she sat alone at parties and had to watch him smooching over his latest passion, for there always was one. Sometimes she felt that he had given up trying to conceal from her the way he was behaving because he was testing to see how far she would let him go before she snapped.

She wanted to go home to New York. She wanted her old life back. She kept a calendar on which she struck off the tedious days one by one. If she asked, Theo would have allowed her and Liza to go home early, but she did not want that. Like a masochist she preferred to see what was going on. One day, she told herself, I will get even with him for all this, for every insult he is heaping on me.

The only thing that prevented her from sinking into deep depression was the music she played with Donald and the courtly way he behaved towards her. She knew her friends Jess and Jackie sympathized with her situation, but she was not one to unburden herself of her miseries. They supported her without saying anything. Both of them found it hard, she could tell, to be civil to Theo who disliked them because he sensed their hostility.

'I don't know what you find so interesting about that pair. You're always together. Are you sure they're not deviant in some way?' he said to Joan.

'Deviant?' she asked, as if she did not know the meaning of the word.

He nodded. 'Come on, Joan. They're always together and they're both married to odd chaps. Perhaps they're a pair of lesbians.'

'That's rubbish! Jackie's pregnant with her third child for goodness sake.'

'Even lesbians want children. They pair up like queer men – one's the woman, the other's the man. The one with the odd eyes hasn't any children, has she? Watch out or you'll find yourself dressing up in a shirt and tie next.'

'Would you divorce me if I did?' she asked.

'Probably not. Mrs Roosevelt got away with it I believe,' he laughed.

The rains stopped and the temperature dropped so that it was possible to wear a sweater in the evenings, but Joan found herself feeling more and more tired. She was losing weight fast and everything was an effort. Sometimes she was even too ener-vated to read to Liza, far less play with her. Jackie saw this and made sure that at the pool Joan's daughter joined in games with her children and often suggested that Joan sleep a little under the umbrella and leave Liza to her.

'You're looking very tired. Do you sleep well at night?' she asked.

'Not really. I get up about two o'clock in the morning and read. I'm doing Dickens at the moment.'

'Is your stomach OK?'

'I get odd pains. I often feel nauseous as well and seem to spend a lot of time on the lavatory,' Joan admitted.

'Get yourself to Breach Candy. You've probably picked up some of the horrible dysentery bugs that are everywhere around here. Alex is very good at treating them, but it's important to knock them on the head early. He has a surgery this afternoon. Leave Liza with me and go along there now. It's only a hundred yards away.'

The surgery was quieter than usual because the return of ambient weather cheered people up and took away their aches and pains. Alex smiled in a friendly way when he saw Joan but at the same time he was assessing her with a professional eye – grey skin, weight loss, haggard eyes. He'd seen how miserable she was when Theo was chasing skirt but that wasn't all that was ailing her.

She sat at his desk and listed her symptoms. Classic amoebic dysentery, he thought.

'You'll have to give some samples – blood, urine and faeces – and we'll check you out, but I suspect you've been infected with the Bombay bug. You're lucky to have escaped it for so long. Most people come down with a raging attack after only a few months here,' he told her.

'We've been in Bombay for almost a year,' she told him.

'You must have a cast iron inside then. How's your husband?'

'He's thriving. What about my daughter?'

'Funnily enough children seem to cope better than adults. They get stomach upsets but they pass quickly.'

'Can you cure the Bombay bug? I don't want to go on feeling like this forever,' she said.

'We can treat it. Enterovioform does the trick sometimes. But there's dozens of different infections and once they're in your system, the bugs are often there forever. Treatment is better now than it used to be though. In the old days people with bad attacks used to be taken on sea trips to Hong Kong; the voyage often settled them down. There are still some intractable cases today though and then the only cure is to return to a less taxing climate.'

Her mind was racing. If she was sent home she wouldn't be

too sorry. But she knew that would mean the end of her marriage. Do I really want that? she wondered.

Alex was watching her closely. 'I'll take you to my friend in the pathology lab next door and perhaps you can give some samples now,' he said.

'Is it so urgent?' she asked.

'Don't worry. We've got onto it early.'

'What do I do after I've given the samples?'

'I'll give you a prescription for pills and you must watch what you eat. An invalid diet for you, my girl. Yoghurt is good and so is coconut milk.'

'There's plenty of coconuts but I've never seen any yoghurt here,' said Joan.

'Tell your cook the Parsi diary sells it. He'll know where that is. You can make your own once you have the culture. That's probably the best way. Don't worry. And go on making music. I can see what pleasure it gives you.'

When Joan did not turn up at rehearsals for several days, Donald grew more and more concerned till he dropped by her flat one evening to find out if there was something wrong. He could have asked Theo, but there was a strong undercurrent of dislike between them and they avoided each other. He chose the time for his call on Joan carefully, hoping Theo would have set off for the rehearsal before he got there.

As he hoped he found Joan alone, on the sofa surrounded by books and looking wan. He wished he was able to hold her hand but could not assume that sort of familiarity with her. Instead he sat facing where she lay with a concerned look on his face.

'Have you been to see Alex?' he asked.

'Yes. I have some sort of amoebic dysentery apparently. It's being treated and I think it's a bit better, but Alex said that some-times the only way people can be cured is by going home,' she said.

Donald had worked in Bombay for nearly twenty years and during that time had suffered from a range of bizarre diseases from fevers to fluxes. 'Oh we can't spare you! I've had every dysentery known to man as well as dengue fever, a dash of malaria, prickly heat, hookworm, scabies, even a mild dose of cholera I think and I'm still here,' he reassured her. She laughed, which pleased him.

'Seriously, in the old days people used to be sent to the hills to recover from their ailments,' he told her.

'Alex said they took sea voyages but I get sea sick I'm afraid.'

'A few days in the hills would put you back on your feet. If I'm off colour I go to a place called Matheran, on the top of the Western *ghats*. It's always cool and breathing the air up there is like drinking champagne,' Donald told her.

'I can't travel far at the moment I'm afraid,' Joan said.

'It's not too far away – only about four hours' drive. You have an air-conditioned car and your driver will know the way to Matheran. It's the first hamlet on the ghat. The view is out of this world,' he enthused.

Joan was interested. 'Is there a hotel?'

'God, no. There's a club at Mahableshwar that was built for sick army officers in the 1850s and hasn't changed since but that's another three hours' drive further on. I have an Indian friend who owns a bungalow at Matheran though and he allows me to stay in it if I've been off colour. Every time I've gone there I've been cured. It's like going back at least a century in time. You take your own servants, food and bedding, but it's furnished and there's a caretaker and a sweeper to empty the lavatories. I'll ask him if you can go,' he stood up, convinced that this was a brilliant idea.

Joan was staring at him in surprise. 'Empties the lavatories?' she asked.

He laughed. 'Those hill station bungalows have no flush loos. There's little rooms at the back of the bedrooms where they keep china potties for you to use. When you've performed, you shout and a special servant, the sweeper, comes along and takes it away.'

'That is like the nineteenth century,' she said, with a little laugh.

'Would you like to go?'

'What if I got ill again when I was there? I can't go alone.'

'Take anyone you want with you. The bungalow sleeps at least eight. You could have a party. I'd go with you but that would cause gossip and the pressure's on with the revue now anyway.'

'I wonder if Jess and Jackie would like to go. We could take Jackie's children. Liza gets on very well with them.'

'You'll need at least two cars for bedding, food, servants, all that sort of thing. Travelling in India isn't easy.'

She clasped her hands, 'Oh I want to go now. I really want to go. I've read the memoirs of the Eden sisters who were in this country in the early nineteenth century, and your friend's bungalow sounds like the sort of places they lived in.'

'It's certainly primitive,' he agreed.

Jess and Jackie were in the Gym having a coffee next morning when they saw Joan come hurrying along the veranda towards them.

Jackie stood up and said, 'It's great to see you out again. Are you feeling better?'

'Yes, much better. Liza's at school and I took the chance of finding you here because I have a project to put to you both.'

They looked expectant. 'What sort of project?' asked Jess.

'It's been suggested that I could do with a few days in the hills and Donald knows someone who has a wonderful bungalow with a spectacular view at Matheran that he says I could have. Do say you'll come with me.' Jackie was pleased to see that Joan's excitement about getting away from the city had brought some colour back into her cheeks.

'Is Donald coming too?' asked Jess, who had not missed his infatuation with Joan and did not trust his motives. He was known to keep a secret little flat somewhere in central Bombay that he used as a tryst for his various affaires. Perhaps he intended to extend his activities to the top of the *ghats*.

Joan shook her head, 'No, he's not coming; he never even hinted at that. He's busy with the revue and suggested I ask you because I don't want to go on my own. I'd really like some time away though and Alex says that going to the hills will do me good. Donald thinks we should stay a week at least.'

'We drove through Matheran that time I persuaded Sam to take me to Poona. I saw a lovely bungalow perched right on the edge of the hill top. I wonder if that's the one,' Jess said longingly. The idea obviously appealed to her very much.

'I know Matheran. We used to spend some of the hot weather near there in Mahableshwar when my father was posted in Bombay in the forties. It's very primitive. There's nothing to do except play cards and read, or if you're an artist, you can paint pictures. My parents drank and had affaires,' Jackie said.

'Donald says we'd need to take an extra car for the servants and all the stuff we'll need. Theo can arrange that for me,' Joan told them.

Jess furrowed her brow. 'I can't take the sturdy bugger because Sam and Perry need it. So your car would have to carry you, Jackie, three kids and me as well as your driver. And we'll need to take the children's *ayahs* as well, remember.'

'It's a very large car,' said Joan.

'Not that large. I might be able to get Peter's car,' said Jackie.

Both of her friends looked at her bulging stomach at the same time and said in chorus, 'But you couldn't drive it.'

'I'll drive,' volunteered Jess.

'You won't need to. Theo's company has a huge shooting brake that would take us all if we squeezed in. I'll ask for that. When will we go?' Joan said.

'Do you feel well enough to travel?' Jess wanted to know.

'Not quite, but nearly. Alex says another couple weeks of treatment and I'll feel like myself again.'

Jess now looked at Jackie. 'But what about you? Will you be safe enough to travel over those rough roads? The potholes are like pits.'

Jackie laughed. 'I come from tough stock. My ancestors had their babies in less sophisticated places than Matheran. Besides, I'm not due till January.'

'Exactly when in January?'

'The fifth, but I have text-book deliveries, I really do. I won't be early and if I was I'd be able to tell you what to do. Let's go for it.'

'When?' They chorused the question and Joan said, 'But we have to find out if we can get the bungalow first.'

'If we can, when?'

'Not Diwali, that's out,' Jackie said.

'When's Diwali?'

'The first weekend of November this year. It's the Hindu New Year, a festival of lights dedicated to the god Rama and the goddess Lakshmi. It's lovely, a bit like harvest festivals at home with lights and fireworks everywhere. The roads will be mobbed.'

'So we'll start planning for the middle of November perhaps? In about three weeks' time?'

'If possible. It'll be lovely in the hills then. We'll have blankets on our beds and perhaps a log fire.' Jackie remembered comforting log fires in various hill stations when she was growing up. The fires were part of their magic.

'I'll ask Donald,' said Joan.

I just wish he wasn't involved, thought suspicious Jess darkly.

Erik had been in the USA for the past two weeks and she missed seeing him, especially because she had no idea if he'd ever be back. Every time a stranger's car drove along their lane in the evening she had to steel herself against jumping up and running to the gate. Sam never said when, or even if, Erik was coming back and so it was like magic when they returned from the city one evening and saw his car parked in their drive. He was sitting on their veranda with a glass of gin and soda on the table in front of him and stood up grinning when they trooped in.

'I hope you don't mind me helping myself to your hospitality but your bearer insisted. I'm on my way to Singapore but thought I'd drop by Bombay for a couple of days to bring you a bottle of real gin. There's something from New York for you too, Jess.' On the table stood a bottle of Gordon's Export with its distinctive yellow label decorated with black juniper berries. Erik gestured at it, then reached under his chair and pulled out a Macy's carrier bag. Inside was the biggest bottle of eau de toilette Jess had ever seen. There was enough scent in it to last her for a year, even if she splashed it all over herself every day.

'Miss Dior!' she gasped in disbelief, clutching the elegantly boxed bottle to her chest.

'I hope you like it,' said Erik.

'I love it, love it! Thank you so much.' They beamed at each other and she felt as if sunshine was glowing all around her though it was dark outside. *This is ridiculous. I'm a twenty-seven year old woman and haven't felt so giddily in love since I was at school,* she thought.

The appearance of real gin delighted Perry who said, 'We'll take this to the revue party tomorrow.' Though this was the first time he'd met Erik, he was so won round by the gin that he added, 'Why don't you come with us?'

'OK,' said Erik, without a moment's hesitation, and for once Jess felt herself really looking forward to a party.

Like a child anticipating Christmas, she began counting the hours and when the next evening came round she dressed in a tight-fitting green cocktail dress with a flying panel at the back that she had never worn because it always seemed too dressy for the parties she attended nowadays. It came from Greensmith Downes, Edinburgh's most expensive dress shop, and outclassed all her other clothes which were made by a jobbing Indian tailor who sat on the veranda with his portable sewing machine and ran up dresses, copying them from magazine illustrations.

They had arranged to meet Erik outside the flat where the party was to be held and, as they drove into the city, Jess's heart was thumping because she was afraid that he would not be there. He was not a party animal as far as she could see. But there he was, waiting in his car outside the address they'd given him, a 1930s block of flats on Marine Drive. Without thinking, as soon as she went into the flat, she headed directly for the sea-facing balcony and found a cane sofa that could seat two. Erik followed her and sat down by her side as if he too knew exactly how he wanted to spend the evening. Sam provided them both with gin and lime and disappeared into the mob as usual, but they were not to move from their sofa. They did not even get up to go for more drinks, but sat entranced, talking and talking, finding out about each other like people exploring a mysterious and fascinating new country.

For once Jess did not have to ask questions. She was so engrossed that she didn't even notice Jackie coming onto the veranda to look for her. Jackie stood in the open doorway watching the couple on the sofa, then turned and walked away with an amused look on her face.

Erik told her he was married but had been living apart from his wife for five years. 'She doesn't like me travelling so much, so she stays in Manhattan in our apartment. She works as a magazine illustrator, a very good one. We have one daughter who's fourteen now. I see them when I go back, but we live separately because I have my own place in Greenwich Village – just a couple of rooms but that's enough for me and I'm not much there anyway.

'My marriage broke up because I'm never at home and she found someone else. I go from crisis point to crisis point you see. When I came back from the war, I spent some time working on oil fields with Red Adair's team. Then my present company hired me to diagnose problems like flare ups and blow backs and make sure they are circumvented as much as possible. When we're building new sites I'm called in and that's what I'm doing now.'

'I've heard about Red Adair,' Jess said.

'There's nobody else like him. I can't do what he does but because of what I learned from him I can tell other people what to do and specially what not to do.'

'Do you actually tackle fires?'

He laughed, 'Not if I can avoid it.'

Jack Bradford appeared, looking for Jess so they could dance together as they did at all the parties. He paused in the open door and saw the couple with their heads together and it struck him that it looked as if there was an invisible wall around them. With a shrug and a wry grin, he too walked away thinking, I can stop having a crush on Jess then.

About midnight, they got up to lean on the balcony rail and stare out over the slowly heaving silver water of the bay. It was dotted with tiny dug-out fishing boats, each lit by a tiny flare in the bow and containing only one man who was coming back to port with his meagre catch.

'I love the sea,' said Jess.

'So do I. The sea's in my blood. When I sailed little boats like those, it was the happiest time of my life though I never knew if I was going to survive another day. I got wounded once but the Nagas nursed me back to health with their own medicines and herbs. The taste of the stuff was foul!'

She turned and stared at him. His face was enraptured. 'Do you still sail?' she asked.

He shook his head. 'There's not much chance in New York

and my family are in the Midwest, in the corn belt. We went there from Norway when I was eight.'

She laughed, 'I thought you were a Viking the first time I saw you. I bet you're descended from a berserker.'

'The sea's in my blood, that's true. When I was small we lived on the edge of a fjord where there was no road and everyone came and went by water. To this day, when spring comes, I get an irresistible urge to travel. I want to get into my longboat and go somewhere, anywhere.'

'I'm the same. I long to travel so much that it actually hurts sometimes,' she said and told him the story of running away as a child.

'There's a touch of the pirate about you, those dangerous eyes of yours give you away,' he said.

They were staring at each other silently when Sam appeared, swaying like a tree in the wind, and saying, 'Come on, Jess, we're off. It's nearly two o'clock.'

Without saying goodbye to Erik, she followed him. There was hardly anyone left at the party except three or four men around the drinks table finishing off the contents of the bottles. Jack was among them and, when he saw her, he came across to say in a slurred voice, 'That guy's too old for you.'

He was very drunk; the first time she had ever seen him in that condition. Sorry if she had unthinkingly given him any encouragement without realizing it, she said jokingly, 'I'm too old for *you*, Jack. What you need is a nice young girlfriend.'

'How to find one though?' he said mournfully.

'I'll ask around,' she told him.

During the following week Sam said that Erik had flown off to Singapore where his company were planning another refinery which he hoped wouldn't divert too much money and interest from the one they were building at Trombay. 'But he's coming back next week and he'll be able to tell me more about it then,' he said. For different reasons they were both wishing that the refinery in Bombay would be Erik's first priority.

Meanwhile Jess was diverted by the plans for the trip to Matheran and went to meet Joan and Jackie at the Gym but when she walked towards their usual table she thought they looked unusually grim.

'What's up?' she asked as she sat down.

'You are,' said Jackie.

'Me? Why?'

'There's two reasons, but the main one as far as we're concerned is that American man.'

'You mean Erik?'

'Is that his name? Was it necessary to make it so obvious that you and he are having an affair? I thought that you were above that sort of thing and that you'd never fall into the India trap. I know what you've said about people who do. Remember what your Ritz hotel friend told you about women losing their sense of right and wrong when they go past Aden.' Jackie was genuinely disappointed.

Jess leaned forward and said earnestly, 'I'm not having an affair with him, although I wish I was. I've never felt about any man the way I feel about him but I'm not going to do anything stupid. If you only knew! All this has taken me totally by surprise.'

'I hope it hasn't taken your common sense as well. He's nothing to look at. What's so special about him?' said Jackie.

'He makes me feel as if a bolt of electricity is going through me whenever I see him. How do you explain that? We can talk for hours and never repeat ourselves. He's marvellous. Sam says he won a Purple Heart during the war—'

Joan interrupted her, 'A Purple Heart! Is that what he said? That's like your VC, and anyway you can only be awarded it if you die in action. He must be telling lies if he said he has a Purple Heart.'

'He's never mentioned it. Sam heard from someone else.'

'But who said it?' Joan and Jackie were onto the case like two terriers.

Jess bristled. 'He's not a liar. I've never met anyone I'd believe more than I believe him.'

Jackie tried to soothe her by stroking her arm. 'Oh heavens above, you've got it bad, but the mysterious American isn't all we're worrying about. You're in trouble for another reason as well. Lilias and her gang are out for your blood. You'll have to come clean about your newspaper articles. You are a dark horse.'

Jess looked from face to face. 'I'm sorry about that. I didn't think it would ever get out and it's easier to work if people don't know what you're doing. Was it Lilias's sale that blew it? I felt so outraged about that I just had to write it.'

Jackie nodded. 'Gloria's contacts at home told her that the *Daily Herald* ran a big piece about rich expatriates selling off half-full bottles of toilet water at enormous prices to local people – all very disapproving and left wing, of course. The trouble was that other newspapers picked up the story and there has been a lot of adverse comment in them too. Lilias is furious and so is Gerald's company. She says she'll sue.'

Of course it had to be Gloria who found out, thought Jess, but what she said was, 'I'm proud of that story. It's my best scoop.' But when she saw that her friends were not impressed, she went on, 'Lilias can't sue. I didn't write anything that isn't true.'

Jackie nodded. 'That's right. Gerald's company lawyers know that too. They've told her she's to clear out immediately though she said she wanted to stay on to perform in the revue, but they insist that she goes home and she's off tomorrow. That means Shackleton's out for your blood as well.'

'How do they all know I wrote the story?' Jess asked.

'For goodness sake, it didn't take much guessing. All that stuff about the hat with Gloria. You didn't cover your tracks too well. You're hate object of the month and Gloria is going around saying you're a Communist and should be deported. Apparently you're friendly with Krishna Menon and all right wingers loathe him.'

'Krishna Menon invited me to lunch and I enjoyed his company. He's a very clever, entertaining man. That was another scoop for me because the *Daily Herald* was the only newspaper he'd talk to when he was standing for the last election here. He said when he was a student he used to buy our paper because it ran a series of Dickens stories in it every week. It was a pleasure and a privilege to write about him,' said Jess. She was suddenly aware of how seriously she took her work. It mattered a lot to her.

'Oh Jess, we're not criticizing you and we don't want you to get into trouble. We are both backing you up, but please don't go rocking the boat again. As well as scandalizing about you writing for the newspapers, the gossips think you're starting an affair with a redneck oil fire fighter who doesn't even own a dinner jacket and that's giving them more material to work on,' said Joan earnestly.

'He doesn't approve of dinner suits and bow ties. He's a left *wing* Democrat,' protested Jess.

'I guessed as much,' said Joan sadly.

Next morning the friendly postman looked worried as he handed Jess a letter with red underlinings on the envelope. 'He is writing again,' he said sadly.

She turned the letter over in her hands. It was addressed to Perry Duncan Esquire and on the back was inscribed the name of the owner of their bungalow who lived in south India.

'He's written before?' she queried.

The postman shook his head sadly. 'Yes, your landlord. For many weeks he has been writing and he always uses red ink on the address. Your bearer takes them from me because they are addressed to his sahib.'

'How many have come?' she asked.

'At least six. Today your bearer has not caught me so I brought it to you, but I am meant to deliver it to Mr Duncan. I will be in trouble if he does not get it.'

With a strong feeling of disquiet Jess took the letter and said as light-heartedly as she could, 'I'll make sure he gets it. Leave it with me and I will personally give it to Perry.'

The letter lay on the table by her chair all day and every time Mohammed came in, he tried to lift it, but she snapped, 'Leave it.'

'It is my sahib's letter,' he protested.

'I'll give it him,' she said shortly and stared him out till he backed away. She knew she'd scored a victory, but it gave her little satisfaction because every time she looked at the letter, the red ink underlinings looked as if they had been stabbed into the paper by an angry pen. She felt afraid for some reason.

When Sam and Perry arrived home, she waited till they were sitting on the veranda with their beers before she passed the letter across to Perry and said, 'This arrived for you today. It looks urgent.'

He stuck it into the pocket of his bush shirt and said, 'That bloody man! If he doesn't stop bothering me I'll tell him that his bill will go to the bottom of my pile.'

'He's written before?' she asked, falsely naïve.

'Several times. He has a damned nerve.'

'Aren't you going to read it?'

'Why should I bother? It's always about the same thing.'

'What does he want exactly?'

'He's fussing about the bloody rent.'

'Well, he is our landlord after all. Do you owe him money?' Jess's temper was running high. She looked at Sam for support but he was sipping his beer and staying out of the argument.

'He knows very well he'll get paid. The way he goes on you'd think we were living in a palace not a ramshackle place. We even had to put in the water heater ourselves. He's lucky to have good tenants who look after the place.'

Jess leaned forward in her seat. She could feel a pulse throbbing in her neck and her heart was thudding. 'How – much – do
– you – owe – him?' she asked slowly.

'*We* only owe back rent,' said Perry pointedly.

'*We* owe him nothing. *How much do you owe?*' She was almost
shouting and had to fight to keep her temper.

'A few months' rent.' He drawled it out languidly as if he was
dealing with a fish wife. She wanted to get up and hit him.

'How many months?' This time she dropped her tone and
fought to keep what she knew was a shrill note of hysteria out of
her voice.

'I can't say exactly.'

'It'll be in the letter. Open it and let me see.'

She must have looked dangerous because Perry suddenly
climbed down and took the letter out of his pocket to hand it
across to her. She ripped open the envelope and pulled out the
single sheet inside. It was covered in fine copper plate hand-
writing but every third or fourth word was underlined in red –
PAY IMMEDIATELY – LEGAL PROCEEDINGS – LEAVE MY PREM-
ISES BY THE END OF THIS MONTH seemed to leap out at her
from the page. She gasped when she came to the last paragraph.
'You now owe me 26,000 rupees and I am initiating legal
proceedings to recover the money'.

'He's going to law over twenty-six thousand rupees,' she
gasped and burst into tears.

Sam was suddenly galvanized into action and jumped from
his chair to put his arms around her. 'Don't cry. It'll be OK,' he
said consolingly.

'No it bloody won't,' she snapped, then looked across at Perry
and said, 'The rent's two thousand chips a month, isn't it? You
haven't paid anything to this poor sod for over a year.'

Then she asked Sam, 'Were you paying our share of the rent
before I settled the petrol bill?'

'Yes,' he said.

'So that means you were giving it to this man here and he was pocketing it. Do you realize that we've been laying out our share of the living expenses all this time and he hasn't passed any of it on? There's no way that we can raise so much money now. His letter gives us a month to quit the premises. I think that's decent of him. It's more than we deserve.'

'He's only trying to scare us,' interjected Perry, and she turned on him like an angry cat.

'You shut up. I am scared and you should be too. What are you going to do about this?'

'I haven't any money,' said Perry.

'Neither have we,' said Jess. Even in her fury she realized that this was her opportunity to get rid of Perry and live with Sam as an ordinary man and wife. It would be a chance to get Erik out of her head too and try to make a success of her hasty marriage. Her mind was racing and she decided to look on the noticeboard of Breach Candy pool to see if anyone going home on leave was offering a flat to rent. She'd have gone there immediately if she could. The ideal place to move to would be something small, too small to have room for Perry as well. She'd miss their pretty bungalow with its leafy garden, but there was another bonus to leaving, she'd get rid of Mohammed.

For once even Sam was angry at Perry. 'For God's sake, you must have known he'd cut up rough eventually if you stopped paying the rent,' he shouted.

'I didn't refuse to pay, I just didn't answer his letters. He knew he'd get his money in the end.' It was Perry's old excuse.

'Like the petrol wallah,' said Jess, who was determined that there was no way she was going to bail them out of this problem and she knew they recognized that.

'I don't know what you are getting so worked up about,' said Perry, calmly going back to his beer.

She stood over him. 'I'll tell you what I'm getting worked up about. We're going to be out on the street like beggars in three weeks' time. That's what I'm getting worked up about. But I'm going to find a place for Sam and me and you are not coming with us so you'd better start looking too.' Furious, she flounced out of the room and no one tried to stop her.

It took six days to find a flat. Every morning she took the car and followed up noticeboard advertisements from the pool and the Gym. Some of the places on offer were too grand and therefore too high rent and others demanded large deposits against damage or breakages.

Eventually, when she was almost in despair, she found a one-bedroom apartment on Nepean Sea Road that was being sub-let for six months by a Danish couple called Baumgarten. Though tastefully furnished with some beautiful pieces of glass and pleasant watercolour landscapes, the flat was tiny – only one small sitting room with a box-like kitchen off the back, a bedroom with an adjoining bathroom and a glassed-in veranda looking down into a building site where exhausted looking women and children carried around huge blocks of stone and sacks of cement while men lay sleeping in the shade. Mrs Baumgarten saw Jess looking down at the building site and said, 'It'll be finished soon and it won't spoil the view because there's no view to spoil.'

She was a kindly, motherly person who warmed to Jess because she recognized her anxiety and exhaustion. 'We're asking twelve hundred rupees a month. Can you afford that?' she asked.

'I was hoping to find a place for a thousand,' admitted Jess. They had been giving Perry a thousand but they would still have other overheads. They would have to eat as well as pay for gas and electricity, not to mention servants. Jess would have been happy to live servantless but that would put them beyond the pale – even the neighbouring servants wouldn't like it.

The servant question was also on Mrs Baumgarten's mind because she said, 'We want any tenant to keep on our bearer and sweeper. They've been with us for fifteen years and we don't want them to go off and find another place while we're away because they might not come back. They earn two hundred and twenty rupees a month between them. We don't have a cook because I do my own cooking, but the bearer Sushi can cook for you. You will have to pay him a little more and he's quite good at it. We pay for a *dhobi* of course, as well.'

Jess couldn't cook, but she nodded, thinking that she'd have a go at it. A sweeper was necessary because he would be an untouchable, the only caste who could clean a lavatory or polish a floor. Of course, everybody also had a *dhobi* who laundered their sheets and towels. She remembered writing a story about a British employee of the High Commission who imported a washing-machine as a Christmas present for his wife and all the *dhobis* working for English people went on strike and his machine lay unused for a year till he went home and took it back with him.

Seeing that her prospective tenant was rapidly doing sums in her head, Mrs Baumgarten felt sympathetic. She remembered being young and hard up herself. 'How much can you afford exactly? You look as if you'd be a reliable tenant and I'd be happy to let you have the flat,' she said.

'I think our entire monthly budget will be just over about three thousand rupees,' said Jess, deciding to dig into some of the *Daily Herald* money if she had to. A rent of 1,500 would take up half of what would be available.

'Good tenants are more important to me than money. I could let you rent the flat for a thousand a month providing you keep Sushi,' said Mrs Baumgarten.

'Oh that's kind. It's a deal,' said Jess and stuck out her hand.

Mrs Baumgarten smiled and said, 'Call me Greta. We're leaving in three weeks and will be gone for six months. If you need the flat urgently, you can move in the day after we go.' Jess did a bit of rapid calculating. In three weeks they would be back from Matheran and their month's grace at the bungalow would be almost up. It was the ideal time to make the move.

'That's wonderful,' she said enthusiastically, Then a thought sobered her up. 'But how much deposit do you want?' she asked.

Greta said, 'You don't look as if you're going to run away with my furniture. My husband said we should ask for a thousand rupees against damages as well as the rent, but we were young and poor once ourselves so if you can always pay a month's rent in advance, that'll be fine.'

'That's very kind of you. How will I pay the rent – to your bank?' Jess asked.

'No, to our landlord. He lives next door; he owns the whole block. He likes to be paid in cash on the first of the month. Perhaps you noticed his nameplate when you rang my bell.'

Jess shook her head. 'I didn't look,' she said.

'Stop and read it on your way out,' said Greta with a giggle.

That was it. They had a place to live and which they could afford.

On her way out Jess walked across the little hall and read what was engraved on the landlord's brass nameplate. It said BABUJAI OFFICER B.A.HONS (FAILED). She felt her sense of humour returning. *We'll be all right living next door to Mr Officer*, she decided.

Delighted at finding a place to live as a couple for the first time, she drove to Jackie's flat in Cuffe Parade and found her friend at home, eating lunch with her children. 'I've found a flat. I've found a flat!' she crowed, running into the room.

Jackie said, 'Good! Sit down and eat with us. We're having a very good chicken salad made by our lodger's cook who is far better than ours. Improvement in the food is the only good thing about having him in the house.'

Jess suddenly felt starving so sat down and helped herself to salad. 'Has Sullivan been giving you trouble? I thought he was a gent.'

Jackie grimaced. 'There's good gents and bad gents. Mr Daniel Sullivan falls into the latter category.'

'What's wrong with him exactly?'

'It's the company he keeps. I don't think I've seen a single Englishman come to call on him and there's often young Indians hanging about and they're real ruffians.' Jackie looked worried.

'You mean rough trade? Do you think he's homosexual?' Jess asked.

'I hope not, but some of his callers are very low caste. They come and go late at night although thankfully not during the day. It's very worrying.'

'But has anything specific happened? Do they make a lot of noise; do they get drunk?'

'No. What I find worrying is how silent they are. They slip in and out in the middle of the night. I don't sleep well so I hear their feet on the stairs and the door opening or closing. Peter says I'm imagining things but Prabu is terrified and he must have reason. I'm expecting him to disappear one day. I think the only reason he stays is because he would find it hard to get another job. The *ayah* has started sleeping on the floor between the children's beds and when I ask her why she says it's more comfortable for her than the servants' quarters at the back.'

'You're lucky to have servants' quarters. The flat I've just found for me and Sam is so small it hardly has room for us, but taking it means I'll get rid of Perry.' Jess sat back in her chair and grinned at the thought.

'I'm amazed you've put up with him for so long. It can't have been easy for you,' said Jackie with feeling.

There was a note in her friend's voice that made Jess defensive for some reason that she did not understand, and to her own surprise she found herself defending her adversary.

'It's not been all bad. He can be good company when he

chooses, and in a way he's been an education for me because he knows about lots of things that I don't know. He's got very good taste and goes out of his way to make his home attractive by arranging the furniture and hanging the pictures in a very clever way. Though he lives almost entirely on roast mutton and rice pudding, he's very knowledgeable about food and cooking as well, and he's musical. He loves opera. He has stacks of records – things like *Aida* and *The Barber of Seville* that I'd never heard before I came out here. My background in music stopped at Gilbert and Sullivan, I'm afraid, but now I'm fascinated by Bach.'

'That's because you're a quick learner. You'll have the chance to arrange your own furniture soon,' Jackie said with a smile.

'That reminds me. I'm on my way to Crawford Market because I want to buy flowers for the nice Danish woman Greta Baumgarten who's renting us her flat. She's not asking for a deposit and I'm sure that's because she knows how hard it would be for us to find more money. I love the flower market. Why don't you come with me?' said Jess.

Jackie considered this for a few moments and then she said, 'I think I will. I haven't been to the flower market for ages and a couple of vases of flowers would cheer this place up. I can afford them now that we have Mr Sullivan's money coming in. We'll go when the kids are having their afternoon nap.'

It was quiet at the market in the afternoon. Sammy recognized the Studebaker and jumped up from a group of small boys to run towards it waving, grinning and calling, 'Memsahib, memsahib. I'm your boy!'

Jess stopped the car and got out. Other boys came rushing over with Sammy and when they saw there was someone else in the car they started pleading with Jackie to enlist their services. A taller, insolent-looking boy whom Jess had seen before and did not like, pushed the smaller ones away and headed for the car door. The moment Jackie stepped out onto the tarmac however, he visibly drew back for he seemed to recognize her. Instead of offering his services, he turned to walk quickly away as if he was afraid that she might recognize him too.

'That's odd, do you know him?' Jess said. From past experience she knew how persistent and eager for business the insolent boy could be.

'I've never seen him before,' said Jackie indifferently. She seemed immune to the pleadings of market boys.

'We only need one boy because we don't need much, only two bunches of flowers and you can get them for both of us,' Jess told Sammy who beamed at getting double custom.

'What you are needing?' he asked.

'I'll have a good bunch of gladioli made up into a spray. What do you want, Jackie?'

'Zinnias. Masses of zinnias. I love their wonderful colours,' said Jackie.

On their way home that evening, Sam went with Jess when she rode up in the lift to give the flowers to Greta. Unfortunately she was not at home but her bearer allowed them to have a quick look at the flat which did not take long because it was so small.

Back in the car Sam said, 'It's very nice really.'

Jess knew that he was putting a good face on things. He was going to miss their spacious bungalow and the large tree-filled garden which was the perfect place for parties. She hardened her heart and stopped feeling sorry for him. If anyone should feel remorse it was Perry, who was sitting in the driving seat of the car looking superior.

'Not a very salubrious block,' he said.

'They're building next door, but that won't go on forever,' said Jess firmly.

'And the flat's nice inside. The bedroom's air conditioned and the furniture is very Scandinavian. Most attractive,' said Sam loyally.

'That's just as well, because all the furniture in our bungalow belongs to me,' said Perry.

Jess said nothing but thought he was welcome to it. What wasn't made of cane was very bashed.

'What do you plan to do with it?' she asked.

'I'll put it into store because I've been offered a room to rent at Donald and Marcia's. I'll take Mohammed with me,' said Perry, as he put the car into gear.

The others stared at him. It was well known that Donald and Marcia lived in a state of open war with insults and china being flung around day and night.

'Are you going to be their lodger?' Jess asked, suppressing a laugh. The thought of fussy Perry and the superior Mohammed living in Marcia's rather grubby household which was run by the conniving Nanny was almost unbearably funny.

'I'm *not* a lodger. I'll be their PG,' said Perry.

'Oh a paying guest! I suppose that *is* a step up the social ladder,' said Jess. She felt more light-hearted than she had done for months. Ahead of her was a week in the hills with Joan and Jackie and then a return to a new place to live with Sam and a chance to put her marriage together. Perhaps they would get to know each other and she'd manage to rid herself of her passion for Erik who had again vanished from their lives. She did not know whether she wished he would come back or not. Yet every night when she went to bed she fantasized about him and wondered what it would be like lying beside him instead of Sam.

'Tomorrow I'm going to make a start on packing our stuff,' she told Sam when they were changing for dinner – something that Perry always insisted on even when there were only three of them in the house.

'There isn't a lot to pack. Just our clothes,' he said.

'There's all my books. I'm not leaving them behind. And I want the little things I've picked up in the Thieves' Market....' She'd found an amber-coloured Victorian decanter and a prettily painted Delft jug, both bought for the price of five rupees, and she treasured them.

'I only have some photographs in an album that I wouldn't like to lose. I think it's on the shelf behind the dining table,' Sam remembered.

'Probably pictures of the rugby team,' she laughed.

'That's right,' he agreed.

She spent next day sorting out bed linen and sending their towels and sheets to the *dhobi*. They came back immaculately clean and pressed and for the first time she felt a housewifely surge of pride as she laid them in the bottom of a suitcase. Playing houses in Greta's little flat might be fun. Perhaps she'd even get pregnant. She sat back on her heels beside the big suitcase and considered that prospect. If it happened, there would no longer be any conflict in her life. She'd forget Erik, force him out of her mind. It would be like coming to a cross-roads and choosing a different way. It was the lap of the gods thing again.

All her good intentions disappeared on Sunday, however, because when she got up and wandered into the dining room looking for a cup of coffee, Erik was sitting on the veranda. Reeling, she put out a hand to steady herself on the table and felt as if she'd been hit on the chin. For a few moments she even wished he'd stayed away, but delight at seeing him overcame that feeling.

'Have you been here long?' she managed to ask.

He grinned. 'A few hours. I like the morning. Mist on the trees reminds me of the jungle.'

Barefoot, she padded over the marble floor and sat down to stare at him. 'Is it true you have a Purple Heart?' she asked.

'Yes.'

'But I thought you had to be dead to get one.'

'In the early years of the war they gave them to people who'd been badly injured. Shed blood. I got one of them because I was posted dead and then turned up again with a lot of scars. Why do you want to know?'

'I just wondered.' Then she sighed and said, 'We're having to leave here,' and felt a surge of regret at the change they were about to make. The bungalow was so beautifully peaceful.

'Why are you leaving?' he asked.

'Perry hasn't paid the rent for about a year. The landlord has given us notice to quit. It was decent of him not to throw us out on our ears without notice.'

'Would money help?'

She shook her head. 'No, Sam and I have found a flat to rent for six months and that will take us up to the time we are due to go home on leave. Perry is going to be a PG with people in Breach Candy. Mohammed is going with him.'

He laughed. 'Do they know what they're in for?'

'They'll find out,' she said.

He and she stared at each other silently for a bit and she felt her throat tighten. Oh God, this is awful, she was thinking. I want to throw myself at him. I must be going mad.

'I have another sack of oysters with me. I bought them at the fish market when dawn was breaking. I've also got a bottle of real champagne. Your bearer put it in the fridge. I've taken the liberty of telling couple of guys from our head office to come round at noon. They're visiting firemen.'

'Visiting firemen? Has there been an accident?'

He shook his head. 'No, I mean they're executive types who usually sit behind desks. They've only flown out for a couple of days to see what we're doing here and I want to show them the good work Sam has done at the refinery. They're the guys who sanction big contracts and India scares the shit out of them. They're living in the Taj but even it intimidates them because it's not like New York. I've sent a taxi to bring them out.'

Jess jumped up. 'I'll tell Sam. He'll be pleased.'

When a ramshackle black and yellow taxi came clanking into

the drive, two tall men in lightweight grey suits and dark glasses climbed out of the back and stood staring around as if they were in the middle of a jungle. 'Gee, this is a pretty little place, Jess,' said one of them to Jess when he shook her hand. It amused her that every time either of the visitors addressed her, he repeated her name and did the same with Sam and Perry. She had no idea what they were called, however.

Erik was sitting on the veranda steps with an open sack of oysters between his bare knees for he was wearing ragged shorts.

'Mohammed, bring me a knife and a hammer,' he called, and when the utensils were produced he proceeded to attack the oyster shells and lay the opened ones onto a large tray by his side. She was sure he was being deliberately haphazard and unhygienic. 'Help yourself everybody,' he cried, and Sam, Perry and Jess fell on the fat, luscious oysters with enthusiasm.

'They're lovely. They're so fresh you can taste the sea, do try one,' Jess said to the youngest of the visiting firemen but he recoiled.

'I wouldn't risk it! What about ptomaine poisoning? I haven't eaten anything except tinned invalid food I brought with me since I landed in this city four days ago,' he said.

'Aw, come on, boys. Try an oyster. You're not in Hoboken now,' cried Erik, holding an open shell up to his mouth and swallowing its contents whole.

Jess looked at him with admiration. Only he could say that. If I ever write a book about living in India I'll call it *You're Not In Hoboken Now*, she told herself. Just then Mohammed appeared, ceremoniously carrying the bottle of champagne wrapped in a white napkin on a tray with five of Perry's best glasses.

The visitors recoiled from champagne too so the others held their glasses high, looked in delight at the bubbles rising up through the wine and toasted each other. 'To us!' cried Erik holding his glass towards Jess.

The bubbles in the champagne tickled her nose making her sneeze so no one thought it odd when tears flowed down her cheeks.

Joan

Donald held out a 500 rupee note to Ginny and said, 'You've won. All bets are off!'

She looked down at the money and sneered, 'You've lost it, Donald. You'll never be Champion Stud of Bombay again.'

He shrugged. 'I don't care what you say. I just don't want Joan dragged into it.'

'Joan! What's so special about her? She's just a woman like the rest of us. She's not the Virgin Mary, though you're carrying on as if she is.'

'She's not like the rest of you,' he said firmly.

'She's not all that different or she'd never have married Randy Theo. Don't you wonder what their married life is like? Do you think he sits around with a dreamy look on his face while she plays the piano to him every night? No, he's out screwing other men's wives, probably because of her piano playing.'

'Knock it off, Ginny. Just take the money. You won the bet,' he said wearily.

She took the note and tucked it into her brassiere between her breasts. 'If you ever want it back, you know where it is,' she said, and flounced away. Within half an hour she had told all the other women in the revue that Donald was starry-eyed about Theo's wife and had put her on so high a pedestal that he wasn't even going to make a pass at her. The news spread from them to the bridge players in the Gym and from there to the gossiping circles at Breach Candy pool.

'What makes Joan Ridgeway so special?' women asked each other. Some of them even asked their husbands if they found the American girl attractive and were surprised when the answer was 'Yes'.

'It only goes to prove that women have no idea of what men find attractive,' said one amazed woman, following an oblivious Joan with her eyes as she made her way along the Gym veranda.

The gossip was carried to Marcia by Nanny who had an intricate network of informants among the household servants of the European community. Who was even thinking about sleeping with whom was known to her before it was recognized by the people involved.

'Your man has fallen in love, baby,' she told Marcia, when she woke her at noon with a cup of black coffee.

Marcia sat up and removed the lace-trimmed eye pads she wore at night.

'Are they talking about it now?' she asked, for she knew what Nanny was talking about.

'All are talking, talking, talking!'

'Damn and blast.' Though both of them continually complained about the other, Donald and Marcia were a pair, like ham and eggs, or salt and pepper. You could not mention one without the other. If one of them was going to fall in love with someone else, Marcia was determined she was not going to be the one who was seriously betrayed. She would not be the one to be left.

'What can I do, Nanny?' she asked. For a moment she sounded pitiful.

'I'll put a spell on her,' was the first suggestion.

'The last time you put a spell on somebody I didn't like, you got rid of her all right because she inherited a lot of money and went to live in Argentina with a polo player,' said Marcia, bitterly.

'Drink your coffee, baby, and we'll think of something,' said Nanny soothingly.

At tea time she was back with more information. 'The American woman's bearer says that she knows her husband has other women, but she loves him so she pretends it isn't happening. She told her mother what she suspected and her mother scolded her, telling her that all men behave like that and she had to put up with it because it would pass. She does what her mother tells her.'

'She's a fool.'

'If you make her face up to the truth about him, she'll be very upset. Already she goes to the hospital because of her nerves,' said Nanny.

'I don't give a damn about her nerves. Do you think I should sleep with her husband and then tell her?'

'You will have to be crafty. Her *ayah* says that she is taking her little girl to the hills next week with her two women friends. The husband is not going. You can get into his bed then.'

'Oh that won't be difficult. Fighting him off is the problem for most people and I've heard he's a wham bam man who doesn't even say thank you at the end.'

'Think of it as revenge,' said Nanny.

The three Js were excited about the trip to Matheran which was now only three days away.

'Theo is being so helpful,' Joan told her friends.

'What's he done?' asked Jess, suspiciously.

'I'll have my own car and driver and Theo's offered us the shooting brake with another driver for our servants and the baggage.'

'That'll be a big help. Peter was worried about our car going on such a long trip. Its brakes are rather dodgy and the *ghat* road is very dangerous,' said Jackie.

Jess nodded, remembering the hairpin bends they had negotiated on the trip to Poona.

'As far as servants are concerned we'll only need one *ayah* and my second bearer who is much more pleasant than Yusuf. He's a good cook too and so's the *ayah*. There's a caretaker in the bungalow apparently, and a little bazaar in the village where we can get fruit and vegetables so we don't need to take basic food. If there's anything special you want though, like breakfast cereal, you'd better take it with you,' Joan told the others. She felt energized by the prospect of getting out of Bombay.

'I'm taking two essentials – Orange Pekoe tea and two cans of asparagus spears,' laughed Jess.

'I'll take Marmite and lots of baked beans, the kids love them,' was Jackie's contribution.

'And I'll take a bottle of gin and some playing cards so I can teach you two to play bridge,' said Joan.

Jess

Next morning Jess went to the grocer in Crawford Market for the tea and the asparagus. As usual Sammy came running when he saw her and then she remembered the strange way the tall boy had acted at the sight of Jackie. She'd forgotten about that till now.

So that Sammy could earn some kick back money, after visiting the grocer, she went with him into the fruit market and bought a basket of oranges and another of limes. They'd need the limes for their gin, she reckoned.

As he was walking back down the broad main aisle with her she said to him, 'Did you know the friend who came here with me the other day?'

He looked at her sideways. 'Your friend, *memsahib*?'

'The lady who came here with me last week. That tall boy who bullies the little ones seemed to know her.'

'You means Ashok?' Sammy was dodging the question.

'Is that his name? I could see that he recognized my friend and didn't want her to see him. Was he once her market boy?'

'Oh no!'

'Then how does he know her?'

'Ashok is a bad boy,' said Sammy, almost in a whisper.

She was not surprised. Ashok had a villainous look. 'Tell me how he knows my friend – and you recognized her too, didn't you?'

'Ashok took some of the market boys to look at her house.' Sammy was still whispering.

This time Jess was surprised. 'Did you go?'

'Yes, I saw her house. It has a pretty garden.'

'Was she there?' she asked.

He shook his head and said, 'No, we hid in the bushes and watched her come home. *Memsahib*, do not go to that house. It is a bad house.'

She paused in the aisle and bent down towards him, saying, 'Tell me.'

'It's not the *memsahib* that is bad; it is the man with the yellow hair who lives there. He is a bad man.' Sammy was obviously frightened so she stood up, patted his head and gave him a handful of coins as she said, 'Thank you. Take my basket to the car and don't worry about this. I won't tell anyone what you said.'

As she drove away Jess was thinking – the man with the yellow hair had to be Sheridan. Peter's hair was very dark, thank God, so it wasn't him getting into trouble again. She had only met Sheridan once or twice and found him slightly repellent so she was not surprised that Sammy thought him bad. Jackie had told her that their lodger would be moving on soon so Jess decided not to tell her friend about what she had been told. The whole thing was unspecific and probably only market gossip.

Next morning, when she was packing her case for the trip on the following day, she went in search of a book to take with her and found Sam's photo album lying on the bookshelf beside Dickens's *Great Expectations*. She pulled it out, glad that she had not forgotten to retrieve it before they left the bungalow and, as she was carrying it back to put beside Sam's packed clothes, a flutter of loose photographs fell onto the floor.

She bent to pick them up. They were the usual rugby pictures, lines of muddied men posing as a team. She'd seen many of those photos and they all looked the same. Why did Sam want to keep them? The last photographs still on the floor were slightly smaller and lying face down. When she picked them up she looked, gasped and then looked again.

Carrying them she hurried into her bedroom and closed the door before putting them on the top of the coverlet to have yet another look. They were black and white pictures of Sam and Perry dancing together. Both were barefoot and wearing brightly patterned bush shirts so they were obviously at a party. They were also obviously very drunk and they were dancing cheek to cheek in what looked like a state of sheer rapture. Perry, who was shorter than Sam, had his cheek on Sam's chest and his eyes were closed. Sam's eyes were closed too and he was holding Perry's hand with the fingers entwined in his.

The second photograph was even more specific because it showed them kissing – obviously at the same party because they were wearing the same shirts.

Jess sat down on the floor and said aloud, 'They're lovers!'

How can I have been so blind? she wondered.

Her father had said some strange things about Sam when she announced that she was going to marry him, but he had never actually come out with the accusation that Sam was homosexual though now, looking back, she realized that was what he'd meant. His chief spoken objection to the wedding was that Sam was marrying Jess for her money – or her father's money to be more precise. To prevent that he'd disinherited her.

My God, he was probably right about everything, she thought.

Strangely Jess found that as she looked again and again at the pictures, she actually felt sorry for the two men. Am I too shocked to feel emotion? she wondered. But no, she wasn't shocked really. In a way she wasn't even surprised. It was like finding a key and opening a locked door. But what am I going to do? she asked herself. She was still sitting on the floor surrounded by scattered photographs when Perry and Sam came home from their offices and she heard her husband's voice calling for her.

When she didn't appear, he opened their bedroom door and asked, 'What are you doing? Are you all right?'

She looked up and said 'Come in. I've something to show you.'

'Join us on the veranda. We're just having a beer,' he said.

'*Come in* and close the door,' she said firmly, so he did as she said and sat on the bed looking down at her on the floor. She was barefoot and still wearing her daytime shorts and cotton shirt and her hair was uncombed. Something was wrong, but she didn't look ill or angry.

'Look at those,' she said handing the two photographs over to him.

He looked and said after a moment, 'We were drunk and fooling around. It was one of those parties that go on for days....'

'He's in love with you,' she said.

'Aw come on, Jess—'

'And I suspect you're in love with him.'

He stared at her silently and she went on, 'You realize that those photographs would be enough to put you in jail at home.'

'You're not going to do anything with them, are you?' he asked.

'Of course not. But I wonder why you kept them. Didn't you realize they were dangerous?'

'I didn't think.'

She groaned, 'That's your problem – not thinking.'

'What are you going to do?' he asked.

'I don't know. I'm going to Matheran with the girls early tomorrow morning and I'll think about this when I'm away. But tell me one thing: were you in love with me when you married me?'

'I fancied you – I do fancy women you know.'

'I'm aware of that. It makes it worse somehow.' For her the fact that Sam and she made love so much seemed to be a betrayal of Perry. Surely I'm not going to start feeling sorry for *him*? she asked herself in surprise.

'Did you love me?' she persisted.

'I liked you a lot. And I've come to love you now, I think. I don't think you loved me madly either when we got married, did you?'

'Not really. I thought I did, but I don't think I'd ever been in love with anyone really.' Not like I am now, she thought. Suddenly she was engulfed with doubt and for the first time felt like weeping.

Am I totally hopeless at reading people? she wondered. Am I capable of telling good from bad and right from wrong. Is Erik another of my terrible mistakes? What am I going to do?

But she knew what she was going to do first. She was going to Matheran to think about it.

Joan

Theo watched his busy wife from his pillow and said, 'You're in a very good mood this morning. Are you so relieved to be rid of me for a week?'

'No, darling, I'm already looking forward to coming back a new woman, energized by fresh cold air. You won't know what's happened to you when I get back.'

I can hardly wait,' he said.

He helped waken Liza and carried her to the car wrapped in a cotton blanket. Then he kissed Joan with more affection than he had shown for months and the two cars drove off in convoy to collect Jackie, her children and their *ayah* before heading for the suburbs and Pali Hill. Jess was waiting on her veranda when they drove up and Jackie said to Joan, 'Doesn't Jess look terrible? I think she needs a holiday in the hills more than either of us.'

'She's been out of sorts for weeks. I can't make out what's wrong with her. It's that oil man who looks like Fred Flintstone,' Joan agreed and laughed.

'Fred who?'

'He's a cartoon character on television at home, a Stone Age man with his hair sticking up at the back like that man who hangs around Jess and claims to have a Purple Heart.'

'Let's hope she's probably only got a passing crush. I can't imagine her really going overboard for him,' Jackie said.

When everybody was stowed into the cars and young Simon was allowed to sit in the big shooting brake with the servants and the baggage because, as he said, he didn't want to travel with his mother like a baby, they headed for the hills.

In Joan's car, the passengers dozed as they drove into the dawn across miles and miles of flat paddy fields where the rice was already being harvested because the rains had stopped. The only traffic they met were bullock carts carrying the grain or enormous lorries brightly and intricately painted all over with beautiful patterns. Their drivers commandeered the middle of the road and when they went swooshing past missing their car by only a few inches, Jess was glad that she did not have to drive and face up to them.

After three hours, their climb began and the road snaked above them, more twisty than anything Joan had seen on her only trip to Switzerland; loop upon loop of bends, back and forward like furled string, reaching to the top of what looked like an unscaleable cliff face. What made it more hazardous were brakeless lorries that came sweeping round corners at what seemed like a hundred miles an hour. All of them had people clinging to their open tops.

The higher they climbed the cooler it became. Jess, who was sitting in the front beside the driver, shook herself, breathed in deeply and said, 'Isn't this wonderful! The air tastes like champagne.'

Joan smiled and said, 'That's what Donald said. And you look better already. Did you have a sleepless night?'

'Yes, I did. I was excited about coming away I think.' She was not going to tell them that she'd lain awake pondering her situation. Sam was not in the bed with her and she did not care where he was sleeping.

'Me, too,' said Jackie, 'I was so worried about leaving Peter. I'm afraid he'll go out gambling again when I'm not there. Sheridan has been bringing men home and I think they play cards or something. There's often quite a lot of shouting but Peter says he doesn't hear it.'

Jess turned in her seat and stared at her friend. 'Shouting?' she asked.

'Not shouting exactly. It's more of a rumble with raised voices every now and again.'

'When's that man going away?' Jess asked.

'Soon. In a couple of weeks. Peter said he'll be off before I have the baby. I'd like his room for a nursery because Simon wants a bedroom to himself now. He's starting to feel very grown up.' Jackie shifted in her seat and the others were immediately concerned, remembering her pregnant condition.

'Are you all right?' Joan asked, and Jackie laughed.

'I'm fine. I'll let you know if I go into labour, so don't worry.'

At that point Joan's driver turned his head to say, 'We pass the holy man soon. You must throw out some money for him.'

This immediately diverted them. 'Holy man? What sort of a holy man?' Jess asked, and it was Jackie who told her, 'I'd forgotten about him but we always had to give him money when we drove up the *ghats*. He sits on one of the corners and people going up give him money to make sure that they make a safe return.'

Jess said, 'It can't be the same man as was there when you were a child, can it?'

'Probably not, but he'll be just as frightening. My father would never drive past without giving him something.'

Joan began rooting around in her handbag. 'We must give him money too then. How much does he need?'

Her driver, who had grown fond of her during the months he had been driving her around and who was well aware of the life Theo led, chipped in saying, 'Not too much money, *memsahib*. Fifty pice will do.'

Fifty pice was half a rupee. 'That's not much to keep us all safe. If I give him ten rupees will that do for both the cars?' said Joan.

The driver was horrified. 'Ten rupees is wrong. You will spoil the rate for other travellers if you give him so much. One rupee in small coins for each car will do,' he said sternly.

A few minutes later, he announced, 'Be ready. The holy man is on the next corner. I will go slowly and you must throw your money out of the window.'

Though the car was air conditioned and the windows ought to be kept tightly closed, they rolled them down on Joan's side and hung out eager to see the *sadhu*. He was a tall man with long tangled greying hair that cascaded over his shoulders and down below his waist. Completely naked except for a string worn cross ways across his chest, his skin was a strange greyish colour because he rubbed himself all over with ash every day. On his forehead between his eyebrows was a mark like an upturned fish hook.

Joan and Jess threw a cascade of small coins at him as the car passed and he gave no sign at all of noticing them or their generosity, not even as much as a blink.

'What if the money all rolls down the hill and he doesn't get any of it? How will he know which cars to protect?' Joan asked but Jackie reassured her, 'Don't worry, he'll know exactly who we are and where all the money is. He'll have it collected in seconds.'

'I hope he sends up a prayer for us. I could do with some guidance,' said Jess, with feeling.

'Don't build up your hopes too high. All he's guaranteeing is that we'll come safely down the hill again,' said Jackie with a laugh.

'That's something at least,' said Jess.

'I feel as if I've gone back a century in time,' said Joan, in an awed voice when she stepped into the bungalow that perched like a bird's nest on the edge of a rock face.

The others following her were equally awed. 'It's a time capsule,' said Jess, looking round.

'And a dirty one,' added Jackie, running her finger along the top of a table and using her fingertip to write her name in the dust The generations of bossy *memsahibs* who had gone before her showed in her voice when she called out, 'Boy, boy!' and a shuffling man in a dirty *dhoti* appeared and started making gestures of obeisance when she began berating him in fluent Hindi.

'What did you say to him?' Jess asked, as he went out of the room backwards like someone in the presence of royalty.

'I said that he must have been told we were coming so why did he not clean up the place and I hoped he'd lit a bonfire for hot water for our baths. He'll do it now.'

'You've gone back in time too. I can just imagine you holding out in this place against a bunch of mutineers,' laughed Jess.

Jackie shivered. 'I've been in places like this before,' she said.

'You know the ropes then. Lead on, boss,' said Jess.

Joan was leaning over the bungalow rail staring down into the valley below. 'Come and look. It's magical. I've never been in a place so beautiful,' she said, in an entranced voice.

The others walked over and stood beside her. Far, far below them the plain that led to the sea was spread out in a vast panorama, crisscrossed with paddy fields where people labouring like ants pursued their back-breaking lives. The sight silenced them all because it made them feel like gods staring down from heaven. 'This is something I will never forget,' said Jess.

Jackie was the first to break away. In an uncharacteristically fussy bustle, she began hurrying around, ordering the servants to make up the beds and hang mosquito curtains. 'Have you brought paraffin for the lamps?' she asked her *ayah*, who shook her head.

'Then tell that idle caretaker to go out and fetch some.' She sounded quite unlike herself and Jess was surprised at the difference that had come over her normally easy-going friend.

Perhaps, she thought, coming into a bungalow like the places she'd lived in a child was bringing back unwanted memories, or turning Jackie into her mother.

She put a hand on her friend's arm and said, 'Come and sit down. You must be tired after that long drive. There's beer in my cool box. I'll pour you a glass. And don't worry, everything's going to be fine.'

Reluctantly Jackie sat down in a long reclining chair and put her feet up. 'I'm sorry. I don't know what came over me. I was just so annoyed at the dirt and the laziness of that man.'

'It doesn't matter. We have our own people to look after us and anyway we're well able to look after ourselves. The Raj is finished, Jackie.'

At last Jackie smiled. 'I'm being silly, aren't I? Let's all sit down and start to enjoy ourselves. Would you like to play cards? I only know snap; the children would enjoy that.'

For Jess the drawing in of the evening, playing cards with her friends, was pure enchantment that drove all thoughts of Sam and Perry out of her head and left her in a state of almost transcendental tranquillity and happiness. The vast bowl of the sky that filled the horizon in front of them was gradually lit up by streaks of wonderful light – purple, orange, deep blue, scarlet and brilliant yellow merging together like a vast palette as the sun set far away over the invisible sea. As darkness crept like a thief over the plain beneath them, they went to stand on the veranda again and saw here and there, far beneath them, a few tiny trees dotted with lights burning in their branches. Five or six of them were here and there over the plain like isolated Christmas trees with candles in their branches.

When she spotted them, Jess called out, 'Look, down there's trees with fairy lights in them. Divali's over, isn't it. Perhaps it's another local festival.'

Jackie looked up and said, 'No, they're death lights. They light them in villages when someone dies. The family put them in a tree to help the spirit to fly away.'

'What a beautiful thing to do,' said Joan softly, but when she looked over at Jackie she saw that she was shivering again, so she went into her room and brought out a shawl which she draped over her friend's shoulders. 'Are you all right?' she asked anxiously.

'Yes, I'm fine, but shout for that man and tell him to bring out the lamps. I don't like sitting in the dark.'

When the lamps were set on the table, they gave out a comforting hissing noise but every now and again a venturesome moth flew too close to the flame and was burned up in a little flash that made Jackie flinch.

Joan signalled to Jess with her eyes and they left the veranda to meet again behind the bungalow and whisper together n the flickering light of an enormous bonfire that had been lit by the servants and where Joan's boy was stirring a vast pot like a witches' cauldron hanging over the flames. It smelt delicious and cheered them up a lot but Jess was still anxious about Jackie.

'Something's wrong with her. I've never seen her so touchy. Do you think she's having labour pains and not telling us?' she asked in a worried tone.

'Gosh, I hope not. Let's wait till the children are all safely in bed and then talk to her. If there's any problem we can load up everything and go home, although I don't think it would be safe for her to make that journey again without at least a night's sleep,' Joan said.

The children were easy to settle because they too were tired and excited and when the deep purple darkness settled around them like a scented velvet cloak and stars like diamonds glit tered in the sky above their heads, the three women were able to sit down at last and talk in the flickering lamplight that seemed to soothe them all. There's something about oil lamps that makes women look extra beautiful, Jess thought, as she looked at her friends – Joan so blonde and patrician with her finely boned face, and Jackie, definitely a high-born Indian princess.

She started the questioning. 'What's the matter, Jackie? Don't say it's nothing because we know something is wrong. You must tell us what it is.'

Though Jackie looked strained, she started by reassuring them, 'I'm not in labour if that's what you're afraid of. It's nothing like that. I can't understand what's wrong really, but the moment I stepped into this bungalow I had the strangest feeling of apprehension. It's difficult to explain.'

'Was it the dirt that upset you? You really turned into a *memsahib* and got that old boy going. He's been sweeping and cleaning like a maniac for the past hour,' laughed Jess.

But Jackie did not join in the laughter. 'No, I took my feelings out on him, I'm afraid. The truth is that when I stepped into this place and saw the dusty rooms with all that old-fashioned, bashed furniture, I felt as if I'd gone back to my childhood. I've been in so many places like this in the past, old *dak* bungalows, furnished by the army about 1850 and never changed. It was when one of you said something about going back in time that it really hit me. Then I remembered....'

The other two said nothing. The feeling of going back in time delighted them both, but it obviously upset Jackie.

She looked at their faces and saw they were wondering what is was that upset her so much. 'You see, I've suddenly remembered something I thought I'd forgotten. When I was about eight we arrived in a bungalow exactly like this one on the trunk road to Jhansi. I was with my father and mother and my baby brother.'

The others sat silent knowing there was more to come but for a few moments Jackie looked as if she was far away, almost in a trance. She stayed silent for what seemed like an age till Jess finally asked, 'What happened there that upset you so much? Can you talk about it?'

Jackie nodded and then said, 'I remember running in and out of the rooms. There was a big sitting room with a huge table and chairs round it. It had doors onto the veranda like this one here. I went in one door and saw another girl about the same age as me coming in the other and then going to sit under the table where she began playing with a doll. I was pleased to see her because my brother was too little to be much company and my parents were quarrelling as usual. I climbed under the table beside her and asked her name. She was English and she told me her name was Sophy.'

There was another long waiting pause till Jackie began again, 'I asked if she lived in the bungalow and she said they were passing through like us. We sat together playing and she gave me a ribbon from her doll's dress. Her own dress was very pretty and I thought it was a party dress because it was long and white and had a very full skirt. I was wearing shorts, I think. When my *ayah* called me to go and have my bath, I crawled out from under the table and left my new friend. I tried to go back to find her but I was being put to bed whether I wanted to go or not and when my father came to say goodnight I was crying and I told him I'd met another girl who was my friend and I wanted to say good-night to her too. He was very surprised and he called the caretaker to ask if there were other people staying in the bungalow. Like me he wanted some congenial company I think, but he was told there was no one else there.

'I started to cry and said *What about Sophy?* My father cuddled me and said I'd imagined her, but I showed him the ribbon she'd given me, and insisted that I'd made a friend. The servant then started talking to my father in a local language I didn't understand and they both looked at me in a funny way. My mother appeared to put me to bed because I was still crying and saying I wanted to see my friend again.'

Joan, sitting forward intent on the story, asked, 'Did you ever find out who she was?'

'Yes, I'm afraid I did. When we left that bungalow early next morning, I was still going on about Sophy and my father's temper snapped. He told me I'd seen a ghost. That made my behaviour worse, I'm afraid. I was hysterical and my mother accused my father of being insensitive – you can imagine the row that ensued and Sophy became unmentionable in our family. Then a couple of years later my father told me that the caretaker had told him he'd seen the ghost of a child who'd been killed in that bungalow with her parents during the Mutiny. Father looked up the records and Sophy's death was documented. Apparently her ghost often turned up if there were children staying in the bungalow. The whole thing upset me and my mother terribly especially because my little brother fell ill with a fever in Jhansi and died there three days later. I've always thought that seeing Sophy's ghost was an omen of disaster. My mother never got over losing her baby. She started drinking seriously then and it killed her when I was eighteen.'

They clustered round her and Jess said, 'No wonder you made yourself forget.'

'I never think of it now and I realize I'm being silly by letting it upset me. Looking back I sometimes wonder if I've made the whole thing up. It was all so long ago,' Jackie said but Jess stopped her by saying, 'Then stop thinking about that now. It's past and it didn't happen in this bungalow.'

Joan agreed, but more sympathetically, 'If the memory upsets you too much we'll go back to Bombay tomorrow,' she told Jackie.

The response was vehement. 'No, no, I don't want to go back. You and Joan like it here and we all need a holiday in a cool climate. I'm being silly. I haven't thought about Sophy for years. I'd forgotten all about her. It was just coming here that brought it back because these old *dak* bungalows are all the same, built to a plan and furnished to a plan. Nothing ever changes. I'll be all right now.'

Jess interrupted, 'If you're not we'll take you home, so don't argue. I probably should be at home anyway because there's something I haven't told either of you. I'm going to leave Sam.' It came out just like that. To her own surprise, Jess had made the decision.

Her friends stared at her in amazement and Jackie asked, 'But what's happened? Why so sudden? You've never said a word about it.'

Jess shrugged. 'I've only just made up my mind. I came away to think about it and I've thought. I'm leaving him. That's definite.'

'Why? It's not because of that Democrat fire fighter is it?' asked Joan.

'He's got nothing to do with it. He doesn't even know I've been thinking about it. Anyway I don't know where he is or if I'll ever see him again.'

'Will that matter?' asked Jackie.

'It'll matter like hell, but I'll be able to live with it. I'm pretty tough. The main thing is that I'm pulling out of my marriage and going home. I'll miss both of you but I can't stay.'

In a puzzled voice Joan asked again, 'Why?' Her mind was full of the admonitions she'd received from her mother when she suggested leaving Theo and she wondered if she should pass them on to Jess, but none of them seemed to apply to her friend's case.

'It's over because Sam's not in love with me and never has been really. He's in love with someone else,' Jess told them bleakly.

'Oh Jess, for heaven's sake. It's probably just one of those awful Bombay flings that men out here get involved in. I know what Theo's been up to, but my mother told me that if I put a good face on it, I'd win out in the end and keep my marriage together. Since I left home I've been wondering what he's doing and who he'll be sleeping with while I'm away but I have to pretend not to notice. It's been such a struggle, acting as if nothing's happening,' Joan's voice broke when she told her friends about her own secret misery.

Neither of them was really surprised and they were very sympathetic. Jess wanted to say, 'Leave the rat', but she knew that Joan didn't want that advice. Besides, she thought, who am I to tell anyone else what to do? I thought I was worldly wise and fairly cynical, but I walked into marriage with a man who loves another man. If it had been happening to someone else, I would have been onto the situation instantly, but I didn't see it when I was involved. Perhaps because I didn't want to.

'I find all this hard to believe. Sam and you have always seemed to be a good couple and he's very proud of you. Who do you think Sam's in love with and how sure are you?' Jackie asked.

'He's in love with Perry.' It came out flat and matter of fact and was met by silence. Jackie made no comment because she remembered the jokes cracked by Sam's friends when he had come back from leave with a wife. Till then it had been suspected that he and Perry were a couple though Sam was known to chase women as well. Perry had no regular girlfriends though he was a favourite with hostesses, filling the role of the useful single man with impeccable manners for dinner parties. No wonder tongues wagged when Jess turned up.

When she made friends with Jess, Jackie and Peter discussed their suspicions and Peter said that Sam was probably trying to become normal. He'd always been less obvious than Perry.

'Marrying is probably his way of going straight. Perry will hate it,' Peter said, and till now Jackie believed that Jess had triumphed and Sam had put his past behind him.

Joan, who knew nothing of the old gossip, found Jess's story more difficult to accept because she'd often seen Sam smooching with other women at the rugby parties and thought that might be the rock that Jess's marriage would founder on. 'Are you really sure, Jess?' she asked doubtfully.

Jess nodded. 'I'm sure. He told me. He admitted it after I found a photograph of them kissing at some party before we were married.'

Shocked, Joan sat back in her chair, and said feebly, 'Maybe he's changed.'

'I don't care if he has. As far as I'm concerned my marriage is over. I'm not jealous or anything like that. I've grown up, I think,' said Jess, getting up from her chair and going to lean on the veranda rail. Far down on the plains there were still a couple of trees with death lights shining in them and from all around came the mysterious noises of a tropical night, the rustlings and mysterious susurration of swaying branches that might be caused by either a soft-footed panther or a careless mouse. From the overgrown garden came the heady smell of jasmine, the one Indians called Rhat ki Rani or Queen of the Night because it only gave off its sensual smell when darkness fell. She breathed in deeply, felt unshed tears prick her eyes and thought I will miss this, until I die I will always remember this.

Now she understood very well why Erik still yearned for the Burmese villages he'd lived in during the war, and suddenly felt an overwhelming surge of gratitude to Sam for bringing her to India and giving her the opportunity of finding a place that touched her heart so much. Strangely there was no anger in her towards him or to Perry. She blamed herself more than them.

She turned back to her watching friends and smiled, 'Cheer up, girls. I'm going to bed and I know I'll sleep like a log.'

She was right. They all slept deeply and woke to the sharp cedar-like smell of an upcountry morning. As soon as they opened their eyes, the children, still in night clothes, rushed outside to watch monkeys scampering away into the undergrowth. The women came out to breakfast on the veranda in their wrappers and sat talking about trivialities all morning. They never touched on serious issues and it was as if the revelations of the previous night had not been aired.

Only the advent of another evening of tropical scents and mysterious noises from the garden made them once again talk about their dilemmas. This time it was Jackie who told them about her problems with Peter, about his idleness and his gambling which was apparently as bad as ever. In their marriage she was the one who worried about lack of money and it preyed on her mind all the time.

'I thought that taking Sullivan as a paying guest might solve the problem, but it hasn't and besides he's so very strange that I don't like having him in the house. He's due to leave soon and that'll be a relief but the money problem will be worse than ever,' she said despairingly.

There seemed to be no solution to that problem and at ten o'clock they went to bed, tired out by doing nothing all day.

Next morning, when Jackie did not appear at breakfast Jess went into her room to ask, 'How are you today?'

Jackie sat up behind the mosquito net and said, 'Much better I think. I'm sorry for moaning so much last night. I love Peter and I'm sure we'll work it out. I was overtired.'

Jess stood casually in the doorway with her shoulder against the door jamb and said, 'We've all done a bit of moaning since we left home. It's probably done us good. Stay where you are and I'll fetch you in a cup of tea. Joan is up already and off taking photographs of the view.'

When the tea arrived, Jackie swung her legs from the bed to stand up, but as she threw back the thin coverlet she gave a gasp, 'Oh my God, there's blood on my sheet.'

Jess rushed over to look and said, 'It's maybe squashed bed bugs who've been feasting on you all night.' But she knew there was too much blood for that.

Jackie stepped out of her pyjama trousers and picked them off the floor, looking at them before she handed them to Jess. Both women stared in dismay at the stained crotch. 'You've been bleeding,' said Jess.

'It's a show,' whispered Jackie, and sat down heavily on the bed.

'Have you any pain?'

'No.'

'I'll get Joan.' The fact that she had never been pregnant made Jess feel incapable of dealing with this crisis so she ran out to fetch their other friend to help. Joan came in, looked at the stains and said reassuringly, 'I had a show like that when I was pregnant with Liza. I went rushing to my obstetrician but she was very reassuring. It's quite common apparently. You're not passing any more blood, are you?'

'No, it's stopped,' said Jackie, who was visibly shaking. Both Joan and Jess remembered how insouciant she had been about the possibility of going into labour in Matheran but it was a different story now. I bet there's not a telephone for miles, thought Jess though she was unsure what good it would do even if they did find one.

Joan took charge and said to Jackie, 'Drink your tea and lie down. It was a long journey to get here. You're probably just tired. We'll need to keep an eye on you for a bit.' Her tone was falsely confident but she flicked her eyes at Jess and they went out into the garden to whisper to each other.

Jess said anxiously, 'I don't think we can mess about with this. She'll have to be taken back to Bombay but it's after ten o'clock already and she can't cross the plain in the midday heat. We'll have to wait till evening when it's cooler and then drive as smoothly and slowly as possible. I'll take her on my own and leave you here with the children to come down later.'

Joan shook her head. 'No, we'll all go in convoy. My *ayah* will be able to help if Jackie goes into labour because she's had five children herself and certainly knows what to do.'

'Have you any sleeping pills?' Jess asked, and Joan nodded, 'I brought some. They're fairly mild.'

'We'll give her a couple to make her sleep on the journey.

She'll have to lie on the back seat. Thank God both of those cars are so huge. We can all get in. Ali, your driver can take us with Jackie and the kids can go in the servants' car. We'll leave all the food and the camping stuff behind to make more room.' Jess felt more capable when she was making practical plans.

Jackie was persuaded to take one of Joan's pills and fell into a peaceful sleep while plans were being made for their return journey. When she woke everything was ready for departure and the sun was sinking over the plain that spread beneath them. No one had the time or the inclination now to enthuse over the view again however.

Joan asked Jackie anxiously, 'Have you had any more bleeding?'

Jackie shook her head, 'No, thank goodness. It's all right.'

'Then get dressed. We've made a bed for you in the back of Joan's car and we're taking you home.'

'Oh no, I won't go. I want to stay here or I'll have ruined the holiday for everybody.'

Jess folded her arms firmly, 'You'd ruin it far more if we had to act as midwives, so it's back to Bombay for you and we're all coming with you.'

As always Ali was most caring and took care to avoid pot holes so that Jackie could have the smoothest ride possible. On their way down the *ghat*, they passed the holy man, still sitting cross legged with his eyes closed. When they drove by him, Jess leaned out of the window and threw out another handful of coins. 'I know you only have to pay on the way up but this is an unusual situation and every little helps,' she said.

Their progress was slow and it was four o'clock in the morning when they reached a village called Thana where there was an enormous encampment of some sort. There the main road onto Bombay island crossed a muddy stinking creek on a long concrete causeway.

Joan looked out at a cluster of lights on their left and cried,

'Look, there's a police station. It must have a phone. I could phone Theo and tell him to go to Jackie's flat and warn Peter that she's on her way home. He could alert Alex as well.'

'That's a good idea. She'll need a doctor,' agreed Jess. Jackie was still sleeping but they did not want to give her any more of Joan's pills which had turned out to be quite strong.

Joan tapped the driver on the shoulder and asked, 'How long will it take us to reach the city from here, Ali?'

'At least three hours, madam,' was the reply.

'Do you think the police would make an emergency phone call for us?'

'I can ask,' he said gravely, and pulled up the car in front of the police station. A constable in navy-blue shorts and shirt and carrying a rifle walked forward and pointed it suspiciously at their cars as the second car had pulled up behind them.

Ali rolled down his window and shouted out a request which was relayed back into the building. In seconds an officer in a smart khaki uniform appeared and walked across to speak to Joan in excellent English which he was delighted to display. He was eager to help and offered to call an ambulance to take Jackie to the police hospital but because she was not in labour they refused that offer. It was best to get her home.

'I only need to make a phone call to my husband,' Joan told him and he escorted her into his office where he pulled out a chair behind an enormous desk and lifted the receiver of a large black Bakelite phone as he asked, 'Tell me your telephone number please.'

She reeled off her number and was amazed at how quickly it began ringing out. Most Bombay calls took ages to connect. It rang and rang for what seemed an age and she was beginning to be afraid that Theo was not in his own bed when she heard his angry voice shouting, 'Who the hell is this? Have you any idea of the time?'

She took the phone and said urgently, 'Theo, it's me. We're on our way home because Jackie's been taken ill. We'll be with you in three hours. Please get a message to her husband and ring Alex at the hospital. She's been bleeding and she needs a doctor.'

There was a silence as he took this in and then he repeated, 'You're coming back now when you were meant to be away for a week? Anyway I'm ill myself and I don't know where her husband lives. I don't know her address.'

Joan was unmoved by his protests. 'Wake Yusuf and send him in a taxi with a note to Peter at number seventeen Cuffe Parade, first floor. He'll find it. He probably knows it already anyway. And, most importantly, telephone Alex at the hospital.'

'Why don't you take her there first?'

'What a good idea! But we must let Peter know too. Do it now, Theo, I know it's very early and probably a nuisance but it's an emergency and we are very worried about her. You say you're ill. What's wrong with you?'

'I've a very sore throat. This is a darned annoyance but I'll do it,' he said ungraciously and hung up.

After what seemed an interminable age, at last they were driving into the city suburbs. Does this city ever sleep? Jess wondered staring out of the car window at hurrying crowds of people and wandering cattle on the streets as they drove along.

The children's car went to Joan's flat with the *ayah* who would put all the children to bed and look after them till things settled down and the others went directly to Breach Candy Hospital as the sun was rising. When they trooped into the hospital's main concourse heading for the lift, a nurse was waiting with the news that a bed was ready for Mrs Innes and Dr Paisley was getting up to check her over. The three women looked so exhausted that the nurse could not make up her mind which one was the patient and when they entered the private room where there was a neatly made up bed with pristine white sheets, all of them wanted to hop into it.

Alex arrived at that point and Jackie asked him, 'Where's Peter? Does he know about this?'

'Yes, he knows we're expecting you. He'll be with us soon. There's been some sort of problem with your lodger I think, but nothing for you to worry about. Just get into bed now and try to relax,' said Alex soothingly, but his manner changed when he turned to Jess and Joan. With an abrupt gesture he almost shooed then out of the room and back downstairs. It was obvious he was hiding something and Jess asked him, 'Peter's OK, is he?'

'He's fine. It just took him a bit of time to get things organized,' said Alex, in a non-committal tone that set Jess's journalistic antennae twitching, but she was too exhausted to ask any more about Peter or his lodger for the meantime.

Because they were left with only one car, Joan insisted that Jess go home first, so they backtracked to Pali Hill where she was dropped off at the bungalow. It took the driver some time hammering on the door to rouse anybody inside. Sam and Perry were sharing the air-conditioned room where the air conditioner was so very noisy that they heard nothing and it was Mohammed in a ragged *dhoti* who eventually unbarred the door.

Jess did not take time to explain anything to him, only staggered past him into her own room and collapsed fully dressed into bed where she slept till late afternoon.

After she had dropped off her friend, Joan could at last go home herself. When Yusuf opened the door to her, Theo could be heard shouting in an obviously bad mood, 'Is that you, Joan? Where have you been? I'm not well and you're wandering around like a mad woman! What do you mean by leaving crowds of kids here, all yelling and screaming at once!'

Joan felt completely exhausted as she walked into the bedroom and held up a hand to stop him in mid complaint.

'Later, I'll tell you later. Are the children all right?' she asked.

It was Yusuf who answered, 'The children are all safe and well, *memsahib*.'

Like Jess, Joan slept till after noon and, when she woke, Theo was not in the bed but she heard the shower running and guessed he was there. She stretched out, pleased to be in clean starched sheets without an insecticide-drenched mosquito net hanging near her face. Trips away were interesting and the land-scape of the Western *ghats* spectacular, but it was more comfortable to be back at home in an COOL bedroom where the sheets were changed daily by the ever attentive Yusuf.

She sat up and saw the telephone on the floor by the bedside table and thought Theo must have extended the lead so he could have it nearby if she tried to keep in touch with him when she was away. Like her he would have no idea how cut off you became when you ventured out of the city. But why had it taken him so long to answer when she rang from Thana police station? He must have been deeply asleep. He'd certainly sounded startled.

Lifting the receiver she rang the hospital and asked to be put through to Jackie only to be told that her friend had been trans-ferred to the maternity ward. Her heart sank and she heard her own voice quavering when she asked, 'Is Mrs Innes in labour?'

'Are you a relative?' Joan recognized the voice and realized it was Gloria at her most efficient on the other end of the line.

'No, I'm Joan Ridgeway, one of the friends who brought her in last night. I hope she's not in premature labour.'

'Oh it's you, Mrs Ridgeway. I didn't recognize your voice,' said Gloria.

Joan knew she was lying, but she repeated, 'How is Mrs Innes?'

'I'm afraid we only give out details to relatives,' said Gloria smugly. 'I'm afraid all can tell you is that Mrs Innes is comfort-able but not receiving visitors at the moment.'

You bitch, thought Joan and hung up.

'I'll get dressed and go to fetch Jess. Between us we'll force Gloria to let us see Jackie,' she said to herself.

But first she had to see to the children. They were in Liza's playroom, happy and clustering round the doll's house. Neither of Jackie's pair seemed to be worried by the absence of their mother because they were enjoying themselves so much among Liza's paradise of toys and books.

'I'm going to see your mummy now,' she told them and they accepted that without question. To the hovering *ayah* she said, 'I won't be gone long. Keep them happy and give them anything they want.'

She went back to her bedroom to have a shower and found Theo back in bed, apparently asleep. When she tried to rouse him he only shrugged her hand off his shoulder and said, 'Leave me alone. I feel rotten.'

Annoyed she went into her drawing room where Yusuf was waiting with a glass of orange juice. A tray of coffee and toast sat on the table by the sofa.

'You must eat, *memsahib*,' he said and she realized that she was starving. It had been almost twenty-four hours since she'd taken anything except water. The worry about Jackie had driven all thoughts of food from her mind. She sat down on the sofa and lifted her coffee cup, noticing Yusuf watching from the door into the kitchen. When she emptied her cup he came across carrying the coffee pot and a saucer on which something lay in a little glittering heap.

Solemnly he refilled her cup and then laid the saucer on the tray beneath her nose. She stared down at it for a second not realizing what she was looking at. 'What...?' she began to say and then closed her mouth tightly for she recognized it. Tumbled in a heap on the saucer was Marcia's charm bracelet. There was not another like it in Bombay – or in the world probably.

She looked up at her bearer and saw a flicker of sympathy in his eyes. Perhaps he liked her after all and it was Theo he disliked so cordially.

'How did that get here?' she asked.

'When I made your bed yesterday morning, I found it beneath the pillow,' he said.

Was Marcia in the bed when I phoned Theo? When she heard I was on my way back, Marcia must have slipped it under the pillow hoping I'd find it. She probably didn't realize that Yusuf would strip the bed completely, Joan thought. Donald's wife's hostility towards her had not escaped her notice.

'Thank you, Yusuf,' she said and stood up with the jangling bracelet hanging from her hand. What a showy, vulgar thing it is, typical of Marcia, she thought.

Fury at Theo filled her and she could not bring herself to go back to the bedroom and confront him. That would take too long.

Walking with a firm tread, she grabbed her handbag and headed for the front door and the lift. She pressed the lift bell and, when it arrived, the doors opened but she did not get in. Instead she left them open and walked down to the floor below where she purposefully slid the bracelet between the ratchets of the closed lift gates, pushing it carefully so that none of the trinkets caught on the metal slats. Then she stood and waited till she reckoned it would fall down twelve floors. She did not hear it touch ground. When she turned she saw Yusuf watching her from the top of the last flight of stairs.

'Please close our elevator doors now and when Mrs Maitland Smith asks what happened to her bracelet, tell her I threw it down the lift shaft,' she said and calmly waited till the lift arrived beside her. With dignity she opened the door, stepped inside and rode to the ground floor where her car and driver waited. Her mind was racing as she settled into her seat.

Theo had made love to Marcia in their bed. It was the final insult. A terrible thought came into her head. I hope he dies! It's the only way I'll be free of him. Terrified by the enormity of the idea, she drove it out of her head.

At Pali Hill there was no sign of Jess and Mohammed said that she had already gone into Bombay in a taxi but he had no idea where she was going. Joan headed for the hospital and tried again to see Jackie, but Gloria was still on duty and visitors were barred. All that was said was that Jackie was 'quite comfortable'.

'What exactly does *quite comfortable* mean?' she asked.

'It means satisfactory,' snapped Gloria.

Joan went back to her car and sat for a few moments wondering what to do. She was not sufficiently friendly with Alex to ask him for the information that the rest of the hospital staff was denying her, but Jess was his friend. She had to find Jess. Where could she be?

The only other thing to do was go to Jackie's flat and ask her servants where Peter was. If he was not in the hospital, he might be at home or in his office.

'Take me to Cuffe Parade,' she told Ali.

To her surprise there was a crowd of people clustered round Jackie's gate and a blue uniformed police constable barred access to the garden. Ali turned in his seat and said, 'You cannot go in there, *memsahib*. These are rough people. I will ask what is happening.'

Solemnly he got out of the driving seat and approached the policeman. They talked for a few moments while she sat in a state of agitation, and when he came back he said, 'There was a killing there yesterday. Someone was stabbed. The police are investigating.'

She put both hands over her mouth and gasped, 'I hope it wasn't the *sahib* who was killed. It wasn't Mr Innes, was it?'

'The policeman said Mr Innes is not hurt but he must stay in the flat while the police take statements. We should leave here now. These kitchen stabbings can sometimes be dangerous, tempers run high and vengeance is taken.' Ali was obviously concerned about her.

She sat back in her seat feeling stunned and thinking, What terrible luck! When Jackie is in hospital, mayhem breaks out in her kitchen but thank God neither she nor her children were here when it happened.

All she could think to do was return home and take care of the children, to make sure they were all safe.

To her surprise Theo was still at home and in bed with all the curtains drawn when she re-entered the flat. She stood in the bedroom door and stared at him bleakly. 'Why are you in darkness?' she asked.

He half raised his head from the pillow and groaned, 'Because I'm ill. I've told you already.'

'What's wrong with you? Is it still a sore throat?' She did not sound sympathetic and knew it.

'I can't breathe,' he told her. She walked across to switch on the bedside light and saw that his lips were blue. This was serious, he was indeed ill.

'I'll phone for a doctor,' she said. His breathing sounded very laboured but he managed to say, 'I don't want that drunken sot of a rugby player that you like. Phone the company and they'll send someone out from the installation,' he said.

The doctor who arrived an hour later was a smooth young Indian who spoke with an American accent because he had qualified in the States. After he had finished examining Theo, he walked into the sitting room where Joan was waiting and told her, 'Your husband is very ill, Mrs Ridgeway. I suspect he has poliomyelitis and it has infected his lungs and his breathing.'

She gasped. 'My daughter is here and so are my friend's two children. It's very infectious, isn't it?'

'It's passed on orally. But I think the infectious state is passed as far as your husband is concerned. I understand from your servant that the children only came back from the hills last night. I believe it's polio because a secretary in your husband's office died of it last week and I understand he knew her.'

She stared at him. Tales of Theo's exploits among the company's secretaries had reached her so she knew what he was saying. 'What can you do?' she whispered.

'An ambulance will take him to the company hospital at Trombay where he'll be well looked after. If necessary he'll be flown to the States.'

She stood up and said, 'I'll go with him.'

The young man put up a hand. 'No, stay with your daughter. Perhaps you and she might even check into a hotel to be away from any infection. Think about going to the one at Juhu. It has a beautiful beach.'

She stared at him in surprise. What difference did a beautiful beach make? 'Exactly how ill is my husband?' she asked, in a challenging way that told him not to treat her like a fool.

He understood. 'Very ill indeed. If he was at home he would be put in an iron lung. Unfortunately we do not have such a facility in our hospital and I would not want to put him in one of the city infirmaries. I doubt if they have any iron lungs available anyway.'

She did not ask the next obvious question because she did not want to hear the reply.

Everything seemed to happen in a rush after that. An ambulance arrived and, while Joan stood watching helplessly, Theo was carried out of the bedroom on a stretcher, wearing a breathing mask with an oxygen cylinder by his side. As he was being negotiated through the flat front door, she squeezed into the gap beside him, stroking his hand and looking down into his face, but his eyes were closed, his lips were an even brighter shade of blue and his hair was matted on his brow with sweat. He did not seem to be aware of what was happening.

'Darling Theo, darling, you're going to be all right,' she told him but there was no reaction, not even a flicker of the eyes.

The doctor was still with them and he told her, 'I'll keep in constant touch with you. If you leave this flat and go to the hotel, let me have its phone number.'

'I'm staying here,' she said. She could not bear the thought of being more than an arm's length away from her own phone.

'Probably you're safe enough. I guess if you and your daughter were going to catch it, you'd be infected by now. It's an unpredictable disease and there's every chance you'll be perfectly well,' he said as he hurried out after the stretcher, shouting to the bearers about keeping the oxygen mask in place while they negotiated their way into the lift which was only just big enough to hold them all.

Joan's decision to stay in the flat with Liza was taken on impulse, but it did not stop her worrying about the danger of Jackie's children being infected. It was irresponsible to expose them to that risk. Determinedly she dialled the Breach Candy number again and when Gloria answered with the usual deflecting words, she snapped, 'Listen to me! I must talk to Mrs Innes. It's about her children. They're here in my flat and my husband has just been diagnosed with polio. I have to find out where her children should go. Her flat is surrounded by police and no one is allowed in.'

The silence at the other end told Joan that Gloria was shocked but knew far more than she was letting on. 'That's terrible. I'll find Dr Paisley and he'll phone you,' she said in a less hectoring tone.

'Do it immediately,' ordered Joan.

'Immediately,' agreed a chastened Gloria.

Alex rang back within minutes. 'I've just heard about Theo. Where is he?' he asked.

'He's been taken to the company hospital at the refinery and they'll fly him home if it is necessary,' Joan told him. Unlike Theo she realized that there was more to Alex than he displayed at rugby parties and wished it was he who had charge of the case because the young man she'd just seen was too slick for her taste.

'I'm sure he'll be looked after very well there. You mustn't worry. He's young and very fit.'

'His secretary died of polio last week apparently,' Joan told him.

Again a pause and Alex told her, 'There's cases all the time but they don't all die.'

'I have Jackie's children here and I'm worried that they might be infected in this flat, but I can't get hold of Jackie or Peter or even Jess. I don't know who might be able to take care of them. There's police all round Peter's flat because someone's been stabbed there.' Her voice broke.

Alex tried to calm her. 'You mustn't worry. Jackie knows about the stabbing but it has nothing to do with Peter. It does mean that neither she nor the children can go back to Cuffe Parade though because friends of a man who died are out for revenge and have made threats against the family, just because it happened in their house apparently. The police have been here and told her to stay in the hospital and we can't let anyone in to see her.'

'For God's sake who's going to attack her?'

'It's a possibility, they say. Naturally she's frantic about the children but she thought they were safe with you. She's been trying to contact you but your phone is perpetually engaged. I was coming round to see you myself because we're anxious not to upset the children. We haven't been able to get hold of Jess because she's never at home. She has been in here kicking up a row, but Gloria's shut her out because she's afraid that Jess'll run off to the cable office and send off a story about the whole thing.'

'I'm sure she won't do that,' said Joan.

'Maybe not, but Theo falling ill has changed the situation completely. It'll be best if you bring the children here so they can stay with their mother who's coming up to stay in my flat till this is all over. Bring them to the hospital and don't let them out of your sight because there's been threats against them too.'

'It sounds dangerous,' said Joan shakily.

'It is very dangerous, I'm afraid,' Alex told her.

It took Joan a huge effort to act bright and cheerful when she went into the nursery and said to Jackie's pair, 'Come on, folks, I'm taking you back to your mummy.'

Simon, who realized something was wrong, looked worried. 'Is Mummy at home?' he asked.

'No, darling, she's in the hospital, but she's better now and she's waiting for you there. Chop, chop, get your things together and we'll go there.'

Liza was sitting on the floor surrounded by toys and she pulled a face. 'Do they have to go away? I want them to stay here,' she said.

'You're coming with us,' said Joan. There was no way she was going to let her precious daughter out of her sight.

By now she trusted and respected Ali her driver and the feeling was returned. Darkness had fallen when he drew the car up to the main entrance of their block. He bundled Simon and Anna is so quickly that their feet did not seem to touch the ground. Then he did the same for Liza and in a commanding tone told them all, 'Lie down on the seat!'

Amazingly they did as he said without protest. Joan quickly climbed in beside them and found a cotton sheet lying in her seat which she realized was to drape over them. 'Play at tents,' she said, as if it was a game.

The car was driven off at a tremendous rate and went dodging dangerously in and out of the traffic on the short run to the hospital. At the entrance, Ali stopped almost on the doorstep, jumped out leaving the engine running and grabbed the little girls, one under each arm, saying over his shoulder to Joan, 'Bring the boy.'

The hospital porters had obviously been waiting for them and they quickly closed the main doors then ushered them into a small private lift. Ali's urgency made Joan realize how much more servants, who served so soundlessly and without expression, knew about the people they waited on than the people knew themselves. Whatever trouble Peter was in, it was obviously very serious and all the servants knew about it.

The lift carried them to the top floor landing where Alex's wife Mary was waiting. She gathered the scared looking Simon and Anna into her arms and soothed them, 'Come in, darlings. Mummy's here.'

Joan and Liza followed her into the flat where an ashen-looking Jackie was huddled in an armchair with her children climbing all over her. When the two friends saw each other at last they burst into tears.

'I heard about Theo being so ill. It's awful, but he's young and strong. He'll pull through,' sobbed Jackie.

'That's what Alex says, but you have trouble too. What's this about someone getting murdered in your flat?'

'Two people actually – one was a man we didn't know and the other was poor Prabu. He seems to have been stabbed in a sort of revenge attack and they're threatening to get us as well. That's why I'm hiding,' Jackie clutched her children as she spoke.

'But where's Peter?'

'He's still in the flat. We don't know why the police won't let him out. It's awful, Joan, I've not even been able to talk to him. He must be in a terrible state.'

'But why won't they let him out?'

'Alex is trying to find out. It's all Sullivan's fault, of course. I knew that man was bad. I wish I'd never laid eyes on him.'

'Where is he? Is he shut up in the flat too?'

'No he isn't! Trust him, he's halfway to London by now. His company flew him out in the middle of the night before the murders were discovered. He got onto his boss as soon as it happened and they whisked him away. That's what influence gets you! The police are keeping Peter because they think he was involved as well and there's nobody to smuggle him out of the country. It makes me furious when I think that Sullivan is getting away scot free.' Jackie was openly weeping now.

Joan sat down and shook her head. 'It's beyond me. Is there anybody who knows exactly what happened?'

Mary who was leaning on the back of Jackie's chair with a hand on Jackie's shoulder, said, 'Alex has driven over to Cuffe Parade and when he comes back, we'll have more information. He gets on well with the police because of rugby and one of the chief inspectors is a special friend. They're meeting up in Jackie's flat now.'

Joan sank into a chair and said, 'This is all too much for me. Has anybody seen Jess?'

Mary nodded. 'She completely lost her temper and has been rampaging through the maternity ward looking for Jackie, but Gloria has such a dislike for her that she won't tell her a thing and she goes storming out again before Alex can catch her. He's left messages for her to come here, but heaven knows when she'll go home to get them.'

'Thank you for bringing the children back,' said Jackie to Joan.

'My driver Ali was marvellous. I couldn't have done it without him.'

'You look exhausted. Have you had anything to eat?' asked Mary sympathetically.

'Eat? I think I had orange juice in the morning. It seems years ago. What time is it now?'

'Eight o'clock. Alex should be back shortly. I'll get some dinner for you and a drink if you want one,' Mary said.

'What I need is coffee, as black as possible, but I can't stay for food because the refinery doctor was going to phone back to tell me about Theo. He should be at the Trombay hospital by now so I mustn't be away for long,' said Joan, obviously fretting to get back home.

The coffee appeared and she gulped it standing up before taking Liza by the hand and running back to the lift. The faithful Ali was waiting in the car by the entrance and he held the door open for her the moment he saw her silhouette through the glass door. As they were driving out of the car-park, she saw Jess's 'sturdy bugger' nosing its way in but she was too intent on finding out about Theo to stop.

'Have there been any telephone calls?' was the first thing she asked Yusuf when she was back in the flat.

'Yes, *memsahib*. The doctor phoned and so did your mother-in-law.'

'What did the doctor say?'

'He told me nothing, but your mother-in-law said to call her immediately because the company has telephoned her about *sahib* being sick.'

Joan's relationship with Theo's mother was coolly friendly, but because she had nothing really to tell her, she put off making the return call. Instead she lifted the phone and dialled the doctor's number. It was answered at once by a girl who trilled, 'I will tell Dr Banaji that you called.'

'But I must speak to him now. It is urgent,' said Joan.

'The doctor will call you back,' said the girl and hung up.

Frustrated, Joan banged her hand heavily down on the table and hurt herself so badly she wondered if she had broken a bone. While she was nursing it to herself, the phone rang again and she forgot the pain as she reached out to lift it up.

'Joan?' said a voice. The accent was the same as Theo's and for a moment she thought it was him.

'Yes, yes, I'm here.' She said.

'It's Randolph. I want to come round and drive you to the installation so you can see Theo.' Randolph was Theo's managing director, a very powerful man indeed who lived in an enormous ranch-style house in the middle of the refinery site.

'You're coming now?' she asked, looked down at her creased,

sweat stained skirt. She hadn't had time to have a shower since she woke.

'Yes, my dear. I'll be with you immediately.'

She didn't argue or ask for time to have a bath because Randolph's orders were always obeyed. In five minutes exactly he was with her which made her suspect that he'd made his call from one of her neighbour's flats. Apologizing for her dishevelled state, she said she wanted to take Liza with her, but he firmly advised against it.

'It's not a good idea. A hospital sick bed is not a place for a child so young,' he said firmly and the servants backed him up.

'Baby is tired and hungry. She will be safe with me,' the *ayah* reassured Joan who followed Randolph to his car, wondering what was waiting for her.

It was as bad as her worst imaginings. As she walked into the hospital, everybody seemed to fall away in front of her. She had never been there before and was surprised to see that it was like a home town medical centre, a long, narrow building with a central corridor off which individual rooms opened. It did not seem capable of providing the facilities Theo needed. In the middle of a phalanx of men, she walked along the corridor acutely conscious of the all pervading silence and shivering in the fierce air conditioning. Theo's room was at the far end, the last of all.

As the door was opened a new sound took over. It was the hissing of a respirator and a terrible gasping and groaning that was coming from Theo who seemed to be choking for breath. There were wires everywhere connecting him to machines that glowed and blinked for, despite its low key appearance, the hospital was equipped with the very latest in medical machinery. She ran from the door towards his bed and grabbed his hand.

'Oh my darling!' she gasped and put her forehead on his upper arm.

A hand pulled her upright and the doctor's voice said, 'Take care. You mustn't dislodge anything.'

She looked up and said, 'He is going to live, isn't he?'

Dr Banaji looked at Randolph who spoke from the doorway, 'Theo's very ill, Joan.'

'I know that. I can see that. But he's not going to die. He's so strong. He can't die. Why can't you put him in an iron lung? There must be one somewhere.'

'He's fighting very hard,' Randolph told her.

She swung round and asked the doctor directly, 'Can't you save him?'

'It's too late for an iron lung,' he said bleakly.

'You can't mean he's going to choke to death? There must be something you can do?' The realization was beginning to dawn on her that she'd been brought here to say goodbye to her husband.

'We can help him,' Dr Banaji told her.

A terrible silence fell on them all after those words were spoken. Joan let them ring through her head before she repeated, 'Help him.'

'Do you want us to leave you alone with him for a bit?' Randolph asked her gently.

She nodded and the men withdrew, leaving her by Theo's bed with his hand in hers. She knew that this would be the last time they would be together in life and it was terrible watching and listening as his breath went rasping in and out. Though she had no idea if he could hear her, she talked.

First, she told him how much she loved him. 'I remember how I felt when I walked up the aisle to marry you. I was blissfully happy because there has never been another man in the world who could equal you. I love you so much, Theo, don't leave me.'

She told him about Liza and how she was going to inherit his good looks. 'She'll be tall like you and she has your beau-

tiful hair,' she said, brushing the fringe back from his clammy
brow.

'When you're better, we'll go back home and have another
baby. Maybe a boy this time. We'll call him Theodore Ridgeway
the Third. He'll go to Yale like you. You'll be a senator by then.
Maybe even President. What a handsome President you'll make.
You're even better looking than Jack Kennedy and you know
what a fuss is made about him.'

She was still talking when the door opened and the doctor's
head came round it. 'I think you should leave him now, Mrs
Ridgeway,' he said.

She bent to kiss Theo on the forehead. It was impossible to
kiss his lips because of the tubes. 'Goodbye, my darling. See you
soon,' she said, and bravely walked out.

Randolph took her arm and guided her back along the
corridor to a corner room furnished with deeply cushioned
armchairs and decorated with bouquets of artificial flowers.
'Why artificial flowers when there's so many beautiful ones
growing outside?' she asked inconsequentially. It was obvious
she did not know what she was saying really and Randolph did
not answer, for he was occupying himself with pouring her a
drink from a flask by her chair.

'What is it?' she asked, lifting the glass.

'Scotch. Drink it up, Joan.'

She did as she was told and felt the alcohol throbbing down
through her veins. 'I haven't had any food all day,' she said.

He got up and rang a bell. 'Bring sandwiches,' he told a
uniformed nurse who answered.

'What time is it?' Joan asked.

He checked his watch. 'Nearly seven,' he said. At that moment
the doctor came into the room. They exchanged a glance before
both looked at Joan. 'I am very sorry, Mrs Ridgeway,' Dr Banaji said.

She shook her head. 'Oh no, there must be some mistake.
Theo's all right, isn't he?'

'I'm afraid he's dead,' was the flat reply.

To their horror she threw back her head and gave a long howl like a wolf. It took them so much by surprise that both jumped towards her but too late to stop her reaching out for her glass which she gripped by the stem and hurled at the wall where it splintered into pieces.

She was standing in the middle of the room screaming like a woman possessed, 'He can't be dead! I didn't mean it! I didn't mean it.'

Randolph and the doctor thought she was referring to the tacit consent she had given to Dr Banaji helping Theo to die.

'He couldn't have lived, Mrs Ridgeway. His death would have been traumatic,' said Banaji alarmed.

'I didn't mean it, I didn't mean it!' Joan screamed on and kept on breaking glasses as if she was demented. People came running along the corridor as Randolph and the doctor advanced on the howling woman, grabbing her by the arms and holding her down in a chair.

'Give her something,' Randolph snapped, still fighting with her, and Banaji ran from the room, returning with a hypodermic syringe which he jabbed into her arm. Almost instantly she slumped back with her eyes rolling upwards. Two nurses came in to lead her away and put her to bed.

Hours later she was still unconscious when a telephone call came through from the States for Randolph. He looked exhausted. He took it in the hospital office where others were involved in making arrangements for the repatriation of Theo's body. When he put down the receiver he looked round at the people beside him and said, 'My God, what terrible news!'

'What is it?' asked the senior nurse, an American woman from New Hampshire.

'Someone's shot John Kennedy. He died in Dallas at one o'clock this afternoon.'

She put both hands over her mouth and said, 'It's a tragedy!'

Theo's death paled into insignificance compared to the latest bombshell.

It took some time before Randolph realized that Kennedy and Theo Ridgeway had died at almost exactly the same time.

Joan had still not returned home in the morning when Yusuf and the rest of the staff heard about Theo's death. They huddled in the kitchen looking stricken, not because they loved Theo, but they liked Joan and were also concerned about their jobs. The *ayah* was anxious that no word of the tragedy should reach Liza though the child was too young to appreciate the finality of death.

'We must not say anything to Baby. Her mother will want to do that,' she said.

Nonetheless, they all indulged Liza's whims by feeding her chocolate and the second boy ran around the house carrying her on his shoulders pretending that he was a horse. He was interrupted in mid gallop over the terrace by the arrival of Marcia's Nanny who demanded of Yusuf, 'Where is my madam's bracelet?'

'What bracelet?' he asked.

She called him a few obscene names in Hindi and said, 'You know very well what bracelet. She's sent me to fetch it.'

'Go and get it. It's at the bottom of the lift shaft.'

'What?'

'My *memsahib* threw it down there when I found it.'

'That bracelet is worth a crore of rupees. You'd better get it back.'

'I can't get it back. If you want it, you must get it back.' Yusuf's ears had pricked up at the mention of the value of the bracelet. A hundred thousand rupees would buy enough land in his village near Ahmedabad to allow him to live in comfort for the rest of his life.

As soon as Nanny departed to find help, he recruited a small boy, switched off the electricity supply to the flats when the lift was almost down at the ground but had enough space under its floor for the boy to slip though. It didn't take long. Before a few angry residents thought to go out to enquire why their air conditioners had been switched off, the boy, thickly smeared with stinking mud, was up in the Ridgeways' flat being showered down by a delighted Yusuf who had Marcia's bracelet safe in his pocket. It was not worth as much as Nanny said, of course, but it made enough to buy him a house and a big compound. The boy got a hundred rupee note that delighted him too.

When Nanny returned with a lift technician, Marcia was with her. The man stopped the lift, dismantled its floor, climbed into the pit and found nothing though he scraped around for a long time. In a fury Nanny hammered on the Ridgway door. Yusuf answered it with a severe look on his face.

'You thief, you badmash. I'm sure you never gave the bracelet to your *memsahib*. You've kept it. We'll have the police on you,' she screeched. Behind her, Marcia added her own recriminations, revealing a fluent grasp of Hindi obscenities.

'Go away. This is a house of mourning. We have just been told that our *sahib* has died,' Yusuf said and firmly closed the door.

On the landing the two angry women stared at each other wondering if they'd been told the truth.

'He can't be dead. He was spritely enough two nights ago,' said Marcia, but she knew it was unlikely for Yusuf to make up a story like that. The first place she went to for confirmation was her husband's office in Hornby Road. Bursting into his office, she said, 'I've just heard that your American woman's husband had died. Can you find out if it's true?'

Donald had wonderful contacts, his job was in PR after all. He lifted his phone and rang around. By the time he'd made two calls, the story of Theo's death was confirmed – the time and the cause as well.

'He died of polio, the kind that paralyses the breathing,' he told his wife, when he put down the phone.

She gasped and put her hand to her throat. He gave a cruel little smile and said, 'You'd better go home and lie down. It's passed on orally I believe. Where has your mouth been recently?'

As soon as his wife had left, Donald went to fetch his car and drove to Trombay. The guard on the gate at first refused to let him in, but he knew Randolph and demanded to speak to him on the security phone. 'I'm a friend of Mrs Ridgeway. I've come to take her back to her flat,' he said, and Randolph told him, 'She's in a horrible state, half mad, I'm afraid. Come and try to calm her down. We've got to get her to talk some sense because his family wants the body to be flown home and that has to be done as soon as possible, of course. She and the child should go with it.'

Donald found Joan sitting up on the bed with her arms linked round her knees rocking to and fro like a mental case. When she looked at him she did not seem to know who he was.

'Joan, sit still. Listen to me. I've come to help you. Randolph's making arrangements for Theo to be flown home for burial, but that must be done quickly in this climate. Do you want to go with him?'

'I didn't mean it. I didn't want him to die,' she moaned.

'Of course you didn't. Nobody thinks you did.'

'What am I going to do?' she asked him pitifully and he longed to hold her but knew that would be wrong.

'You and I will go back to your flat. You'll have a shower, collect your daughter and get on the plane to go back to New York. It's waiting on the tarmac for you now.'

He put out a hand and pulled her to her feet. Amazingly she went with him. Trailed by anxious nurses, they walked to the door.

'Tell Randolph to get us a car,' Donald ordered and, when it arrived, he helped Joan into it. His own car could stay at the main gate till he had a chance to come back for it.

They did not speak during the ride into the city, but when

Donald handed his charge over to her *ayah*, he said, 'Go into the shower with her and make sure she is all right.' He would not put it past Joan to try to harm herself. As he sat in the white drawing room, Yusuf laid a copy of the first edition of the Bombay evening newspaper on the table. In huge letters on the front page was the news of Kennedy's murder. He read it in a state of shock. What a horrible coincidence. Theo and Kennedy on the same day at almost the same time, he thought.

From somewhere along the corridor he heard the child's voice greeting her mother, 'Mummy, where have you been? I've been playing horses but I want to go swimming.'

Joan's voice was a low mumble and he stood up when she came into the room leading her child by the hand. The *ayah* had dressed her in a severe looking black shift with a string of pearls round her neck, a blonde version of the tragic Jackie whose picture was in the newspaper in front of him. He tried to push it under a pile of magazines so that she could not see it, but she read the huge headline and gasped, 'Is Kennedy dead too?'

'Yes.'

'What of?'

'He was shot.'

'Oh.'

'Are you ready to go now?' he asked.

'To the pool?' asked Liza.

'No, sweet, to the airport. You're going on an airplane,' he told her.

'I haven't said anything to her. I'll tell her later. She thinks Theo's sick,' Joan told him.

'That's best,' he agreed. Then he asked, 'What do you want to take with you?'

'Oh nothing. It can all be sent on. We have enough at home. If you telephone my mother for me from the number I give you she'll meet the plane and bring thick coats for me and Liza. It's winter there, you know.'

She seemed quite rational and composed and he nodded, saying, 'Yes, of course.'

'Let's go then,' she said almost gaily.

Donald turned to Yusuf and said in Hindi. 'Play fair by your *memsahib*. Pack her things carefully and don't steal.'

Yusuf stared him in the eye man to man before he said, 'I would not steal from her. She is a good woman.'

After he stood on the airport tarmac and watched her plane take off with its mournful cargo, Donald knew that he would never see Joan again. Wearily, suddenly feeling his fifty years, he climbed back into his car and drove to the Gym where Shackleton was drilling his troupe. A man on the stage dressed as an Indian bearer was answering the telephone without realizing that it was his *memsahib* on the other end of the line. '*Memsahib* not in,' he kept saying while the woman at the other end screamed at him, 'This *is* your *memsahib*.' It ended with the servant uncomprehendingly hanging up. That sketch was a favourite with the Gym audience and it was played every year but, as Donald watched it for the hundredth time, he felt a strong surge of resentment and shame. That was the way his compatriots thought about their Indian servants but he remembered the impressive Yusuf who had everybody well summed up. The revue audience didn't want to hear about servants like him because they couldn't be condescended to.

The two grand pianos stood at the side of the stage. Joan's music was still on the rack of one of them. Donald walked across to his seat and played a discordant chord. 'You've just lost your best musician,' he said.

There were already rumours circulating that something had happened to Theo but no one knew the full facts yet, so Shackleton stared at him and asked, 'What do you mean?'

'Mrs Ridgway has flown back to New York with her husband's body. I've just seen her off.'

'Damn and blast,' Shackleton snapped, 'How am I expected to

mount a review when people keep dropping out all the time? Lilias, Ridgeway and now his wife! It's not good enough.'

'I'm sure Savage and Ridgeway wouldn't have gone and died if they knew how much it was going to inconvenience you,' said Donald sarcastically.

'We can cope with only one pianist. We've done it before,' said Shackleton.

'Well, you'd better find one soon because I'm quitting,' Donald told him. Though Shackleton flew into a fury, raved and shouted and stamped around the stage like Donald Wolfit at his most histrionic, there was no changing Donald's mind. He couldn't face doing the show without Joan by his side.

As he gathered up his sheet music and turned to leave the hall, Ginny, in her black fishnet leggings, ran after him and put her arm around his waist, before she said sincerely, 'I'm so sorry, I knew how much you felt for her.'

He shook his head and kept on walking. Behind him Shackleton was still screeching, 'That's it. This show is jinxed. The only thing we can do is call it off. It must be the first time since the Mutiny that the Bombay Gym hasn't staged an annual show.'

There were so many things to discuss that the gossips did not know where to start. Kennedy's assassination was of premier significance but Theo's death sent a thrill of terror around the expatriate society and the hypochondriacs among them noted every variation of their own physical condition with dread and terror. The situation that caused most speculation however was the strange case of Daniel Sullivan and Peter Innes and rumours about it were rife.

Jess had returned to Pali Hill at night ignorant of the news of Theo's death and without any accurate information on Jackie's situation. Denied access to both Jackie and Peter all she'd heard were rumours. Hints of homosexual liaisons were mingled with stories of gambling schools had that got out of hand and murderous retributions because of refusal to pay sums owing. Neither Perry nor Sam were any wiser than she was and they managed to sink their own estrangements as they sat up till late discussing what they knew. At midnight, when she decided to go to bed, Sam got up with her but she said, 'I'd rather sleep alone.'

'What are you going to do?' he asked.

'I'm going home. I feel as if I've put my career on hold while I've been here. My friend Andrew has moved to the *Daily Express* and he thinks he can get me a job there.'

'I wouldn't say you've been exactly idle,' snapped Perry.

'The problem is that I think I've exhausted the possibilities here for the moment,' she told him.

'Granted,' he said.

She turned back to Sam, 'You know we've agreed to take the Baumgartens' flat in four days' time, it's only right if you do that, but I won't be there because I've cabled my father and he's sending me an air ticket.'

'First class, I presume,' said Sam sarcastically and she was glad he was showing a bit of spirit.

'We always travel first class. It's only since I married you that I've had to travel steerage,' she snapped back.

As she was leaving the room, she paused at the door and said to him, 'I'm not going to do anything about divorcing you. We can stay apart for the number of years the law allows and then you can divorce me for desertion. I don't care.'

'Thanks,' said Sam and she laughed thinking it was a very low key way for a marriage to end.

Before she left the room however, the phone rang and Sam answered it. Alex was at the other end. 'Is Jess back yet,' he asked.

'She's here.'

'Tell her Jackie's in trouble and wants to see her. Have you heard about the Ridgeways?'

'No, what's happened to them?'

'Theo's dead and Joan's been whisked off to the States in a private jet with their little girl. If you can get over here now we'll fill you in on the whole mess.'

All thoughts of sleep disappeared and the three of them piled into the Studebaker and went back into the city. Alex and Mary's normally tidy flat was in a state of confusion and Jackie lay with her feet up on a couch, ashen faced and visibly twitching with nerves.

Jess went to sit beside her, take her hand and ask, 'For God's sake, what's happened?'

'Peter's under suspicion of murder,' she gasped.

'That's ridiculous,' said Jess.

'I know that, but Sullivan told his boss that Peter arranged a killing in our flat and it's difficult to disprove because Sullivan's fled the country.'

'What's Peter meant to have done?' The three newcomers asked the question in unison.

'Organized the murder of the man who was blackmailing Sullivan apparently,' said Mary.

Jess groaned, 'This is all too much. First Theo dies and Joan's flown out of the country in the blink of an eye and now this! You'll have to start at the beginning.'

Alex took over the story. 'It seems that Sullivan, Jackie's PG, was a paedophile with a taste for little boys.'

'And there's plenty of them in Bombay,' said Sam.

'Exactly.'

'Did he prey on the market boys?' asked Jess, remembering the strange behaviour of the sinister boy at Crawford Market.

'He did. There's some sort of ring that supplies boys from there to people like him but one night a boy was brought in and treated so badly that he died....'

Jess shuddered imagining the desperate lives led by the little boys, some of them no older than five or six, who lived in the market car-park. However she could not believe that the ineffectual Peter was involved in procuring them. He was lazy and feckless but he wasn't wicked.

'After the boy died, they got rid of the body but the men who control the gangs started to blackmail Sullivan. He paid up at first but the demands got bigger and he hit on the plan of hiring a pair of thugs to kill his blackmailer when he came for his final pay out. It was all arranged to take place in the Cuffe Parade flat when you girls were away in the hills.'

Jess asked, 'Did it work?'

'Yes, they killed him all right, but it was a messy business. What Sullivan didn't know was that the blackmailer brought some friends with him and they were waiting in the garden. When they saw what was happening they went to help him but Jackie's bearer tried to hold the door against them and he got stabbed. Then everybody bolted. Sullivan looked out for himself first and immediately got onto his boss who rushed him to Santa Cruz airport and put on a plane for Europe. He was lucky there was one leaving for Geneva at that time and bribes got him on board. He never gave a thought to the dead men or to Peter.'

Jess could imagine the anger of Jackie's long suffering cousin when he was confronted with Peter's latest disaster.

Alex was going on with the story, 'Peter called an ambulance and the bodies were taken to the Victoria Hospital so the police got involved, but by the time they got to Cuffe Parade, Sullivan had gone and only Peter was there. Even the rest of the servants had run away. No one likes getting mixed up with the Bombay police, even when they're innocent.'

'So Peter's the only witness,' said Sam.

'Absolutely. But Sullivan apparently told his boss that Peter was the one who was procuring boys and arranged the killing. He was trying to pass the buck and he seems to have been believed, but connections and influence are involved as well, of course. As far as the police are concerned, they have to get some-body and Peter's the fall guy.'

'I know he didn't do it. He was only involved with the gambling that went on. Sullivan brought people in to play cards as well,' sobbed Jackie.

'The police know about that too. Apparently Peter lost a lot of money to the blackmailer and that also gives him a motive,' said Alex ruefully. 'And that's not all, though it's bad enough. The associates of the dead blackmailer are out for revenge. They've threatened to kill Jackie and the children. They don't know that she wasn't married to Sullivan and they can't get at Peter because the police are guarding him. He's under house arrest really. We have to keep her and the kids shut up here and not let anyone near her.'

'What a bloody mess,' said Jess with feeling.

'Indeed, and it's even more complicated. The police have advised me that Jackie ought to be flown out of Bombay at once, but airlines won't take pregnant women who are near their delivery. I'll tell a lie and post date her expected date but she can't travel alone. The show of blood in Matheran wasn't huge but it was a warning. I can't travel with her because my assistant is on holiday and Gloria can't go – anyway Jackie doesn't want her. We have to find someone else, for the police are insistent that she should be sent out of danger. They've told me that the men who are making the threats are very dangerous and violent. They certainly wouldn't hesitate to kill a woman or children.'

'I'll go. I'm going home soon anyway and my father has cabled me a ticket,' said Jess suddenly. She didn't give a thought to how she'd cope if Jackie went into labour. Surely there would be someone with medical knowledge among the rest of the passengers in the airliner.

'Oh thank you, Jess,' said Jackie in a heartfelt voice and none of the others tried to argue her out of her offer.

There was only one snag: Jackie wouldn't consider leaving

until she could speak to Peter. Alex knew that she had to go as soon as possible so he undertook to persuade his friend in the police to let her see her husband.

'Maybe you could give the police some information that might be useful. I picked it up from one of the boys at Crawford Market,' Jess suddenly said to Alex.

He looked at her with interest because he respected her sharpness of mind. 'What is it?'

'When I go to the market I always use a very ugly little boy called Sammy to carry my basket and about a week ago Jackie went with me to the market to buy some flowers …' She looked at her friend and asked, 'You remember, don't you, Jackie?'

'Yes, I remember, but what has it to do with this?'

'There was a bigger boy called Ashok there that I don't like and he acted very oddly when he saw you. I could see he recognized you though you obviously didn't know him. Afterwards I asked Sammy about him and he said that Ashok often took small boys to your flat. He knew who you are and where you live.'

'Market boys went into my flat?' asked Jackie aghast.

'Yes, that's why Ashok knew you. He'd seen you there. I'm pretty sure he knows a lot about this, but tell your police friend if they round the boys up, I don't want Sammy hurt.' She knew from Sammy that the police often beat the market boys and sometimes rounded them up and drove them off the island, leaving them by the side of the road to survive as best they could. The most enterprising of them jumped onto the first train going into Bombay and were often back at the market before the police vans.

Then Jess had another idea. 'In fact, please don't pass on my information till about nine o'clock tomorrow. I'll try to get hold of Sammy before that and give him some money to go home, wherever that is, so he'll not be here when the police make their round up. It's Ashok they need anyway,' she said.

'It's a deal, but nine o'clock's the deadline,' said Alex.

That night Jess slept in Alex's flat. She asked Sam to lend her the Studebaker and he and Perry went home in a taxi. At six o'clock next morning, drinking coffee in Alex's flat, she said to him and Mary, 'I'm going to have to borrow some money off you, I'm afraid. I've got to find enough to make sure Sammy can live when he gets away. I think he's a Bihari because he's so black and it would be good to give him enough to get him back there and impress his family, if he's got any. If you give me some of your housekeeping money, Mary, I'll give you a really huge bottle of Miss Dior eau de toilette with an atomizer that has never even been opened. I was given it as a present a couple of weeks ago. You like perfume, don't you?'

Mary always smelt delicious and she did like perfume. The thought of Miss Dior made her eyes light up. 'How big is it?' she asked.

Jess made a shape with her hands, the size of a brick. 'That big. Lilias would have sold it for five thousand chips at least, but I'll give it to you for five hundred,' she said. That was more than enough to send Sammy home in style. He'd probably hitch a lift on a train by riding on its roof anyway.

Alex was eating toast and he said, 'I'm afraid you're being a bit naïve, Jess. The boy'll probably take your money and be back in the market next week.'

'I'll just have to take that chance, but I don't want to risk Ashok turning on him. When the police rope him in, even if it's only for questioning, he'll suspect Sammy told me about his visits to Cuffe Parade. He always watches me when I talk to Sammy and he's been even worse since I went to the market with Jackie.'

'OK, I'll give you the money for the perfume but don't you want it yourself?' said Mary.

'I'd love it, but poor wee Sammy needs saving. He's so endearingly ugly and sweet and cheerful and he's got nothing going for him. I'll give him the money and then go on to Pali Hill to fetch the perfume for you and bring Sam and Perry into their offices. Trust me.'

'Oh I do trust you, darling, I just think you're a bit crazy,' said Mary with a laugh.

As usual Sammy came running towards her familiar car waving his arms and shouting, 'I'm your boy, I'm your boy. What you are wanting?'

'A bunch of flowers, that's all,' she said, walking fast in front of him past the other boys. Ashok was leaning against the wall beside the market gate and she did not even look his way as she passed him. He, too, looked away.

Halfway up the central aisle with banks of flowers towering over her head on both side, she said quietly out of the side of her mouth to Sammy, 'I am going away and I'll never see you again, but I want to give you something. You must go home to your native village *today* – not tomorrow, today.'

He opened his mouth to say something and she hissed, 'Don't speak, just listen. Get me a spray of tuberoses and when I pay you for them, I've got some money for you. It's rolled up very tight and I don't know where you'll hide it, but I imagine you know a place where it can't be found.'

She'd taken the money mostly in low denominations so that he would not arouse suspicion if he bought anything.

He stared at her and saw how deadly earnest she was, and had a good idea why because the whole market knew about the killing in Cuffe Parade and that Jess was friendly with the woman whose husband was involved.

'Get me the flowers now,' she told him and stood back while he bargained.

'Take them to my car,' she ordered loudly and, when they reached the Studebaker again, the square was packed with cars and people were streaming into the market. She opened the car door and stuck out her hands for the flowers. As they were being passed to her, she ordered, 'Get into my car now and lie down on the floor in front. There's a newspaper on the seat to put over yourself. Go on, do it now!'

He crouched down, slipped past her like an eel and squirmed into the foot space. She put the little roll of money on the floor between the seats and threw her flowers on top of him as she casually hopped into the car, and switched on the engine. Thank God it started at first turn, it didn't always. Driving away, looking as casual as she could, she said, 'We're going to the station now because there's going to be big trouble here soon and you're better out of it.'

A few minutes later she drew up at the front of the Victoria Terminus, a vast, Gothic monstrosity of an imperial railway station built by the British in 1886. 'Off you go,' she said, and Sammy jumped out of the passenger door, made a *namaste* salute to her through the window and slipped into the crowds thronging through the station entrance. She didn't wait to stare after him, only revved up the accelerator and drove away. She hoped for his sake that they'd never see each other again.

Fifteen minutes later a police van with wire mesh over its windows stopped in the middle of Crawford Market car-park. The blue clad constables who jumped out were armed with long *lathis* and, using them mercilessly, they rounded up the boys, including Ashok who tried to bolt but was outrun by a long-legged policeman. The captives were jammed into the van and driven off to be mercilessly interrogated. The few who staggered back that evening were visibly battered and bruised. Ashok was not among them.

When Jess eventually returned to Alex's flat, she discovered that the news of Jackie's plight had spread among her friends. Sprawled in a chair was Colin who looked up when she entered the flat and said, 'I hear you're taking Jackie back to the UK. Have you any place to stay in London?'

She said 'No' because she had not thought that far ahead.

Colin told her, 'I have a flat in Chelsea. You and she can use it till you get yourselves settled. Jackie says she has an aunt in Somerset, but she won't be able to travel there till she gets herself sorted out medically. I've brought the flat key with me because I hear you're off soon.'

'Are we?' asked Jess looking at Alex.

'As soon as possible,' he said, 'We're just waiting for the police to bring Peter here to see her. She won't go without speaking to him and I've managed to arrange it. They should be with us any minute.'

At that moment the flat bell rang and he went out onto the landing to wait for the lift to arrive. Peter was escorted in by a police officer in khaki who treated his captive with scant respect. Dejection was written all over Peter, his shoulders were bowed, his face ashen, his eyes red rimmed as if from weeping.

'Jackie's in our bedroom waiting for you,' Alex told him in a cursory tone that did not hide his contempt.

'I didn't *do* anything,' Peter protested but Alex only waved a hand.

'Jackie's waiting. It's really important that she gets out of here as soon as possible. There's a plane taking off in an hour's time. I want her to be on it because if she goes into labour, there's no way she'll be able to fly.' Peter ran into the adjoining room and closed the door.

Jess looked at Alex and said, 'Is it as urgent as that? What'll I do if she starts?'

'I'm only trying to scare him because he bloody well deserves it, but I do want her to be on that next plane because we might not be able to keep her hidden here much longer and the police say that the mood of the locals is very threatening. They've got the main ones but they can't keep them all forever. That boy in the market you told them about came up with the whole story. Innes is in the clear as far as the murder is concerned, but he was bribed by Sullivan to let things go on in his flat that he should have forbidden.'

'He gambles,' said Jess.

'And he's a weak fool,' said Alex.

'Do I have time to go back to the bungalow and pack some clothes?' Jess asked.

'I'd rather you didn't. It's possible you'll be followed,' said the police officer crisply.

Jess looked down at her crumpled cotton pants and shirt. 'I'll freeze in London in this,' she said.

'Mary can lend you an overcoat. Just leave it in Colin's flat and she'll pick it up when she gets home next year,' Alex said.

Colin reached into his back pocket and said, 'I thought you might have money problems. It can take time to get to banks and change rupees, but I always keep a little reserve of pounds and I've brought you a hundred. Take them, you'll need them.'

Jess thought it was amazing how the most unlikely people turned out to be true friends when crises arose. 'Thanks, Colin,' she said, taking the money. She knew that her father would provide her with cash as soon as she was back in England and free of Sam. 'I'll leave that in the flat for you too,' she promised.

'It's a present so it doesn't matter if you don't,' he said with a grin.

In the room next door, Jackie lay weeping on the bed while Peter sat beside her with his hands on her shoulders. 'Why did you allow it? You must have known what was going on?' she sobbed.

'I didn't pay much attention till he told me he was being blackmailed. Boys came and went and they all seemed happy enough. I don't know when one of them died, or how it happened, but that was when the trouble started. Some thug tried to blackmail Sullivan about it and he brought people in to deal with the blackmailer when he came to get his money,' Peter told her.

She shuddered. 'Our children were in the flat when the busi-ness with the little boys was going on presumably. You should have thought about that and thrown him out on the spot.'

'But we needed the money,' he protested.

She turned her head away from him in horror. 'We didn't need that kind of money. Besides what did you do with it? You gambled it away, didn't you?'

He went on the defensive. 'Only to make things better for you and the children. That's why I gambled. I did it because I love you and wanted to give you things. I know how much your family despises me because I'm poor and have no money behind me. I wanted you to be able to stand proud beside them.'

'Instead of that you've made me into a pariah,' she accused.

'No, I haven't. I've told your cousin that I'm resigning from the company. He thought that was a good idea and said he'd try to fix me up with an office job in London, but in fact I'd already been offered a job in Hong King by a fellow I play tennis with. He's just been made managing director of a textile company with clothing factories out there. It'll be the start of a new life for us, Jackie. We can start all over again.'

She desperately wanted to believe this, but there were doubts. She'd heard nothing about this tennis-playing friend before.

'Is your friend genuine? Does he really have a job for you?'

'Of course he does. He's only been in Bombay for about nine months and he's not one of the rugger buggers. He's an ordinary bloke from an ordinary family. We get on well together and he needs someone to run his personnel department. When I told him about the trouble I had with your cousin, he sympathized and offered me this job.'

Jackie decided not to criticize this version of events and said, 'It'll be something new for you. You've not worked in a factory before,' she said.

He sat up straight and with a firm look on his face. 'I get on with people and I've a good brain. It'll all be common sense. I'm determined to make a success of it. Besides I'll be my own boss, and won't have to obey the orders of men who think they're better than me because they went to fancy schools.'

She knew that they would have been much worse off if her cousin had not gone out of his way to help them, but she desperately clung to her belief in Peter. 'We'll be all right,' she agreed, and put her head on his chest.

'I can't go with you to London tonight because I'm still needed to give evidence, but the police insist you and the kids should be out of Bombay as soon as possible. They've roped in the man who actually did the killing and a couple of market boys as witnesses because they were there too. I know the Gym gossips say I've been arrested for murder, but that's rubbish. I'm not under suspicion for anything, so don't worry. Go home and I'll be with you before the baby comes, I promise.'

It was a horrible surprise to Jackie to hear that people were saying Peter was suspected of murder. She knew that was impossible. What he was guilty of was being tempted by Sullivan's money. When things were happening that should have alerted his suspicions, he deliberately closed his eyes. Also, she thought with cold clarity, her husband had been impressed by Sullivan. He wanted to be useful to him.

'Will you be safe? If people want to kill me or the children, won't they want to kill you too?' she asked.

'Probably, yes,' he admitted.

She stared at him in horror and he reassured her, 'Don't worry. I'm safe with the police. I'm staying in Colaba Police Station till they have all the information they need, then I'll come home to be with you. It'll probably take about a week.'

'But we've no money,' she said.

'Your cousin's company will pay my fare. He's already paid yours but that's part of my contract. Aren't you going to stay with your aunt? I'll write to my father and ask him to send you some money to keep you going till I get back. Then we'll go straight to Hong Kong. The job's waiting for me now.'

Once more Jackie squashed her scruples about taking money from other people. Peter seemed to think it was due to him. An only child, he'd been very spoiled by his mother.

They both wept and clung together when they parted, and at midnight Jackie and the sleepy, fretful children were loaded into the Studebaker with Jess and Sam drove them all to Santa Cruz airport. Alex's friend provided them with a two car police escort. At the terminal, they were ushered through to a safe place so Sam and Jess had to make their farewells at the security barrier.

She kissed him and said, 'Look after yourself, Sam. I'll be at Colin's flat in Chelsea for a little while till Jackie gets the medical all clear and then I'll let you know my address. I don't know what I'm going to do really.'

'You still want a divorce?' he asked.

'Oh yes,' She had no doubt about that. It was very strange that Sam, her husband, now seemed to have become a pleasant friend, someone she could leave behind without recriminations.

'You'll be OK, Jess,' he said, and she took comfort from his words. She'd said nothing to him about Erik and had no idea what would happen. If she never saw him again, she knew she'd survive, because she was the surviving kind, but there would be a big empty hole in her heart that she was sure would never be filled.

It was raining in London and Jess hailed a taxi to take them to Chelsea. Colin's little house was actually nearer the Fulham Road than Chelsea, in a cobbled mews that ran behind a row of large houses that had been turned into flats. When she opened the door Jess was overwhelmed by the smell of dust. Obviously the place hadn't been lived in for a long time, but it was well equipped with functioning electric radiators that heated up quickly and there were bundles of bedding and towels in a linen cupboard. At the end of the street a little basement shop sold basic food and Jess bought milk, tea, bread and breakfast cereal which they ate before falling into bed and sleeping round the clock.

She wakened in confusion, not knowing where she was, and it took a few moments before she could marshal her thoughts and remember everything that had happened in the last two days. Someone was calling her name. 'Jess! Jess!' She jumped out of bed to go into the room next door. Jackie was sitting up in bed looking distressed, with her thick black hair all tangled.

'I think I'm in labour,' she said.

'Oh my God.' Jess looked at her watch. It said ten o'clock and she hoped it was the morning because the curtains were still drawn. She pulled them apart roughly and saw daylight outside. 'Thank heavens! Is there a phone?' she asked, her eyes ranging round the room.

'I saw one downstairs in the little hall,' Jackie said, grimacing as another pain hit her.

Jess ran down the stairs and lifted the receiver. Thank God there's a dialling tone, she thought. An out of date phone book stood on the table top. Alex had given her the name of a friend from his student days who worked in the maternity department of Guy's Hospital and she decided to ring him up. Hospital numbers usually didn't change.

There must have been a desperate urgency in her voice because she was put through when she told the Guy's switchboard, 'I must speak to Dr Armitage. It's a personal matter and very urgent.'

When he came on the line, she plunged straight into the subject. 'I'm a friend of Alex Paisley in Bombay and he gave me your name and said you'd help us. I arrived with a pregnant friend from India last night and she's gone into premature labour. We know no one else in London. Please help.'

He was remarkably calm and unruffled as if strange requests from Alex were nothing new. 'Is she able to travel?'

'I think so. The pains are strong but not continuous.'

'Get her in a taxi and come here to Guy's. Ask for me in the obstetrics department.'

'OK,' said Jess and hung up. While she was out on the street whistling up a taxi, Jackie told the children to get dressed. Awed by the obvious seriousness of the situation, and the signs of distress shown by their mother, they did as they were told, though the clothes they put on were peculiar because they took out the first things that came to hand in their suitcases. Little Anna had on odd shoes, one white and one black.

Before she left the flat Jess had written down its telephone number and when Jackie was being wheeled away on a hospital trolley, she said, 'Ring this as soon as you know what's happening.'

The rain kept on falling and Jess was afraid to leave the house in case she missed a phone call. Fortunately the novelty of television distracted the children and all she had to do was feed them – breakfast cereal and baked beans seemed to be their favourite food.

By eight o'clock at night, Jess had heard nothing from the hospital. When she telephoned she told the nurse that she was Jackie's sister and was informed that the patient was still in labour and the doctors were considering performing a Caesarean section. Shocked, she hung up and was sitting wondering whether she should phone the news to Bombay when the phone rang and a woman's voice said, 'Lady Hemmings here. I'd like to speak to Jacqueline please.'

'I'm afraid she's not able to come to the phone at the moment,' said Jess cagily.

'Tell her it's her aunt Daphne who is planning to come to London tomorrow to collect her and the children. My nephew in Bombay has contacted me with the news about her leaving that dreadful man, thank heavens.'

'She's in Guy's Hospital right now. Her labour pains started this morning and they're thinking of giving her a Caesarean,' said Jess. The idea of such an operation chilled her blood.

'Good heavens, where are the other children?'

'They're with me. They're OK.'

'And who are you?' Aunt Daphne's tone was very patrician.

'I'm a friend who travelled with her from Bombay.'

'My dear, that was very kind of you. I'll come tomorrow and take the children off your hands. Just give me your address. I'll be with you by eleven. I live in Sussex, not too far away.'

'I'll expect you,' said Jess.

'Don't bother about lunch,' said Aunt Daphne.

Daphne arrived on time in an ancient Rolls Royce with a uniformed driver. She said that Colin's flat was 'quaint' and cooed lovingly over Simon and Anna who were sitting patiently waiting for her. When they all drove away, Jess was suddenly overcome by complete desolation and the finality of what she'd done came home to her. Here she was in London, a city she did not know and where no one knew her. She was far more at home in Bombay. No one in her own family knew where she was; she had no job and only a limited amount of money which would not last long once she started dipping into it. Her clothes were outdated and unsuitable for the weather; her friend was very ill and the man she, loved was – where? She had no idea. It wasn't like her to weep but she did shed a few tears.

The ringing of the telephone brought her out of self pity.

'I'm sorry to have to tell you that your friend's baby was delivered dead. She wants you to come in and see her,' said Dr Armitage.

'I'll be there immediately,' Jess told him.

Jackie looked terrible, pallid and exhausted, with strangely lifeless looking hands spread open on the counterpane in front of her.

'It was a little girl. If she'd lived I was going to call her Jess after you,' she said.

Jess lifted one of her friend's hands and gently rubbed it to bring the blood back. 'You went through too much,' she said.

'I know. Will you let Peter know?'

'I've done that already. I sent a telegram to Alex. Your aunt came and took the children away with her to Sussex. She wants you there as soon as you leave hospital.'

'She's my best aunt. I love her. She married a general who was much older than her but they never had any children and she's always taken a special interest in me. She loathes Peter though.'

'She thinks you've left him.'

'Oh dear, that's a pity.'

'When do you think they'll let you out? Your aunt said she'll send her car to take you to Sussex.'

'There will have to be a burial service for the baby first. I don't want anyone but you and me there.'

'If that's what you want. They must have facilities here for that.'

'They do. The ward sister told me. I want to do it as soon as possible. We'll name her and bless her and send her to be cremated.'

'If that's what you want,' said Jess again.

'I want it done now,' said Jackie who obviously had everything worked out.

A nurse brought in the baby wrapped in a white blanket and Jess held out her arms to hold the pathetic bundle. Pulling back the edge of the blanket to see the little face she sighed and said, 'Isn't she beautiful? Absolutely perfect.'

'She's a lovely child,' agreed the nurse who had a strong Irish accent.

Jess had never seen a new born baby, far less a dead one, and was amazed at the definition of its features, by the high bridged nose, the long eyelashes and elegant eyebrows. Little Jess was the image of her mother. Pity, sorrow and anger flooded her mind. Jackie should have given birth to this child in Bombay under Alex's care. Instead, because of Peter and Sullivan, she'd gone through trauma and the beautiful baby had to die and lose its chance of life.

The ceremony was kept short and simple and, when it was over and the child taken away, Jackie collapsed in an agony of weeping while Jess sat dry eyed beside her. She was too angry to cry.

Before she left she sought out the ward sister who was sympathetic and kind. 'When will my sister be able to leave?' Jess asked. It was best to keep up the sister pretence, she thought.

'In a week, I think. She's in good physical health fortunately but very shocked and distressed. You don't look like sisters, do you?'

'We have different fathers,' said Jess.

'I see. Your aunt Lady Hemmings has been on the telephone. She'll send a car and a nurse to take your sister to her house near Horsham as soon as we decide she's able to travel. We've been told to contact her direct.'

'She's Jackie's aunt but not mine,' Jess said.

'So it's all right to contact her instead of you?'

'By all means.' Jackie would be far better looked after in Horsham than she would be in Colin's flat off the Fulham Road.

When she walked out of Guy's elegant forecourt, Jess was lost and stood looking around wondering where to go. John Keats studied at Guy's. He must have known this street, she thought, as she headed towards the river for she had a good sense of direction. Walking soothed her and she wanted to walk and walk, to stare and stare, to soak up London. To her delight she soon found she was in Fleet Street, the place where she'd longed to work ever since she decided to go in for journalism.

The *Daily Herald*'s address was Endell Street, she knew, and she guessed that would not be very far away so she went into a pub and asked the barman for directions. The office was easy to find and when she went up to the uniformed commissionaire, she said, 'I want the news desk.'

'Back door,' he said dismissively, pointing down the street.

Feeling like a Victorian tradesman, Jess meekly asked the man in a little wooden kiosk beside a time clock if the news editor was available.

'Who will I say wants him?'

'His Bombay stringer,' said Jess.

Though journalists are not given to enthusing over each other, Jess met with a friendly reception and the assistant news editor actually said, 'That was a good piece about the half-empty bottles of hair lotion.'

She beamed, happy that she'd made an impression. 'I'm looking for a job,' she said.

They began to back track. 'There's no vacancies at the moment,' she was told. What she did not know was that the paper was paying people off rather than taking them on.

'Is Andrew Gordon still on the staff?' she asked. Andrew would get her in, she was sure, because he had a genius for making friends who went out of their way to help him. 'He went to the *Express* last week,' she was told.

'Where's the *Express* office?' she asked.

'You can't miss it. It's made of black glass and it's right in the middle of Fleet Street.'

Luck was with her. Andrew was at work and when the front office phoned up the news room he came down, delighted to see her. 'My God, what are *you* doing here?' he asked.

'Looking for a job,' she said.

'About time. I can probably get you a few shifts,' he said and hurried her upstairs with him. Within what seemed like a few minutes, Jess was fixed up with the equivalent of two days' work a week. As she had done with the *Herald*, she used her maiden name professionally so she was hired as Jessica Harper. She threw her arms round Andrew's neck saying, 'You angel. I knew you'd save my bacon. Come out and let me buy you a drink.'

He looked at his watch. 'Five o'clock, opening time. We can go across to El Vino's. Women aren't allowed to buy drinks there so I'll have to get them for you but you look as if you could use a gin and tonic. Let's go, and you can tell me about it.'

It took her half an hour to unburden herself and, when she'd finished she felt physically lightened for Andrew was a good confidant who didn't butt in with advice or comments. 'What a story. You did the right thing by bailing out and you'll be fine,' he said at the end.

She wondered if that would be true because there was one thing she hadn't told him. She'd said nothing about Erik.

Back in Colin's house by eight o'clock, she felt painfully lonely. A phone call to her father took him by surprise but, like Andrew, he approved of her decision to leave Sam. 'Don't worry about money. Come home and I'll put you on the company board,' he said.

'That's not necessary. I've found a job on the *Daily Express* starting now.' An avid reader of newspapers, he was impressed.

'Your mother and I will come down to see you then. What's your address?'

'I haven't really got one. I'm in a friend's house in Chelsea but it's only temporary. I'll let you know when I find a flat.'

'Don't stint yourself. I'll pay,' he said. I will stint, whatever that means, she thought, because of him keeping her in thrall by paying for everything was one of the reasons she'd wanted to get away from home in the first place.

Jackie stayed in hospital for a week. Jess visited every day, often snatching the time between assignments, but one afternoon she rushed in to be met with an empty bed.

'Where's Mrs Innes?' she asked a nurse.

'Oh her aunt arrived and whisked her away this morning. Is your name Jess?'

'Yes.'

'She left you a note. I'll fetch it for you.'

The note said that Aunt Daphne had taken over, persuaded the doctors that Jackie would be better off being nursed at home and taken her off to Horsham. There was a Sussex phone number attached. Scrawled at the bottom of the page was an urgent PS: *I've just had a phone call from Alex to tell me that Peter has been sent direct to Hong Kong. The man who offered him the job couldn't wait any longer and insisted he went at once. The children and I will join him when I'm fit enough to travel.*

If Aunt Daphne has anything to do with it, that will be never, thought Jess.

Now Jess was really alone. There was no excuse for her continuing to occupy Colin's flat if Jackie had gone. She'd have to find her own place. Andrew lived with his wife and baby son in Ealing and he offered to find her a place there, but Jess wanted to be more central and anyway she'd come to like the Fulham district where she had landed up.

Anything on the market to rent however, was either too expensive or too miniscule – usually one bedroom with a tiny gas ring in the corner and a chicken coop of a bathroom if you were lucky. Places like that made the Baumgarten flat seem immense.

Standing despondently in the window of Colin's sitting room she was wondering what to do when she noticed a red printed notice that had appeared in the first floor window of the little house opposite. TO LET, it said. The ground floor of that house was occupied by a car repair shop where the men always wolf whistled at her when she went in and out. She wondered if they were leaving.

Without waiting to put on a coat, she ran over the cobbles and put her head into the open garage door. A pair of boots stuck out from underneath a car and she called out, 'Who's letting that place upstairs?'

The feet wriggled and kicked till a man with an oil-streaked face finally emerged. 'It's me boss that's letting it. His mum used to live up there but she's died and he's looking for a tenant who won't mind us working down 'ere.'

'I wouldn't mind,' said Jess. He stood up and wiped his face with a rag. 'Oh it's Miss Cat's Eyes from over the way. Are you moving out?' he said.

'It's not my house. It belongs to a friend and it's too big for me really. How much is the rent for your boss's flat?'

'Dunno, I'll ask him; he's in the office.' He turned on his heel and yelled, 'Oi Fred, Miss Cat's Eyes 'ere wants to know about your mum's flat.'

Boiler-suited Fred came sauntering through from somewhere at the back. He eyed Jess critically and said, 'From over the road, yeah?'

'Yes.'

'Any security?'

'I have a job. I'm on the reporting staff of the *Express*. Jessica Harper's my name.'

'What about the kids from over there? This's not a place for kids.'

'They're not mine. They belong to my friend who's been in hospital. She's out now and they've all gone to live in Sussex.'

'What about the guy who comes to that flat now and again?'

'That's Colin. He works in India and he's the friend who lent us his flat because we'd no place to stay in London, but he'll be coming back on leave soon and will want it himself.'

'He's an odd guy. We see him standing on his head for hours every day in his front room. A bit nutty, we reckon.'

'I suppose he is a bit nutty,' Jess admitted. The men laughed.

'What's the rent?' Jess asked, eager to get to the nitty gritty.

'That's open to discussion. We're just going out to have a pint in the pub along the main street now. Come with us and we'll talk it over.'

A third oil-streaked mechanic emerged from the back and joined them in the pub where they all ordered pints, so Jess had one too. They sat round the table discussing the other residents of their mews and, as she listened, she began to like them all very much, because they were worldly wise and unimpressionable and seemed to miss nothing that went on. They even knew the exact age and possible price of Lady Daphne's Rolls Royce which had greatly impressed them.

Two pints was enough for Jess's patience and she said, 'Come on, tell me the worst. How much do you want for your flat?'

'But you 'aven't seen it?' said Fred.

'I'm sure it's perfect. Your mum lived there, didn't she?'

'Yeah, and all the furniture is the old junk she liked.'

'I like old junk too,' said Jess, thinking nostalgically of the Thieves' Bazaar. There was a note of longing in her voice that did not go unnoticed.

'Five quid a week.'

She stuck out a hand over the table and said, 'Done. Do you want a reference or a deposit? Do I have to take a lease? When can I move in?'

'No references, no deposits, no leases, just the rent in cash. Buy us all another beer and you can move in tomorrow if you like.'

They adopted her and she felt perfectly safe and happy living among Fred's mother's old-fashioned furniture. In a huge chest of drawers with big knob handles, she found embroidered tablecloths, napkins and beautifully monogrammed linen sheets that Fred said his mother had 'acquired' when she worked as a housemaid in a fine house in Belgrave Square.

He said she could use the garage phone that sat on the floor of the half landing between the workshop and her flat and, when she was out, the mechanics took in her mail and any parcels. If anyone came to call, they were quizzed before they were allowed to go upstairs. Andrew, who arrived with his wife and a baby in a pushchair, passed muster, but another old friend who worked as a racing tipster on the *Evening Standard* and favoured flashy pin stripe suits was given a hard time till she vouched for him.

When she offered to pay extra for her electricity, Fred laughed. 'We get it free,' he said. Apparently they'd rigged up an illicit link to an overhead street lamp in the mews and saw nothing wrong in that. 'Everybody does it down our way,' said the youngest mechanic, Lennie, who came from the Isle of Dogs. In return for their protection, Jess wrote stiff letters for Fred who always seemed to be chasing people for unpaid bills. He was pleased because her use of legal sounding phrases seemed to work on his most laggard payers.

Her father came to visit and got on famously with them all. He stayed in the Grosvenor House, anything less he would not consider, and brought a crate of beer to the garage when he arrived to take her out to dinner. Tactfully he avoided the subject of her going home to work for him.

Joan

Joan's father was deeply concerned about his daughter when he helped her off the plane with Theo's coffin in its hold. She was extremely calm, too calm, he thought, and he feared that her composure might crack at any moment and she'd break out into screaming hysterics.

As she settled herself into his car, she said, 'Stop at a drug store, please. There's something I need to buy.'

'We can send someone out to get anything you need,' he said, but she insisted quite calmly, 'Please stop for me, Father.'

He did as she wanted and watched anxiously as she made her way into the shop, returning very quickly with a small package which he hoped was not pills.

Next morning, when she emerged from her room for breakfast, her parents were astonished to see that she'd dyed her hair jet black. Neither of them commented on the change but when they discussed it later, they decided it was some sort of mourning gesture.

Her calm continued through all the arrangements for the funeral and interment, but she took only a cursory interest in the details, spending all her time in front of the television set which was almost exclusively dominated by the death and burial of John Kennedy. She was particularly interested in any news bulletin that showed Jackie Kennedy.

'Do switch that set off,' said Joan's mother finally in exasper-
ation, but her daughter turned and looked at her in surprise,
'But she and I are united in this. We're going through it together.
We're like Siamese twins.'

Just as Jackie took her children to stand beside their father's
grave, Joan insisted on taking Liza to stand beside Theo's. Like
Jackie, she was icily admirable in dignified grief; like Jackie, she
wore simple, black clothes and enormous dark glasses. She
became a Jackie clone.

When she returned home after the burial, she shut herself up
in her room and spent hours writing letters, a sheaf of which
were handed to the doorman of their building to post. A few
days later he said to Joan's mother, 'Gee, Mrs Kennedy must be
tired of getting all those letters from your daughter.'

'What do you mean?'

'Well I've been posting at least five a day from her.'

'All to Jackie Kennedy?'

'Yes, ma'am.'

Joan's parents decided to tackle her on the subject. 'Perhaps
you shouldn't be sending so many letters to Mrs Kennedy right
now,' said her father.

'But I know what she's thinking and I know she'll want to
know what I'm thinking. Our lives are running on parallel lines.
We lost our men almost at the same minute – the same *minute*!
Everything that happens to her, happens to me too.'

Joan's mother looked meaningfully at her husband and rose
to her feet. 'I think I'll go and phone Theodore's mother,' she
said, and left the room.

Between them they organized a doctor to come to see Joan
who received him graciously, just like the First Lady. To him she
repeated her conviction that she and Jackie were living parallel
lives. 'We've lost men who we loved very much though we
know that they had huge character flaws, other women and
things like that, so we need to talk about it,' she said.

'But Mrs Kennedy might not want to discuss such personal matters with someone she doesn't know,' he suggested.

'She knows me! We're like sisters. All I have to do is keep reminding her that I'm here waiting. I write to her several times a day and I've been ringing her up too.'

'I think you should stop for the meantime,' he said in a kindly tone.

'I can't. It's my duty to keep on. It's the only way either of us will come to accept what's happened.'

Things came to a head when a solemn looking man arrived at Joan's parents' apartment and told them that if the bombardment of Jackie Kennedy with letters and telephone calls did not stop, legal steps would have to be taken. 'Mrs Kennedy is aware that Mrs Ridgeway is very upset because of the death of her husband which seems to have taken place at about the same time as the President's, but this must stop,' he said firmly.

Yet Joan would not see sense. There was only one thing to do: her parents had her committed to a very exclusive mental hospital in the wilds of New Mexico where she remained for the best part of a year. When she emerged, she was much more subdued than she had ever been before, but her hair had grown back blonde and she had worked through her grief. There were no more letters to Jackie Kennedy.

LONDON 1964

By the time Jess had been living in the flat above the garage for almost two months, Christmas was over, another year had started and she realized that she was happier than she'd been for a long time. There was only one hidden sorrow that she deliberately avoided thinking about.

Sam wrote to tell her that business was going well and he and Perry were sharing the Baumgarten flat. Jackie phoned to invite her to Horsham but before she could go, there was another call to say that Peter had arranged a flight to Hong Kong for his family and they were leaving in two days. It seemed that Jess's past was well behind her and she consoled herself with the thought that she was essentially a solitary.

I'm not temperamentally suited to living with anybody else and I'm obviously incapable of having a long term relationship with a man. There must be something wrong with me, she thought.

Then, one evening in January when she was coming home from a job, Fred called out to her, 'When you were out, a guy came looking for you at the house across the road. At least I think it was you he wanted but he called you Jess Grey. He was kinda rough looking so we said we'd never heard of you.'

She stopped dead with her heart thumping. 'Rough looking?'

'Yeah, pretty tough. He was a Yank and he needed a shave,' he said.

'So you said you'd never seen or heard of me?'

'Well I've never heard of Jess Grey. You're Jess Harper and he wasn't the kind of bloke you need. He's too old for you.'

'Oh Fred, that's the love of my life and you've gone and sent him away!'

Two days later Jess didn't have a shift so she was cleaning her flat, a task that partially drove away the blues for her. It gave her tremendous pleasure to dust Fred's mother's knick knacks and put posies of flowers in the little vases that stood on every polished surface. Suddenly she heard the unmistakable sound of a black cab drawing up in the mews outside and a door banged. She went to the window and to her indescribable delight saw Erik standing on the cobbles facing up to Fred, 'Come on, I've checked with Bombay and I know Jess was here. You guys must have seen her. Where did she go?' he demanded.

Frantic, she rapped on the window glass with the handle of her feather duster making the men in the street all look up at her. In an instant Erik was transformed from a potential pugilist as his face split wide with the most tremendous grin she had ever seen. Without a glance he pulled a note out of his wallet and thrust it towards the cab driver at the very moment Jess came plunging down the narrow little stairs and flew at him, almost bouncing off his chest.

'Erik!' she gasped, laughing and crying at the same time. 'Oh Erik, I thought I'd never see you again.'

He said nothing, just sank his face into her hair and held her so tight that she thought all the breath was about to be expelled from her body.

Then she stepped back, took his hand and pulled him into the hall. He kicked the door closed behind him with his heel.

The three mechanics all stood in the open garage door watching this and then Fred turned to the taxi driver to say, 'He won't be needing you again, I guess.'

'But he's given me twenty quid and the fare's only one pound two shillings.'

'Don't look gift horses in the mouth,' said Fred.

NEW YORK, NOVEMBER 2004

In the Algonquin Hotel, New York, Jess Harper sat in the foyer reading a newspaper. Like her father she enjoyed good hotels and her choice in New York was the Algonquin because of its literary connections. Her eye lighted on a photograph of a social event at one of the city museums and, though she was alone, she cried aloud, 'My goodness!'

Some heads turned and a waiter sauntered over to ask, 'Yes'm?'

'Sorry. I don't want anything. I was surprised by something I read in this paper, that's all,' she told him.

She sat back in her chair and folded the paper. I only needed a clue, she thought, I needed a lead and here it is. Since the spring she'd been trying to tie up the loose ends of her life and find out what happened to her old friends. The search had become engrossing. In the beginning it was fairly easy because she started off with Jackie who sent her a Christmas card every year so she had an address at least. Sadly she had failed to find any trace of Joan Ridgeway who seemed to have disappeared.

She dipped into her Hermes handbag and brought out her spectacles so that she could take a closer look at the photograph. It was Joan without a doubt.

The caption said that Mr and Mrs Philip Zedek, who had donated a valuable collection of Mexican art to the Brooklyn Museum, were the hosts at a glittering reception and Mrs Zedek was pictured greeting some of the guests.

Joan had weathered well. Still blonde, reed thin and upright, and looking very WASP-like, she was wearing a long, tight sheath with a halter neck and what looked like a collar of diamonds. She must work out, thought Jess, because her upper arms were tightly muscled.

'Get me a residential phone book for New York – I'm looking for a name beginning with Z,' she told the waiter, who came back carrying the book on his tray. Jess began ruffling through the pages and found at least twenty Zedeks in different parts of the city, but she guessed if Joan was rich enough to be donating art to a museum, she would be living in a good class area. But, of course, she might not be living in New York at all. The best thing to do would be to go to the museum and ask to see some of the Zedeks' Mexican art. She might pick up a clue there.

She went to Brooklyn in a cab but unfortunately the collection was not yet on show to the public. When she expressed her disappointment to a curator, she said, 'I know Mrs Zedek you see, but I've lost touch with her and haven't seen her for years, I don't suppose you can tell me her address or phone number?'

The curator shook her head firmly because she was well trained in how to handle patrons' fans and one of the things not to do was to hand out personal information.

'I've not seen her for nearly forty years and I'm flying back to UK in a few days,' said Jess sadly, and her obvious sincerity softened the curator's attitude. 'The best I can do is take your name and a contact phone number and send them on to Mrs Zedek. Then it'll be up to her to get in touch with you or not,' she said.

Jess handed over a business card but then tried to take it back as she said, 'Oh that won't do. It has my maiden name on it and she won't recognize it. Look, I'll write on the back ...' and she scribbled, *Jess (was Grey) from Bombay in the sixties is at the Algonquin for another four days and would very much like to meet you again. Suite 149.*

Every time she returned for the next two days she stopped at the reception desk and asked if there had been any messages for her. There never were and she began to doubt her own certainty that Mrs Zedek, the donor of Mexican art, was the Joan she knew. Perhaps there was a special type of upper-class American women who all looked the same and could only be found in good social circles. Joan was probably one of them.

On her penultimate morning she was packing and checking her flight tickets when there was a tap at her door and she opened it to find Joan, swathed in sables. They stared at each other without speaking for what seemed an age and then Jess stood back, opening the door wider, and said very formally, 'Do come in, Joan. It's wonderful to see you again.'

As always Joan towered over her for Jess was not tall. Joan shrugged out of her fur and let it drop casually over a chair in the sitting room. Through the open bedroom door a jumble of clothes and parcels could be seen covering the floor.

'Are you alone?' Joan asked.

'I'm afraid so. The place is a mess. I've been in Australia and I'm going back to London tomorrow night. Let me order you a coffee.'

'Yes, please. It's amazing you found me and I'm so sorry I didn't get in touch with you as soon as I got your note, but I wasn't sure that I wanted to remember the past. I've tried very hard to forget Bombay. Then I woke up this morning thinking about you and Jackie and the time we went to Matheran and I knew I had to come.'

She was obviously nervous, very intense and agitated. Without comment Jess lifted the phone and ordered coffee, then, taking another look at Joan, she added, 'and a chilled bottle of champagne with two glasses please.'

'I've been looking for you for a long time and it was purely by chance that I saw a newspaper photograph of you at the Brooklyn Museum. Your name has changed, but you still look the same,' she said.

Joan did not return the compliment by saying that Jess looked the same and that made her grin. 'I know I look different. My hair's gone grey and my bust has slipped a bit,' she joked.

'But you still have those inquisitive eyes that bore into people,' said Joan, and when the champagne arrived, she became more like her old self and sat down on her fur coat with her long legs sticking out in front of her. Her shoes were crocodile skin, as was her handbag, and the coat was real fur of course. She obviously was not worried about protecting endangered species and Jess wondered if she was also wearing something made of ivory – probably bangles.

That thought made her remember Marcia's charm bracelet and she laughed as she lifted her brimming glass to toast her friend, 'Here's to us meeting again. Do you remember Marcia and her bracelet? She never got it back and when I saw her last spring she was still going on about it. Her Nanny found out that your bearer Yusuf retired to his native place when you left. She said his retirement fund was the bracelet.'

'You saw Marcia recently?' Joan looked astonished.

'Yes, she worked for years in a secretarial recruitment agency in Bond Street. By the time I found her she was well over eighty, but the rest of the women in the office thought she was sixty. She worked very hard at putting on a good front. We went over the road to the Ritz and drank champagne cocktails. Nanny was still with her and they were living in Finchley, terribly hard up actually. I really admired her guts.' Jess remembered sitting with Marcia in the Ritz bar listening to old stories and the inevitable dirty jokes. Before they parted, Marcia kissed her on the cheek and said, 'I always liked you, Jess. You were right to leave that queer. I hope you found someone else to love.'

Jess bristled at Marcia's way of referring to Sam but she only said, 'I did, Marcia.'

'That's good. I only ever loved one man really and that was Donald. I love him still.'

'She told me that Donald was the love of her life,' Jess told Joan.

'That was hard to guess. I don't regret chucking her bracelet down the lift. It was a vulgar-looking thing anyway,' was the dismissive reply.

'She died about a month after we saw each other. I went into the recruitment agency to call on her again and they told me she'd had a heart attack at her desk. It was only then that they found out her real age,' Jess said.

'What about Donald? He was so kind to me when Theo died,' Joan said.

'I don't think he ever got over you. He left Marcia within months of you leaving and you'll never guess who he married next?'

'No. Who?'

'Ginny! Remember her in the show chorus? Long legs and so tanned that her skin looked like leather, but she was OK really. Her husband was caught fiddling his insurance company's books and was fired, but she didn't go home with him. She stayed and married Donald; then they retired to Spain – probably so she could keep up her tan – and I heard from Marcia that Donald died last year. Ginny's still in Alicante I think.'

Joan was now looking sad, probably because she was remembering the terrible time of Theo's death, Jess thought, so she hurried to change the subject. 'Jackie's well. I've just been to Australia to see her and she's had an amazing life. It'll take me ages to tell you about it. She lives in Perth and she's as good value as ever. We talked about you a lot. She'll be so happy to hear that I've found you again.'

'Philip and I have been thinking about going on a round-the-world trip soon. Perhaps we can visit her too,' Joan said.

'She'd love that. She lives in a very rural area, in the middle of a cattle ranch actually. You'll be amazed because she looks nothing like the Jackie we knew. She still rides out to look at her cattle every day.'

'Her cattle?' Joan obviously found that idea hard to accept.

'She and her son Simon own a huge spread of land and her daughter Anna is married to a man who owns the farm next door. You remember Simon and Anna, don't you? They were such sweet-natured children. Your Liza was very fond of them. How's Liza?'

Joan's face closed down again and once more Jess was afraid she'd said the wrong thing. 'She's known as the Ridgeway heiress, I'm afraid. She's married to a banker now, but she was married to a film actor before and that didn't work out, nor did the first one. We don't see a lot of each other because when I brought Theo's body back I broke down completely and his parents took over Liza. I didn't look after her for a long time. When she went to college, they asked me not to visit her. She married at eighteen for the first time to another law student, but they didn't invite me because they were afraid that I might break down and make a scene. When she was little I did go off the mental rails a lot, but I haven't done it for a long time now. Philip has been such a help in making me face up to my feelings of guilt about Theo.'

Jess was surprised. 'Guilt? What have you got to be guilty about?'

'I sublimated my relief at being free of him and transferred it into exaggerated mourning. Then I had an identity crisis and became convinced that Jackie Kennedy and I were living parallel lives. Jack Kennedy died at almost exactly the same time as Theo, you see.'

Jess could not resist pointing out, 'I reckon a lot of people died that day. People die all the time.'

But Joan did not want to hear that. 'I felt I was suffering the same things as Jackie – we both lost a promiscuous man whom we loved and we felt guilt, not only because we were glad to be free, but we felt that we had let them down somehow – why did they need other women?' Joan was visibly agitated and Jess bit back a crack about some men needing no excuses. She thought Joan was coming out with a lot of psychiatric babble and decided to change the subject.

'Tell me about your Philip,' she said.

Joan leaned forward and took a sip from her glass. 'Philip saved my sanity and my life,' she said.

Jess said, 'That's wonderful,' and prepared to hear more.

'He was a psychiatrist at a clinic in New Mexico where my father sent me when I broke down the first time, just after Theo's funeral and Mrs Kennedy sent a secret service man to tell me to stop writing her letters.'

Jess nodded in encouragement thinking, She's obviously had more than one crack up.

Joan was warming to her theme. 'Philip was only starting his career then, he wasn't long qualified when he went to work in the clinic and I found I could talk to him. He tried to stop them giving me electric shock treatment but it was fashionable then and my parents wanted it for me. It was horrible,' she shuddered.

'I've heard about it,' said Jess sympathetically. One of her newspaper colleagues had gone through that treatment and all her front teeth were burned black by it. Joan's teeth looked all right though, but all American teeth seemed perfect anyway.

'I was very sort of spaced out but basically all right for quite a while afterwards. I forgot about Mrs Kennedy when she married that man Onassis. Why did she do that? My mother said it was for money, but she must have had enough. Thank God, I have never had any money problems. But my parents both died, only months apart, and that hit me badly so I went off again. The Ridgeways wanted me to go back to New Mexico, but I refused and then someone told my mother-in-law about a wonderful psychiatrist who was practising in Manhattan. It turned out to be Philip. He took me on as a patient. We married and I've been all right ever since. I still have therapy once a week, of course. I go to a colleague of Philip's, a man he respects. Have you ever had therapy, Jess? It's so freeing. I have the most incredible dreams.'

'No, I haven't had therapy, but it sounds as if you went through a terrible time,' said Jess sympathetically. She felt very sad, not only because of what happened to her friend but because the woman who sat facing her was not the Joan she remembered. She seemed to have no interest in anyone but herself.

That unspoken thought seemed to occur to Joan at the same time however, because she said, 'But all we're talking about is me. What about you and Jackie? Did you divorce Sam? Is she still with that awful Peter?'

'Jackie and Peter split up and Sam and I divorced quite amicably, just by waiting long enough. He divorced me for desertion and that was OK as far as I was concerned.'

'Have you remarried?'

'No.'

'I'm sorry you didn't marry again. A woman needs a man to back her up, I think. I wouldn't be able to function without Philip.'

'Is it you or Philip who collects Mexican art?' Jess wanted to know, remembering the function at the Brooklyn Museum which had reunited them.

'It's Philip. He started buying from local artists when he was working in the clinic and his collection just grew and grew. We live in an duplex in Sutton Place and there isn't room to show all of it. There's so much he decided to give half to the Brooklyn Museum because one of his relatives used to work there and redesigned it or something. Philip's Jewish. My mother would be horrified if she knew I'd married him.'

'Lucky she died,' said Jess sardonically and immediately regretted her levity fearing that the new Joan was unlikely to appreciate that sort of crack.

Fortunately Joan did not seem to take offence. She leaned forward and said, 'Do you have to go home tomorrow? I want you to meet Philip and I'd like you to come and see the Mexican pictures. We've kept the best. They're wonderful, such brilliancy of colour, very primitive. Change your ticket and stay over.'

Jess shook her head. 'I can't. My son's getting married next week in London.'

'Your son? Were you pregnant when you left Sam?' Joan was obviously surprised.

'No.'

'What happened? You said you didn't remarry.'

'Oh Joanie, I'm a loose woman. I lived with a marvellous man for ten years, but we never married. We didn't want to. He was married already and I was waiting for my divorce. What was the point of going through it all again because we both knew that there was nobody else in the world for either of us so we didn't need to stand up and make promises.'

Joan reached into her handbag and brought out a packet of cigarettes. 'Do you mind if I smoke? You're not talking about that man who had no dinner jacket, are you?' she asked.

Jess laughed. 'Are you still shocked? Yes, I have a son with the Democrat-voting fire-fighter. I didn't mean to have children because I was terrified of going through labour, but when it came to it wasn't as bad as I expected and my son is terrific.'

What's his name?'

'Olaf Hansen. His father registered him as his son. He was tremendously proud of him and they look very like each other.'

'Is he an oil man too?' Joan asked.

'No, he's a sailor. He's first officer of a tanker so oil does come into it, I suppose.' Both of them laughed.

'And is his father still alive?' Joan asked.

'He's dead,' said Jess shortly. That was a subject that she did not discuss more than she could help.

'I'm sorry.'

'So am I.' Jess knew she sounded abrupt so she got up and walked across to the window to look down into West 44th Street.

'Let's go out. The constant heating in this place gets me down. I want to breathe some fresh air and it looks beautifully cold out there. The sky's very blue. We could walk to Central Park.' She looked down at Joan's expensive shoes. Fortunately they were flat heeled.

Joan jumped up saying, 'I love the Park. Let's go and walk. And you must do the talking. Start by telling me about Jackie.'

It seemed as if being out in the open air revived their old companionship and Joan said, 'You said you've been in Australia visiting Jackie on her cattle ranch. I can't imagine that. She never seemed to be much of an open air type to me. Is she still as beautiful?'

Jess laughed. 'More so. She looks like the Rani of Jhansi now – you know, the Indian queen who led her army against the British during the Mutiny. She's sixty-nine but she still spends most of the day on a horse and her hair is long and flowing and streaked with grey, very dramatic. She swears like a trooper too. She has an entourage of old boys who come to call on her and they all want to marry her, but she says once is enough. It was wonderful because when we parted in London in 1964 she was ill and very down in every way. You don't know the story about her having to be flown quickly out of Bombay, do you? You'd gone off with Theo's body and there was no way I could contact you. I tried sending messages through Theo's company, but I don't think you could have received them because you never answered.'

Joan nodded sadly. 'I was in another world and very protected. People only told me what they thought I ought to know and I wasn't taking information in anyway. Tell me what happened.'

Jess told about the drama in the flat on Cuffe Parade and their hurried flight out of Santa Cruz. 'Jackie had an aunt living in Sussex, but she was in no state to travel any further. Fortunately Colin lent us his house in Chelsea and almost as soon as we got there, Jackie went into labour and had to be rushed to Guy's Hospital. I kept the kids with me till Jackie's aunt turned up, but the baby was born dead unfortunately. It was awful.'

'Oh poor Jackie. It's lucky you had a place to live in London,' said Joan.

'Yes, Colin came up trumps by giving us his house. I still hear from him at Christmas and he keeps me up to date with what's happened to people. He spends half of the year in Bombay – or Mumbai as they call it now – with Raju's son, and the rest of his time in England, usually Bournemouth where he goes to watch the tennis. He has a thing about lady tennis players. It was on a Bournemouth tennis court that he met the wife who ran off with the ship's officer.'

Joan laughed. 'I've not forgotten the complications of people's emotional lives in Bombay. What happened to that other admirer of yours, the young man who worked for an insurance company? He used to moon around after you at every party.'

'That was Jack. He's managing director of an international insurance company now. His Bombay boss, Mr Goddard, was a crafty old bloke. He brought out his eighteen-year-old daughter on a visit. She was incredibly pretty and Jack fell for her. They're still married and he's been tremendously successful. I reckon

Goddard noted his potential and decided to arrange a marriage, Indian style. And like most Indian marriages, it worked.'

'Which is more than you can say for ours,' said Joan. 'But go on telling me what happened to Peter and Jackie.'

'While Jackie was in hospital, Peter was still held by the police. In fact he was jolly lucky not to be charged with complicity in the death of the man who was trying to blackmail Sullivan. I'm sure he knew more than he ever admitted. Jackie's cousin must have had a hand in getting him off, but she persisted in taking Peter's side, blind to his shortcomings as usual and he had plenty of those.'

Joan nodded in agreement. 'I remember that he was handsome, but he had a very weak mouth. Why did they eventually break up? Did she see through him in the end?'

'While she was recuperating from losing the baby, he took off for Hong Kong without coming home to fetch her, so she and the children had to fly out to join him. He was working for some chap who was starting a business making cheap clothes and they used sweated labour. Jackie had only been in Hong Kong for a few months when Peter fell out with his new employer too and sent letters to everybody he knew asking for help. He was offered a job in Australia and they were all set to go when he suddenly announced that he'd fallen in love with one of the Chinese machinists and she was expecting his child.

'You can imagine the chaos that caused, especially because he couldn't make up his mind whether he wanted to stay with the Chinese girl or go with Jackie. He went backwards and forwards between them like a cuckoo in a clock. It was Jackie's aunt Daphne who sorted the whole thing out. She flew to Hong Kong and talked some sense into Jackie. Some of her relatives lived in Perth and Aunt Daphne said she would give Jackie an allowance if she went to stay with them to see if life there suited them. She persuaded Jackie the children would have a better future in Australia.'

'And they stayed?' asked Joan.

'They loved it. Peter stayed with his Chinese girl and Jackie divorced him. Soon after that her aunt died and she'd made a will saying that if Peter and Jackie were no longer married, Jackie was to inherit her aunt's fortune which was considerable. As well as having a very nice house, she had a lovely mulberry coloured vintage Rolls Royce. Fred, the man who owned the garage where I lived, bought it. He's given up the garage now and gone to live in Essex, but he hires out the Rolls for weddings and it still looks wonderful.'

'I bet Peter was furious when he found out that Jackie was rich. He'd never have had to work again,' laughed Joan.

'Fortunately Jackie had seen though him by that time, but I suspect she sent him money from time to time because she knew where he was living in Hong Kong with his girl and their children. To this day she still makes excuses for him, but thank God she'd never have taken him back. Someone who knew him in Bombay saw him in Hong Kong a few years ago and told Colin that he looked Chinese. He was taking drugs and still gambling, of course. Then news came that he'd died and Jackie was really sad.'

'The man you love first is the one you never really get over, I'm afraid,' said Joan.

'You're right. Even Marcia said Donald was the love of her life.'

'Is Sam still alive?' Joan asked.

'Sam? Oh yes, he and Perry live in East Grinstead. They give cocktail parties for the neighbours and sit on the parish council. Perry is famous for his dinner parties and his delicious home-made mayonnaise.'

'How do you feel about them?' asked Joan, and Jess looked surprised as she said, 'I'm glad they're happy, but you see Sam wasn't my first love. In fact I don't think he or I were ever really in love at all. Getting married suited us both. I've only been in love once and that was with Erik. I've never felt about anybody in the same way as I felt about him and I never will again. I don't even bother looking.'

'What happened to him?' Joan asked outright.

Jess knew the question would inevitably come up and it had to be answered. Her voice was bleak when she said, 'He was killed.'

'Oh, my dear, how did it happen?'

'Did you ever read about a big oil rig disaster in the North Sea off Aberdeen twenty-five years ago? Erik was a director of the company and he and some colleagues were flown out by helicopter on an official visit to that rig because it was rather a showpiece. He was there when it had a blow back and, being Erik, he weighed in to help. It was the sort of thing he'd done all his working life and he loved it. But the fire was worse than anything he'd ever experienced before, very intense and confined. A lot of men were killed. The few who survived jumped into the sea, but Erik was engulfed.'

Where they were walking there was a park bench and Jess stepped aside to sink heavily into it as if her legs could no longer hold her up. Her whole demeanour had changed and she said, weakly, 'Joanie, I'll never forget that morning. We were still living in the same mews because Erik bought me the house next door to the garage where I'd originally lived. I still live there in fact though it's gone up market now. I was listening to the radio in the kitchen as usual and suddenly the programme was interrupted by a newsflash about an oil rig fire. I knew Erik was there and I *knew* he was dead. I began screaming and throwing crockery about like a mad woman. Our son was at school thank God. My friends in the garage next door heard me screaming and I remember Fred coming in and giving me a terrific wallop to shut me up. When I told him what I'd heard he got me a doctor and then went to the school to pick up Olaf. We never got Erik's body back. They were all so badly burned. It must have been instantaneous.'

Joan reached out and took her friend's hand. 'I am so sorry, so very sorry,' she said.

'Thanks.' Jess's eyes were dry and her face set. All her tears had been shed long ago, but the pain still lacerated her heart.

The two women sat silent in the winter sun for what seemed like a long time till Joan shivered and said, 'Come back to Sutton Place with me and have something to eat. I want you to meet my Philip.'

Philip was a surprise. Theo had been a blonde god, but Philip was short, squat, black-haired and overweight. Theo was disdainful of most people except the few he wanted to impress; Philip was genial, companionable, funny and older than Joan by about ten years. If she hadn't known he was a psychiatrist, Jess would have thought he was an actor or a comedian. She liked him very much and was pleased to see that he was obviously in thrall to his wife. His Mexican art delighted her too with its basic shapes and brilliant primary colours. There was nothing sophisticated or effete about it or him.

He made her feel relaxed because he'd obviously heard about her from Joan and said, 'Are you the friend who wrote for newspapers and caused trouble by reporting how some woman sold her dead husband's after-shave lotion?'

'Guilty,' she said with a laugh.

'Do you still write for newspapers?' he wanted to know, but Jess shook her head.

'You were lucky not to be sued,' said Joan. 'Have you any idea what happened to the woman who sold the after-shave lotion?'

'You mean Lilias? She married a chap she met in a bar. Apparently he wore thick gold necklaces and rings made out of half sovereigns.'

'She could afford more for him,' Joan laughed. She was much easier and confident in her manner when she was with Philip and Jess too began to relax and stop reliving the terrible day she lost Erik. She was aware that Joan was trying to coax her back to equanimity by asking about other people they'd known in Bombay.

'What happened to the doctors?' she asked.

'Doctors? You mean Alex and Shackleton? Shackleton never put on another revue. He said that last one ruined his enthusiasm. He retired and went to live in Ceylon. Alex Paisley, the one who had the roulette wheel, went to Australia – to Brisbane – and became a professor, specialising in heart surgery, I think.'

'Good heavens! Theo wouldn't let me call him in when he got sick because he thought he was a hopeless drunk.'

'Alex was far cleverer than he pretended,' Jess said.

'Did that marriage survive?'

'No, like most of the couples we knew they divorced. I hear from time to time about a coterie of ex–wives from Bombay who all live in the Home Counties and meet up for lunches. They're very respectable now – including the nymphomaniac Pat – Tory-voting and conservatively dressed and reading the *Daily Telegraph*. If they're hard up they'd sooner die than admit it. They're stuck in the past and it's all they talk about. Gloria stayed married to one of the old rugby team and is the queen of the group because her husband is very rich and they live in Virginia Water. She entertains a lot and keeps up with all her old friends and writes letters of consolation when anyone dies. Quite admirable really.'

'I can't believe that I'm hearing you being charitable about Gloria,' said Joan with a chuckle.

'One mellows with age,' said Jess.

Joan put her elbows on the table and leaned forward to say, 'You know I often look back and realize what an important time that was in my life. I changed completely when I was in Bombay.'

'I agree,' said Jess. 'I've never forgotten the old man who used to drink in the Ritz and said that going past Aden had a tremendous effect on European women. He was convinced they were never the same again, one way or another. I'm sure he was right.'

'I think you should write a book about being in Bombay,' Joan said, but Jess shook her head.

'No, but I do have plans for my retirement.'

'Doing what?' asked Philip.

She looked at him keenly and decided to tell him what was in her mind.

'I'm planning to go back to Mumbai for the first time since I left and set up a charity for the children who hang around Crawford Markets. You see I'll be quite rich when the hotels are sold. Olaf has a trust fund from Erik so he doesn't need a lot more money.'

Philip and Joan stared at her with keen interest and Joan said, 'I remember seeing the little boys at the market. They could be such pests.'

'There were girls too, all starving and homeless and they trusted nobody for good reason. They were abused in every way and harried from pillar to post by the police. I was particularly fond of one boy called Sammy. Before I left I gave him enough money to get out of Bombay and I've always wondered what happened to him,' said Jess.

'Running a charity needs a lot of reliable help,' said Philip solemnly.·

'I know. I'll have to rope in helpers and advisers and all sorts of interested people but Sam and I knew a lot of decent Indian people and I think I can still find some of them.' Jess stared at Philip and said on sudden impulse, 'You wouldn't like to help would you?' He was exactly the sort of person she needed and she instinctively knew she could trust him.

'Have you a definite idea of what you want to do really?' he asked.

'Yes, but I realize I'll only be dealing with a small percentage of the problem, like a grain of sand on a beach in a way. I want to get some houses where children can have a settled way of life with a roof over their heads, get some basic education and food every day. I need to find trustworthy helpers. I'm pretty careful with money and I'm not planning anything lavish or enormous. If I can help a couple of hundred kids a year that's better than nothing. I'd like to call it Sammy's House.'

Philip pushed back his chair and left the room, returning a few moments later with a glistening bottle of champagne that was obviously just out of the refrigerator. 'Let's drink a toast to Sammy,' he said, and popped the cork, lightly spraying the women with some drops of champagne as he filled three glasses.

'Does this mean you don't think I'm being unrealistic or senti-mental?' asked Jess.

'I don't think that at all. I've been to India and seen the child beggars so I know what you're talking about. I'm thinking of retiring from practice soon too. Will you let me join in?'

Jess raised her glass. 'I'll have to check your references first,' she laughed.